MAYHEM IN MONTE CARLO

Sequel Novel to:
THE LITTLE BROWN DIAMOND

MICHAEL CHRISTOPHER FERRIER

DEDICATION.

Monaco is a fascinating place, full of extraordinary characters from all over the world. I dedicate this book to my many friends there — none of whom remotely resemble some of the sleazy characters I describe! I also dedicate the novel to those I love most — my four lovely children, seven exciting grandchildren — and above all to my beautiful wife, Diana.

PROLOGUE

Even in early summer, 4:30 a.m. on the French Riviera can be cold and clammy - especially out at sea in a six-meter fishing skiff.

The short, stocky man standing in the back hugged himself tightly to ward off the chill. He stared silently out to sea and then turned and watched the lights of Monte Carlo fade slowly into the background.

He avoided looking down, for at his feet lay the body of a man he once knew and whose company he had occasionally enjoyed—but a man who he had also ended up disliking intensely. But was that good enough reason to find him like this: dead and hidden under heap of greenish fishing nets with a plastic bag over his head to restrain his badly damaged skull?

Even though the man had only met his death a few hours earlier, rigor mortis was already well advanced. Thus, as the slight swell eased the boat from side to side, the body rolled stiffly in sympathy, causing the dead man's shoes to clunk eerily against the brass-lined bulwarks.

At the helm stood a weathered old sailor sucking deeply on his yellow-papered, fat French cigarette. He exhaled with obvious relish, the smoke mingling with the exhaust of the aging single-cylinder diesel blowing back over the transom.

The stocky man coughed as the pungent mixture hit his nostrils. Then he coughed again. The coughing was his stomach's last straw, and he leaned quickly over the transom retching miserably until he could retch no more. He eased backward wiping his mouth with a cloth until he stumbled badly on the corpse.

v

"Shit—fucking shit!"

The helmsman immediately turned to look back and pulled the speed control to neutral.

Now the poor landlubber lurched forward once again as the deceleration caught him unawares. He landed flat on his back, spread-eagled across the cold and lifeless body.

"Shit and more fucking shit. For the Lord's sake, mon—get me off of him!"

"Qu'est qu'il y a?" (What's up?) "You seasick? You've never been seasick before?"

"Aaach no, it's not the sea. This fucking corpse gives me the creeps. How much farther must we go?"

"About another one thousand meters, or so. Keep your cool. Ze water must be profonde, you know. Et pas des courrants. We talked about all that, non?"

"Si, si…Keep going, I'll be all right. I just hate the fact that we are burying a person who must have meant something to someone once. Now he's nothing more than a rolling stiff. Life's cheap, isn't it?"

"Don't look at 'im…And I don't think a soul will miss the animal. He's not worth nutting. Not even the diesel fuel to dump him here! Merde! That son of a beetch…We are doing the world a favor. Keep that in mind, mon ami!"

Twenty minutes later, the engine slowed again and then stopped. Total silence and deep darkness now surrounded them. The only sound was the gentle lapping of the wavelets on the bow and stern. The helmsman took off his French seaman's hat and scratched his thinning grey gray hair. Cautiously, he looked all around.

"OK—I think eets safe. Let's get to work."

In the gloomy darkness, lit only by the dull glow of the red and green navigation lights, the two men started the job they had rehearsed carefully a few hours earlier.

First they carefully removed the fishing nets that had been hiding the cadaver covered in a somewhat blood-soiled white sheet. Then one held up parts of the torso as the other slid and slipped an old canvas sail under the fast-stiffening body. As soon as they were satisfied that enough canvas had been pulled across, the two men hoisted each side up to the center.

One then held the canvas together as the older man carefully threaded a small rope through the holes once used to attach the sail to the mast and then sewed the rope to the other end of the canvas. He pulled the rope tight as he went, like someone might do when wrapping string around a clumsy Christmas gift.

This job done, the 'package' was further rolled and wrapped in water-resistant sealing tape until the end result looked not unlike a modern version of an Egyptian mummy.

"Don't want any pieces of clothing or canvas to rot and float away," the elder man muttered to himself in French.

Now the two men heaved the body up onto the top of the box covering the centrally situated diesel engine. Taped or not, the skull and legs still drooped rigidly off the front and back of the box.

The old man now headed into the protected head of the little boat and slowly brought out six black iron weights of the sort old-fashioned scales once used to measure the kilos of fish caught that morning.

With metal wire, one weight was carefully attached to each corner of the package and another two at both centers. Under the carrying ring, each weight was marked "4 kilos." Thirty-two kilos in all.

The old seaman now tugged heavily at each weight ensuring it would not come off easily and then checked the package one last time to make absolutely sure nothing floatable could easily escape.

Satisfied, he crawled back into the head and brought out two thick planks.

These he pushed under the shoulders and thighs of the dead man, with the other end of the planks resting on the port gunwale. With a bucket on a rope, he now raised seawater and made sure the two planks were wet and slippery.

"OK, my friend, eet is time. Ready?"

"Ready."

"UN, DEUX, TROIS…" And on the sound of "trois" both men heaved the heavy corpse onto the wet planks and then slid the corpse along the wet wood and into the water. The weights banged loudly on the boat's side as the body fled the gunwales.

In the water, the torso floated a minute or so as the air trapped by the canvas and tape tried to escape. Then, hissing gently as the last gasp of bubbles fought their way to freedom, the mummy slowly submerged, tugged down by those weights anxious to find sea-bottom.

The two men stayed silent as they watched the body slowly disappear.

As soon as there was nothing left to see, the old man turned to the helm and returned with his thermos full of coffee.

"Let's drink to the end of that 'espece de crapeau' (piece of toad)."

"Phew, I am glad that's over—we can't thank you enough!"

"No thanks required. Just have some coffee and watch the sun's rise. A new day. And the world has one less idiot to worry about. They ought to give us a medal!!"

They drank the steaming brew, glad of the warmth.

"Now, do not forget our plan. I will drop you off at Cap d'Ail jetty, and you will calmly walk to your hotel Marriott along the seawall as you have done every morning for weeks. I go fishing as if nothing had 'appened at all. Murder is not so difficult, ees eet? Kill a fish to feed a man. Kill a man to feed the fish. Where's the difference? Vive the *le cercle de la vie.*"

The younger man appeared a little taken aback at the stark Gallic logic. Then he grinned.

"True, the circle of life—or death—is not as difficult as you imagine if you have enough motivation."

The old man laughed softly.

"Especially if that motivation is 'l'amour' (love)!"

The younger man winced. Love had played a role but unfortunately not in the way the captain had guessed. He had just helped a friend. A friend who, unfortunately, loved another! The man, in fact, who was now drifting slowly to the bottom.

But the excited old man took his grimace to mean the thrill of romantic intrigue, and so he leant over impulsively to hug the other, happy to feel part of a wonderful 'crime passionelle' so beloved of French romantic novellas.

Then there was silence—only broken a few minutes later by the engine firing up again for the slow trip back.

CHAPTER 1

KILLIN, PERTHSHIRE

Hamish Macintosh pulled his taxi to the side of the road, a few feet short of the little stone bridge. It was drizzling again, but then it always drizzled in this part of the British Isles. It did not bother him.

He buttoned up his treasured Barbour waxed raincoat, checked the car was not blocking the narrow roadway, and ambled up to the middle of the centuries-old crossing. He stared into the black water. The drizzle was not heavy enough to disturb the stillness of the slowly drifting Tay River, which empties Loch Tay, lieing, - darkly brooding - just west of where he was standing.

Hamish could just about recognize his own face mirrored on the surface. For at least four minutes, he gazed at himself, slightly amused how the swirling motion of the flow distorted his image from time to time, making him look alternately ugly or the handsome Scot that he was.

"Dr Jekyll and Mr. Hyde," he whispered to himself. "But I am all Dr Jekyll, no Mr. Hyde—dead, boring."

The old stone bridge was the only crossing of the river between Killin and Aberfeldy in Perthshire in the Southern Highlands. It led directly into the little town of Kenmore, which offered at that time not much more than a warm and comfortable hotel, an old dilapidated castle (now being slowly refurbished as a potential golf resort), a small church, and a small post office cum souvenir shop.

Perth was the nearest big center, but he rarely went there. Hamish rarely went anywhere. There was no need to. His wife hated the trip and preferred BBC or ITV. His daughter had left some years ago to marry an Aussie from Queensland. And he saw little reason to go and visit. He really had little in common with the brash Aussie she married. Like it or not, Hamish was a prisoner of these highlands.

It wasn't always that way. In his youth he and his pal Adam had roamed Europe in Adam's old Morris Minor convertible. And what an adventure that had turned out to be!

Hamish smiled a deep smile and was about to relive once more those heady days, when his mobile buzzed in his pocket.

"Killin Cabs, here…"

Hamish listened intently; it was hard to hear the lady.

"OK, Madam, I will be right over. Sorry your whist game was canceled, No, no—it is no problem, I promise you. It is absolutely no problem!"

Hamish Macintosh put away the phone, switched off his memories, and headed back to his cab.

Five minutes later he tooted politely outside the little stone house, half a mile behind the Kenmore Hotel on a narrow country lane. The door opened and his fare waved happily to him and then turned around to have a few last words with her host.

It was raining a little harder now. She raised her white umbrella and hurried to the opening door of the black cab. Hamish closed the door and wiggled himself back into the driver's seat. Barbour coats are great against the Scottish mist but not so good for sliding in and out of midsized cars.

"Aach, Hamish. I am so sorry to muck ye aboot, but Mrs. Samson is feeling a wee bitty poorly and couldn'a concentrate. So we decided to call it a day. It's the anniversary of her poor husband's death, and I think it was praying on her mind."

"Madam, do not worry. I was just standing around waiting for you. I did not go back to Killin. Business is a bit slow these days—no tourists yet."

"You have nothing to do then?"

"Not really, Madam."

"Well, let's go shopping in Aberfeldy and I'll buy ye a pot o' tea. How's that for a brilliant idea for a rainy day, Hamish."

Hamish thought about it. Then he thought about why on earth he should be thinking about it! What else did he have to do? Why was it so difficult for him to make even the smallest spontaneous decision these days? Why was it so easy for this seventy-something old woman to stay so cheery? She lived alone in her drafty old house, at least three hundred yards from the nearest neighbor. She didn't seem to have that many friends— how could she? Her failing eyesight prevented her driving. And yet, she was always happy and seemingly so delighted to be alive.

"Whatever you like, Madam. I have time."

"Hamish, it is not just what *I* like. What would *ye* like? Do ye fancy a cuppa with an old lady, or do ye not? Come on. Give me some decision will ye? Anyway I feel like giving the gossips some fodder. The Lady out with the Laddie from the Cabbie.

I love it. How say ye, then?"

"Madam, I would be delighted to have some tea with you. Thank you for asking."

"It's aboot time anyhoo," she mused, "you've been driving me for… how many years is it, Hamish?"

"Oh dear, Madam. It must be at least four. I think you are my best customer."

"OK four years…" And a thought struck her. "Hey, if it's four years and I am your best customer, then Hamish, me boy, guess who will be buying the tea?"

Hamish laughed.

"Happy to do so, Madam."

"And stop that *'Madam'* stuff, will ye? It is driving me out of me head. Anyway, as I was saying, you've been driving me around for years and I know less about you than my Cousin Clement—and he lives in New Zealand with a few thousand sheep. Yuck—I hate sheep. Creepy-looking critters, I think."

The lady fell silent rummaging in her bag and muttering to herself.

"Ooch—I didn'a leave my credit card at home did I? Nope—here she is. Bright as the day that McLeish crook at the bank gave it to me. Card, you are going to buy me a new cashmere twin-set today."

Hamish smiled. He loved this happy, contented old dear. The cab entered Aberfeldy. Not much of a town but big enough to offer a few good shops and a tea room or two. Hamish's fare addressed him again.

"OK—you wait at Polly's tearoom and order two pots of tea, Earl Grey for me. I'll just get me a new book or two at MacDonald's. He's an old rogue—books cost at least 20 percent less in Perth, but who wants to drive all that way for a good read?"

"I thought you were buying a cashmere, Madam?"

"First, stop calling me *Madam*. It makes me feel like an old French whore. Secondly, were you listening to an old lady ramble to herself? Not a gentlemanly thing to do is that! Thirdly, since when, Hamish Macintosh, is a lady not allowed to change her own mind, may I ask ye?"

Hamish laughed out loud and dropped the old lady off at the bookstore, did a U-turn in the deserted town center, and parked outside Polly's Tea Emporium.

Before opening the door and entering the little tearoom, he tried to peer in the window. The steamed up panes defeated him. He had wanted desperately to see who was inside. Now, he asked himself why? Was he worried about who might see him with the old dowager?

"Hamish, you have become a stupid, boring fool. Snap out of it."

With new determination, he rushed through the door, tripped on the jute welcome mat, and stumbled against the first table, scattering cutlery and crockery all over the floor with a shattering clatter.

Mrs. Thompson, the owner, rushed out of the little kitchen at the back.

"Good Gracious me, Mr. Macintosh, have you been frequenting my alcoholic competitor at the Frog and Princess?"

"Oh I am so sorry, Mrs. Thompson. I didn't see the mat."

"Aach, there's no harm done. Just one broken cup. It's years old. Don't ye be worrying about nothing, all right? And what can I do for ye?"

"Oh…I will be waiting for Lady Lothmere. She is shopping at Macdonald's, the bookman, and then we will be having a pot of your best tea, Mrs. Thompson. Earl Gr…."

"Aach Oy, Mr. Hamish. I know what Hermoine drinks. What about you though?" she added with a wicked wink. "Chasing the money are we now? Isn't she a touch old for you, Hamish me man?"

Hamish went very red and examined his wet shoes.

"Aach, man. I am only joking you. Sit down by the window there. Not a warm body is out today. I'll be having you all to myself. See if I can wow you before that rich old dear wafts you away…anyway, what is she buying books for, the old silly? She can't see past the end of her nose!"

Speech over, Mrs. Thompson popped back into her kitchen like a cuckoo bird after completion of the top of the hour chimes.

Hamish looked around the friendly little tearoom. Primrose table cloths covered the ten or so little white wooden tables. Very upright reed woven chairs surrounded each table like the Queens Guard protecting their Sovereign.

On the pale green walls were the familiar scenes of the highlands. A bag piper playing on a crag. A stag at sunset. Loch Tay in moonlight. And then, incongruously, a large framed photo of a graduating class at Edinburgh University.

The counter on the left of the door still supported an old cash register, and underneath cooled delicious Scottish scones, cakes, and shortbreads.

A big round bell hung over the door to warn Mrs. Thompson to keep an eye on 'them foreigners' who might dare to pop in. If the customers were Scots whom she knew, she disappeared back into her kitchen as fast as she exited. If not, she stayed and watched in case these strange people from across the channel might spirit away a rock cake or two without paying.

The bell sounded and a dripping Lady Lothmere staggered in. Mrs. Thompson's head popped out of the cuckoo's nest again, recognized the white umbrella, and popped back into the kitchen.

"Hamish, it's getting worse out there. Thank God for Mrs. Thompson. Did ye order the tea? Lapsung Suchong for me. Got to like it in India, don't 'cha know."

"Did I hear Lapsung, Lady? But you always order Earl Grey. I have it almost ready," bellowed Mrs. Thompson from the back room.

"Yes, you did tell me also to order Earl Grey, Lady…!" added Hamish.

"Oh, all right then. You are all so *boring*. Can't a lady ever do something different? But if you've already brewed Earl Grey, it will do nicely then Mrs. Thompson. Thank ye so much." Turning to Hamish she whispered, "See, no one lets a lady change her mind anymore. Life is getting very dull, Hamish Macintosh. Very dull."

She hung up her coat and sat down opposite her nervous driver.

"Now, my man, who are you exactly, Mr. Hamish Macintosh. Tell me your story."

"What story, Lady L?"

"Your story, the story of your life, of course—where were ye born, bred, schooled, married…all that sort of stuff."

"I wouldn't know where to begin. Anyway I am afraid you might find the story a little dull, you know."

"All right then, tell me about the finest time of your life. The most fun you ever had. How's that for a start?"

Hamish looked away, embarrassed.

"Come on, boy. Out with it. I know it's raining hard, but I can't keep waiting all day, ye know? And your tea is getting cold. A cold cup of tea is like a blister on yer nose. No bloody use to no one!"

"All right, Lady L. I think the best time of my life was when I was nineteen and a wee bit."

Once started, his early life flowed out like lava from an erupting volcano. Lady L was fascinated. The tea turned into that blister on her nose. Stone cold—before she eventually remembered to finish it.

CHAPTER 2

FIRE
REKINDLED

The screen door creaked open. There stood Vladimir, framed in the doorway of the seedy little Mexican restaurant, all male, silhouetted against the pouring rain, water dripping off his soaked black hair. Paz felt a cold shiver track down her spine and settle somewhere south of her navel. The shock was total. Like a light switching on in her depressed subconscious.

Recovering as fast as she could, she rushed up to hug him tightly—more tightly than she had planned. Her breasts sunk tightly into his chest.

"Vladimir, how nice to see you. Tell us all your news. Come in out of the rain. You know everybody here, right? Marsha and Elsie, daughters of my ex-husband, Jack; Elsie's husband from London. Tony from New York, but now living with Marsha in Argentina—I mean, they are married, but living in Argentina."

She completed the introductions and placed him next to her at the central table. Natasha, her seven-year-old daughter, sat on his other side and eyed the couple suspiciously.

The group of some twenty-two invitees, who had earlier attended the burial of Peter Palmer, her husband, watched uncomfortably. Slowly, conversation returned to some sort of normality, but it remained strained. Everyone suddenly seemed to find a valid reason to be urgently elsewhere.

The Ashdowns and the Russian Consul from Mexico decided to share a taxi and head back immediately to Miami airport. The Ashdowns were to rejoin their son at their ranch in North Argentina. The Consul was on her way to a well-earned holiday in Poland.

"Traffic can be bad at this time," was the Ashdowns half-hearted attempt at an excuse. "And with security and all that these days, you can never be too early."

Joining the Ashdowns would be Natasha, Paz's seven-year-old daughter. All the family seemed to think a few weeks in the Argentinean sun, riding horses and getting to know her cousin better, would be a very good idea. It would give Paz time to get her head together after the death, clean out the house, and think through her future life—alone.

And it would allow the child to slowly appreciate the loss of her father in an atmosphere of less overpowering sadness.

The Londoners (Elsie and Jack) had already left to join their private jet at Palm Beach airport. He (the ever-busy and driven brewer) explained he had a series of vital phone calls to make and could not leave his empire alone for more than a few hours, no matter what the cause!

The locals then started collecting their coats, kissing Paz good-bye with sincere offers that they were always there for her. And Pedro the restaurant owner disappeared in the back to start the dish-washing sequence.

Soon, Paz found herself more or less alone with the Russian. She settled the bill Pedro had just left her and then turned to Vladimir.

"Well, I guess that's that. End of a chapter. You are born alone. You end your life alone. But I had hoped to share the years in between with a partner. Sad, sad day. But, I guess that's life."

"You're not alone. You have a lovely daughter. The one you thought was mine, remember? You have your family. You have friends, like me. I will always be your friend, Paz."

Paz was beginning to feel a little uncomfortable. This man had once been her lover when they had all shared the so-called Mexican affair some years back. The adventure that had started—and ended—Paz's modeling career—the adventure that had placed her at the center of Mexican politics and resulted in her being idolized by practically all of Mexican womanhood.

And then, through a series of accidents and deaths, the adventure had resulted in her and her team fleeing Mexico only minutes ahead of a police chief determined to incarcerate them.

But that was all history now and best forgotten. Paz had escaped and married the father of her child, the man who had befriended her when she had left home and the man who had indirectly placed her on the path to fame and eventual defeat.

On the way, she had shared a brief project and an even shorter romance with the man now in front of her. She had thought that night of passion may have sired her daughter. It had not. An earlier night with her now-deceased husband had been responsible.

But the time with Vladimir—ridiculously short as it turned out to be—was the only time in her life that she had known real emotion and real physical satisfaction.

Then Vladimir had disappeared out of her life, thrown out of Mexico at the request of the corrupt Mexico City police. He had been sent as researcher to Moscow and then on to the war in Chechnya, which meant being an active agent of the local KGB.

Vladimir had found her again. Why? And why at this sad moment? And why was Paz so excited despite her sadness?

She wished he'd go away so she could sort out her emotions. But going away was very far from Vladimir's plans.

"Vladimir, I must go home now. There are so many loose ends to tie up. Thank you so much for coming. When do you fly back to Russia?"

"I am not going back to Russia yet. When I go depends on you."

"On me, Vladimir? Why me?"

"Because we have so much catching up to do. I have to explain to you why I was forced to leave Mexico. I want to tell you my plans…"

Paz cut him off.

"Vladimir, I am emotionally drained right now. Once again, thanks for coming. It was a great thing you did being here—and a great tribute to

Peter (her husband). But I'm really not up to any more chatting. Call me in a month or so, if you want…Bye, Vladimir."

"OK, I'll go. But it's about five o'clock right now. There is no way I'll get any plane to anywhere tonight. Go home and lie down and let's just have a steak or a fish together tonight. I am booked at the Best Western hotel. Know where that is?"

"Oh sure, it's not more than a mile away on US Highway 1. I'll get the limo to drop you off. I don't know about dinner, though…"

"You want me to dine *alone*? I don't know a soul here. Russians do not eat alone. It is seen as an insult. It means that you are too boring for anyone to want to share a table with you. Am I that boring, Paz?"

"Oh, all right then," laughed Paz. "I'll pick you up at eight and we'll go to Schooners. But don't plan any discos. I am beat."

"You mean there are discos in this one-horse town?"

"Enough, Vladimir. Where's your suitcase?"

"It's already in your limo, Paz."

Somehow this fact made Paz even more uneasy. And even more intrigued.

⎯⎯⎯⎯◦◉◦⎯⎯⎯⎯

Vladimir and Paz sat in the far corner of the outside terrace of Schooners, an old established and excellent fish restaurant not far from the Jupiter inlet. She was wearing a red, boat-shaped cotton blouse with a white lace-bordered skirt. Her hair was brushed back and held in place by a black satin band. She looked fresh again and remarkably relaxed.

Now that she was able to look at him in a less stressful atmosphere, she noticed that Vladimir was thinner and more muscular than she remembered him. His hair, parted in the middle and flowing down each side of his face, was—amazingly—starting to gray here and there. His eyes were colder, more piercing, troubled even, continually looking quizzically down that long, slender nose.

He was also slightly stooped. She hadn't remembered that either. Rather like a priest in constant meditation.

But the same determined masculinity was unmistakeable. This was still the man she had loved so desperately for one wild night all those years ago. He still had the power to raise her pulse; that was obvious.

Paz ordered spice-blackened Dolphin filets, and Vladimir just doubled whatever she ordered. He seemed totally uninterested in what he ate or when he ate it.

What he *drank* was something else. Double vodka on the rocks in a deep glass with a dash of water and half a lemon or lime.

He did not say much either. So Paz, a trifle nervous and unsure of this evening's purpose, kept the conversation alive.

She reminisced about those events in Mexico and how they had escaped the police in the Russian cargo plane. How she married Peter and the life they had built quietly together. About her hopes and dreams for little Natasha. There he stopped her in mid-sentence.

"Were you sad when you found out the child was not mine?" He had grabbed her wrist as she was about to pop the last morsel of fish into her mouth.

Paz didn't know what to say. This was a topic she wanted to avoid. In actual fact, she had been disappointed, but she could not admit it here. Nor did she want to talk about that steamy night in the Mexico City hotel just in case the conversation veered into directions she was desperately anxious to avoid. But how could she say no, she was not disappointed? It would be rude. And a lie. Paz did not lie easily. She decided to flannel…

"It was a surprise, I must say. But it turned out fine. Peter was a great husband and…"

"But were you sad, Paz? Did you wish it had been mine? I have to know."

"Vladimir, I cannot answer that. Please do not force me."

Vladimir slowly released his grip on her wrist and looked directly into her eyes.

"Well, *I* was disappointed. Very disappointed…"

"Vladimir, let's pay and go. OK? I feel a little sick. Too much emotion for one day…" A little tear appeared in her eye and slowly drifted down her left cheek. He saw it and wiped it off with his finger.

"OK—we go." He asked for the check, paid cash, and helped her out of her seat.

"Shall I drive you to the Best Western hotel, Vladimir?"

"I'll drive you home in your car, then I'll call a cab," answered the Russian very forcefully.

She did not resist. She was just too exhausted.

At her front door, Vladimir stopped the car and walked round to the passenger door. He helped Paz out, and together they walked the few steps to the entrance.

Once inside, he scooped her up and carried her to the bedroom. There he placed her carefully back on her feet and held her tightly as she sobbed softly into his chest. They stood together like this for minutes, even though it seemed like hours. The only light was the reflection of the streetlamp down the lane bouncing off the calm river surface and back through the bedroom window.

"Paz," he finally whispered, "get into bed. You need a rest."

He left her then and went into the lanai. She quietly undressed, slipped on her nightgown, washed, and crawled into the massive double bed.

A few minutes later, Vladimir entered, fully naked, stooped to look at her, and then gently entered the bed from the other side. No one said a word. Her back was turned from him. Slowly she felt him approach. Carefully, he turned her on her back and lifted her nightgown as far as it would go. To her surprise, she lifted her upper body to help him complete the unveiling.

He placed himself astride her, one knee on either side of her waist. His eyes darted all over her exposed body and then focused on her face. She stared back.

Still gazing into her eyes, he softly maneuvered his knees between her legs. Then he leant down and gently kissed each breast. She grabbed his head and kept it in her cleavage, moving her fingers softly through his hair.

Finally it was time. He entered her, arms extended, one hand on the bed at each side of her. His thrusts were long, hard, and measured. There was a pause between each action. She raised her arms to hold her breasts. He pushed them back and held her wrists down beside her head.

"Leave them alone—I like to see them move," he hissed.

She felt the waves of passion begin to build. He felt them as well and increased the pace, switching to a regular rhythm.

She let go and rediscovered what had so moved her all those years ago in that Mexico City bed.

Exhausted, he rolled off her and fell asleep. She cried a tear or two, not sure if it was for her recent loss or for her even more recent rediscovery.

CHAPTER 3

HAMISH'S STORY

Hamish never had much time for reading and learning and university. He knew his parents didn't have the money. And frankly, he didn't see the need for a lad whose ambition did not reach much further than the moors and the borders of his native Perthshire.

Adam, his best friend, thought otherwise and decided to try pastures new. He literally forced his way into Edinburgh University where he planned to study law. Adam was the determined one; Hamish was sure he would make it and probably make it big. The only bad part could be that Hamish was not so sure their paths would ever cross again.

So imagine his surprise to pick up the phone and hear Adam on the other end.

"Hamish, what are you doing over Easter, chum?"

"Not much of anything—why?"

"Cos I want to drive to France and thought you might want to join. How say you? You game?"

Hamish did not reply. Leave Perthshire? Go away for Easter, which was only a few weeks away? Go to France, wherever exactly France was? In a car? He did not even have his licence yet nor was he earning more than a few pounds helping out his father in his game-keeping job.

Those were a lot of issues to juggle in thirty seconds for a man not used to facing more than a decision to go right or left on leaving the house most mornings.

"Hamish, you there, chum?"

"Yes I am here—but I dunno what to say. I can't drive, I don't have a passport, and I am just about broke. I'd not be much good to ye!"

"I can drive. I have a car. I have £500 from my uncle because I did well in exams. All you have to do is get your dad to order up a passport. It's easy. Anyway, I miss you…So don't be a prick and just say yes."

"OK, Adam—I'm in…Let me grab a pencil to take down the details."

Three weeks later, shiny new passport in hand, Hamish found himself cruising down the highway from Calais to Paris, Adam gently humming at his side.

"Feels a bit weird sitting in the driving seat and not driving,

dun'it? I forgot only us Scots and the Sassenachs motor on the left."

"And the Aussies. Malaysians, Japanese, most Africans, and goodness knows how many others. We're not that unique, you know!"

The first night saw the little Morris Minor reach the Loire Valley. The lads had decided to camp on the sandy banks of the river, which was flowing wide and shallow at that point.

After a baguette and pate, sloshed down with a bottle of cheap Algerian wine, they bunked down in a little Blackstone tent and remembered their young days hiking up the slopes of Ben Lawers mountain on Loch Tayside. The day and the drive and the wine soon saw them fast asleep.

Adam was the first to sense something was wrong. He sat up sharply in his sleeping bag and opened the tent flap. The distant roar was louder now, like the rush of an oncoming express train.

"Holy shit! Hamish, get your arse out of bed. We are about to be flooded the hell downriver. Move…"

Already water was lapping at the tent edge and against the wheels of the Morris.

"Leave the fucking tent and run to the car. Quick, Hamish. Run."

They made it to the car, and, thank God, it started first turn. Adam reversed up the path as fast as he dared. Both boys watched the rising waters tug at the tent, lift it up, and tear it away from its pegs.

"Hell, there go our sleeping bags. And lunch."

"And Dad's tent..." wailed Hamish. The tent had been his only real contribution to the trip. "What the heck happened?"

"I guess all that rain and drizzle we've been driving through just accumulated and started racing down the river. Good damn thing I woke up!" replied Adam.

"What do we do now?"

"I say we drive through the night and get the heck out of this shit weather."

They re-found the Route Nationale 7 and drove until breakfast in Montpelier stopped them. At the little café, they rolled out the map and stared at the romantic names they read as their fingers traced the coast of the French Riviera.

"Cassis—I've heard of that. There is a drink named after that village. I remember reading how it's some sort of little port hugging the bottom of what I think is France's highest sea cliff. Let's go there. You OK with that?"

"Sure," answered Hamish. "You know I love mountains."

"A *cliff* is not a *mountain*, chum. But OK, let's head there, unless you have a better idea."

Hamish did not have a better idea. And so they reached the lovely little hamlet of Cassis between Marseille and Toulon about 5:00 p.m. that afternoon.

Another baguette, a hunk of cheese, and another even cheaper bottle of wine and both boys were fast asleep on the beach just east of the main port.

The evening chill woke them both up almost simultaneously.

"Heck, I could eat a horse," offered Hamish.

"Me too. Let's go see what this town offers. The secret I've heard is to check out the *Plats du Jour* as they offer the best value. That and/or the *menu touristique*."

Hamish did his best to understand and moved from café to café trying to make sense of the menus posted outside. But the likes of '*Daube de*

Provence,' '*Moules Mariniere,*' and '*Soupe de Poisson*' (Poison soup?) just threw him.

Adam came to the rescue, running over from the other side of the port quay.

"I've found this cute little place where we can get a menu with steak and chips for only eighteen francs. Let's try it."

The steak was good and well worth the expenditure—even for a couple of thrifty Scots lads. But the creamy cheese with tomatoes they did find just a little strange. (*Mozzarella* sounded to them like a Japanese B-film monster!)

They had just paid the bill when Hamish felt a strong hand grab his shoulder.

"Hey guys, you hail from the UK, right? I saw your little car. Wanna join us? We have this huge bottle of rose wine to kill. And frankly the Frenchies are beginning to bore us…"

Pink wine sounded a little gay to Hamish. To him and most of his compatriots wine was red. Or occasionally white. Never pink, for goodness' sake.

But the big hand belonged to a big man, tougher than nails and just as sharp. If he could handle a pink wine, well then so could a couple of Scots chums.

His name was Herb, and he and his pals were on shore leave from the US carrier *Dwight D. Eisenhower,* presently berthed in Toulon for essential repairs.

Alongside Herb sat a jovial sailor from New Jersey and a rather wiry midshipman from Denver, Colorado. Herb swept the boys up and plopped them down on the two spare seats at their table.

"So limeys, how's the action around here?"

"Action? What action?" asked Adam.

"Come on dumb bum, I'm talking about the talent. The goods. The dames. Broads. Malukas."

The boys remained blank.

"Jeez, kids. The girls. G.I.R.L.S., of course. Or should I say, of curse!"

The sailors laughed in unison.

Adam was the first to get it. "Aaach, you mean the lassies. I can't be helping you. We only just arrived."

"Shit, Herb, what ya hassling those kids for? The fat lady told us where to go. Remember? Some dump called Chantal's bar, where Chantal is supposed to reveal all to us poor, hungry sailors. Why don't we just do as she suggested?"

"OK, OK," said Herb. "I thought maybe these handsome young lads could fetch us some pussy without having to dive into some low-life bar!"

"Since when have you become allergic to lowlife, you prissy snake. Your brains are always dangling about six points south of your crotch. Let's just go to Chantal's, OK?"

New Jersey's flawless logic won the day, and ten minutes later the party of five was inching their way down the narrow stairs of Chantal's Nightclub.

Nightclub? Chantal's was no more than a dank cement room, with two lightbulbs, a rudimentary wood bar, and a clutch of tea chest tables with small wooden stools clustered around. A wheezy old cassette player provided the 'ambiance.'

Everyone ordered a beer and eagerly anticipated the antics of "Chantal." Chantal, however, apparently had other priorities that night.

Herb started to get restive. He called the barman over.

"Hey buddy, when do we get to see some pussy around here? We ain't got all darned night you know."

"Poosey? What is poosey? I don't understand."

"We want Chantal to show what she's got. Up here. I've been to sea for three months, and I need to see some boobs. Breasts. These..." And Herb, with round cup movements of his hands, did his best show what breasts were to the confused barman.

"Ahhhh, Monsieur. Le Strip Tease, oui??"

"Ja Ja, le Strip. You got it. Now go get it!"

Herb sat down pleased with his linguistic skills.

The barman slipped through the dirty red curtain separating the bar from whatever went on behind, and soon re-emerged triumphant.

"Chantal she say she come, OK?"

"No, no, you buffoon—it is *I* that wants to 'come'…not Chantal." Herb giggled to laughter all round.

"Chantal no come now?" The barman looked puzzled again.

"Oh go away, you nutter. Yes—we—want—Chantal…"

At that moment, the curtain swept aside and out strode Chantal stepping Arab-style with one foot in front of the other, ensuring that her ample hips swung their maximum.

"OK, who eese zee big mouth that wants to see Chantal's bijoux?"

"I'll own up to that. I have a mouth big enough to eat you right up…." blurted out Herb.

Chantal went straight over to the happy loud mouth, let loose the belt of her robe, grabbed the back of his head, pushed her arms together to narrow the cleavage, and then smashed his face deep into the valley.

Herb gasped, partly in shock, but more from the smothering effect of the softly aging breasts.

He wriggled free and tried to open his mouth to say something.

"Still 'ongry, Yankee sheet? Then try this." And Chantal forced his mouth over her right nipple. "Eat that, baby, and learn not to fook with French ladies."

Chantal then turned her attention to the boys.

"Where you from, kids?"

"We are from Scotland, Ma'am…!"

"L'Ecosse—j'adore les Ecossaises. I love the Scotch."

"Scots, Ma'am. 'Scotch' is a drink."

"You want Scotch? We have Scotch. Pierre le Johnny Black svp."

Adam was panicking now, knowing the retail value of a Johnny Walker Black label.

"No, no—I drink wine. Red and white."

"Sacre Bleu, Ils sont dificile. Pierre du vin rouge et du vin blanc svp. "

Pierre rushed out placing bottles left and right on the little tea chest table.

Chantal now turned sweetly to Herb, a big grin on her face.

"Drink zat up like good leetle boys and I come back and maybe I do zee strip, hokay?"

"Deal lady—you got a deal."

The Scots were not too sure, thinking more of their wallets than their hormonal needs. But the Yanks took the challenge seriously. Wine followed whisky followed wine and sooner than any reasonable person would think reasonable, the Americans started chanting for Chantal again.

Mangling the ageless little nursery song, New Jersey hummed hoarsely *"I love little pussy, it feels nice and warm, and if you don't hump it, a fool you are born."*

Chantal heard the song and reacted. She came. She stripped, she conquered. Within ten minutes she faced them as naked as the day she was born. Everyone cheered.

Calmly Chantal walked over to Herb and lowered herself—still naked—onto his lap. Hamish leant over to Adam's ear.

"I've got me a wee boner, and I can't get it down."

Before Adam could react, Chantal pointed to the two boys and said, "Scotland boys, I want you." The 'wee boner' disappeared as fast as it had risen.

"You speak Engleesh. I want my daughters to speak good Engleesh. You drink much. Pierre portez ma l'addition."

Pierre hastily finalized the bill and brought it over. Chantal grabbed it and held it aloft, thus ensuring her breasts showed off to their finest.

"I tear up bill if you teach my girls Engleesh, hokay?"

"Heh," yelped Herb. "I can do that. Whadda I get if I teach your girls English?"

Chantal ground her bottom a little harder into Herb's groin.

"You enjoy my ass and shaddap. I want my girls learn the King's Engleesh, not Yankee talk. OK boys, I gotta deal, or not?"

"Sure," said a much-relieved Adam, talking through his wallet again. Then come here tomorrow, eleven o'clock. No be late. You no come, I find you and I fuck you, hokay?"

Slowly Chantal got up, pulled hard on Herb's manhood, dropped him a kiss on the forehead, and returned to the red curtain swinging the robe loosely over her shoulders.

That night the boys slept off the booze on the beach and made sure they were ready in good time to make their rendezvous. A quick dip in the cold April Med cleaned them up as it woke them up, much to the amusement of many onlookers who were amazed to see anyone brave such frigid water. But then none of those onlookers were brought up on the banks of the freezing Lochs of Scotland.

At 10:58 a.m. both boys were in front of the little brown door of Chantal's Nightclub. At exactly 11:00 a.m. they rang. Then they knocked. And rang again. No response.

At eleven fifteen they heard a rising chorus of screaming female voices. A few seconds later, they saw Chantal round the corner literally dragging two young ladies behind her, one by each wrist.

"When I say you learn shit Engleesh, you learn shit Engleesh. Pas de discussion. Basta. Basta. Et Basta."

The chain gang reached the little brown door of the 'nightclub,' and Chantal let out a long, loud sigh.

"Zut—young girls like chiennes sauvages. Nutting but problemes…"

She searched for the key, but with one hand firmly clasped on each of the two girls' arms, that was also proving a "probleme."

"Here, you, take this sauvage and don't let her go…" Chantal hissed at Adam.

Adam held on but looked away trying to avoid the icy hatred in those young black eyes.

Door open, Chantal practically kicked the two girls down the stairs. Once back in the dank little cellar, she plopped the four down at a tea chest table, took a six-pack of Cokes out of the old fridge, straightened her back, and ordered:

"I lock door and come back at midi et demi. You Scotland boys speak good Engleesh. You stupid girls learn. Engleesh is the langue maternelle du future, hokay? Don't try run away—I lock door. Hokay?"

She stormed back up the stairs.

Once alone, stony silence descended.

Adam tried the universal icebreaker.

"Bonjour, I am Adam and this is Hamish. We are from Scotland."

No reaction.

"So what are your names then?"

Silence.

Now Hamish started to feel the hairs rising on the back of his head. Highlanders do not take kindly to deliberate discourtesy.

"YOU HEARD HIM, WHAT ARE YOUR NAMES? ANSWER…"

One head turned round a little apprehensively. After all, two young sisters were now locked in a damp basement with two unknown boys from some ungodly country where the men wore skirts.

"Je m' appel Merde, et elle s'appel Zizi!"

"That's better," snapped Hamish. "Listen, Mlles. Merde et Zizi, we are here for an hour or more, so let's make the best of it. Let's see how much you know. Merde, you start. Say something in English."

"Pig."

Hamish started a slow clap. "Bravo, bitch. Very funny."

He got out of his chair, grabbed his bottle of Coke, and placed his eyes about five centimeters from hers.

"We have been paid to teach you English, and I always do what I promise. Speak, or enjoy a Coke shower." And he placed the almost full bottle just above her beautiful, shiny black hair.

"No do that, pig."

"I do what I want. Speak some more, Merde. Where do you live?"

"Oink, oink."

The bottle poured over her head. Merde screamed and swore for a full twenty seconds in rich colloquial French.

"OK, OK, we speak. No more Coca." That was Zizi.

"Right, Zizi. Then let's start with you. Where do you live?"

The Coke started the flow in more ways than one. Adam formed a new admiration for his old friend. The lesson now started in earnest. The girls' English was rudimentary, but it was not hopeless. And they talked…

Midday Riviera time turned out to be more like 1:00 p.m. They heard Chantal turn the key, and then the noon sun poured in, blinding all four sets of eyes.

"Did they do good?" demanded Chantal.

"It took a little friendly persuasion to get things started, but after that we had a great talk. Merde here is a little more fluent than Zizi."

"Merde? Zizi? What you talking about?"

The girls burst into giggles. Chantal looked puzzled and then started to smile as well.

"You stoopid girls. This is Helene and this is Sophia. 'Merde' mean 'sheet,' and 'Zizi' mean…mean (she was searching for a word)…mean 'Dick'!"

Hamish looked stunned. He thought he'd won the war of wills, but Adam started to laugh with the girls.

"Well, Sophia sure is a better-looking Dick than Hamish here!"

That did it. They all dissolved into giggles. The match in the end was "match a nul" or equal. No one won. Or everyone won, however you wanted to see it.

Chantal was the first to recover.

"Well, at least you boys learnt two words of French! Now we go dejeuner my house."

The full French lunch of salad and lamb chops seemed to inspire Chantal. She announced she just had a brilliant idea.

"Scotland boys, you have no house here, so why you no sleep on balcony. You eat here. You talk to girls. They make good English. I make good French food like today. Hokay?"

Hamish looked at Adam, and Adam replied…

"Why not? Sounds great to us. We are not exactly flush for cash, so, yeah, that would suit us fine. Thank you very much."

Over the next few days, the boys saw the sights whilst the girls did their thing. In the evenings they would all go out together with the girls' gang of friends. Sometimes a dinner, sometimes just chatting in the café or on the harbor wall, or even occasionally at the disco.

Hamish, being the shier, would be the most out of it and most often on the sidelines. Helene would then find him and bring him back into the group. She was also the more eager of the two girls to learn English, as she fancied a career in pop singing.

Often the couple would head out on the beach in the late evening to talk. Hamish loved these moments, although he was not yet quite certain why.

One night, after sundown, it turned a little chilly and Helene felt cold.

"We'll head back, Helene, don't worry."

"No, no, Hameesh. I love to see the stars and all zat. Please let us stay."

"Take my sweater then…"

But even with the sweater on, Helene still huddled close—very close—to Hamish for warmth.

Hamish's annoying apparatus started to soufflé in his shorts again and Helene noticed.

"Hameesh, you like me a bit, no?"

Hamish was trying to think of an answer when he felt two soft lips land gently on his own.

"I like you too—a lot. You not stoopid like those silly French boys. I like you much, Hameesh."

This time the kiss was harder and longer. And sweeter.

Hamish had never, ever felt like this, and he was overwhelmed. He was in love.

Some days later, the girls had to go back to school in Marseille, and Adam decided it was time to move on. Tonight would be the big good-bye.

Hamish and Helene sat on the beach in their usual spot. Adam was in the port bar trying to follow some animated conversation.

A shooting star dropped out of the sky. Helene squealed with joy.

"Hameesh, a falling star means you will come back to me. I want you to come back to me. Promise you will come back for me?"

"I will, Helene, I will…"

And Helene gave him a new reason to remember her. A night full of love and tenderness. His very first time, in fact. Maybe hers too…

———◦◉◦———

The little tearoom was getting hot and stuffy as Hamish finished his tale. A little tear welled up in each eye.

Lady L sat still and quiet. The story had moved her greatly.

"So, Hamish, tell me—you never went back for Helene?"

"No, Madam. I never did. I never did…"

"Why Hamish? Why ever not?"

"I guess I couldn't really believe it. It seemed like a film. It ends and you go back to reality. It was the stupidest decision of my entire life. Now it's too late…too damn late…"

Lady L paid the bill, and they left in silence. Not a word was exchanged on the short, rainy trip back to her house.

Hamish saw her to the door, returned to his car, and wept. And wept. All the way back. Twenty-four years of sorrow and anguish finally finding an exit in those eight long, winding miles to his empty home in Killin…

Empty because his wife had left three days earlier to visit their daughter and her newborn grandson in Australia? Or empty because Hamish felt his life was empty, wasted—with or without his wife.

And that seemed to him doubly sad.

CHAPTER 4

THE ROAD TO MONACO – PART 1

Natasha had just turned seven and was doing well at school. Paz rented out the house on the river she had shared with Peter Palmer and took a lease on a little condo nearer Natasha's school and Pedro's Mexican Restaurant, the same eatery where she had entertained her friends and family for her late husband's funeral.

Pedro, the owner, was suffering from colon cancer and was unlikely to be able to run the café again even if he recovered, which was probably doubtful. So soon the management fell almost entirely to Paz, which she found both absorbing and fulfilling.

She thought of herself as relatively well-off and happy, even though the lonely nights disturbed a still young and beautiful Mexican-American. On those long evenings, she would relive the two nights of passion she had shared with Vladimir. She regretted not one moment of her marriage, nor was she imagining a longer relationship with this strange and scary Russian.

But he had been the only man to ever bring her to total fulfilment. She did not understand why, nor did she care. Thinking of him just shortened the dark hours between sundown and sunrise. And that was all.

Therefore, the late-night phone call came as a complete shock. No one ever rang at 12:30 a.m. The phone scared her; off-hour calls in her well-ordered life usually meant bad news. She was shaking as she answered.

"Hi, it's Vladimir. Sorry if it's a bad time, but I had to talk to you. How late is it there now?"

"Vladimir? It's after midnight. Where are you?"

Paz didn't want to prolong the call as she predicted Vladimir might sooner or later disturb her presently ordered existence.

"Paz, I am in Monaco. No, No, not **Mexico**. *Monaco.* On the French Riviera. Don't know it? What about Monte Carlo—have you heard of that?"

Yes, Monte Carlo rang a bell somewhere in Paz's subconscious.

"What are you doing there?"

"Paz, it's a long story. I don't have the time now. I have a wonderful opportunity for you here. Can you pop over and see us? We'll pay."

"Us? Who's us, Vladimir?" Paz was surprised at her own reaction to the collective preposition. Was she jealous?

"Me and my boss. He's a Russian millionaire—maybe even a billionaire. He's great—made a huge difference to my life. Paz, you must pop over and see us."

"Vladimir, I have a life here. There is Natasha's school, and I run that little Mexican restaurant now, you know. I can't just drop everything and 'pop' anywhere. You are crazy."

"Paz...I know you run a restaurant. I have been following your life. I have already made arrangements at the International School here for your daughter. It's all set..."

"Vladimir, slow down. What do you mean you have been following my life? Why are you talking about Natasha and a new school? How dare you? Stop it this instant."

Vladimir cut her off.

"Paz, I miss you. I need you. I know now that I can't live a full life without you. I know I have no right to order you around, but I can't help it. I think of you—of us—every night. Please, Paz, just come…come and see. If you don't like it, you can go home and I'll never bother you again. I will think of you. I will love you. Forever. But I will never contact you again, I promise. Paz? Paz, are you still there?"

Paz was softly crying. She knew she shouldn't say yes, but she felt unable to say no. What was it about this man that so affected her?

She hung up as Natasha entered the bedroom.

"What's wrong, Mama? Was that call bad news?"

"No, darling. Not bad news. At least I don't think so. Go back to bed."

"Then why are you crying, Mum?"

"I don't know, Natasha. I just don't know. Please leave me now…"

CHAPTER 5

THE ROAD TO MONACO – PART 2

Hamish put down his phone just a few hours after Paz hung up on Vladimir. And he was just as shocked.

It was his wife on the line. All the way from Australia. The message was short, simple, and brutal. She was not coming home. At least not for a long time. She loved the freedom of Australia and adored her grandchild.

Possibly she was expecting Hamish to beg her to come back, but he said little.

"Whatever makes you happy, dear. Let us know what you finally decide to do…Jumbo (the dog) and I will miss you. Give my love to Mary and the baby. You all right for money? OK, then, hear from you soon. Let me know your plans."

He sat down by the coal fire, the dog's chin on his knee. He was quite still for a while, then got up, grabbed his coat, and took the dog down to the pub. He wanted to tell someone about his wife and the call, but it suddenly dawned on him that he had no really close friends in that little hamlet to confide in.

So, he had a few beers, watched the football match on TV, and strolled sadly back home.

Walking through the door, he saw the red light of the answering machine flashing. Stupid him—he had forgotten to take his cell with him. Good taxi chauffeurs never stay out of contact.

He listened carefully. It was Lady Lothmere. Please call back before midnight. It was only eleven thirty-five, so he dialed the familiar number.

"Hello, Lady Lothmere? Hamish Macintosh here….Of course. Ten in the morning sharp. And where would we be going? To Rolls Royce Edinburgh? No, Lady, I have no idea where their dealership is. But I'll check the Internet. No, no, it's not a problem…I have no fares booked for the morrow. Good night, Lady L."

In the shower, Hamish wondered why the Lady wanted to visit Rolls Royce. She couldn't be planning to buy a Rolls, could she? She was not even able to drive anymore…

It was a funny thing, but whenever Lady Hermoine L was involved with Hamish, life became a lot more fun and unpredictable. He was looking forward to the new day. Australia and his errant wife were already all but forgotten.

———◆———

"Aach, Hamish, come in and have a coffee. The pot is still hot. I'll be with you in a minute."

He sat down at the rickety wooden kitchen table and poured himself a rich continental brew the Lady loved so much. Looking up to check if the Lady was still finishing her makeup in the bathroom, he carefully watered down the almost black drink until it became a more light brown—a more Scottish idea of what a coffee should be!

A few minutes later the Lady reappeared rouged and lipsticked as Hamish had never seen her before and sporting an Austrian-style tweed fedora with a large and out-of-control pheasant feather. Hamish had to swallow hard not to grin.

"Ready, Lad? Then off we go. Did ye get the address of that dealer, Hamish?"

"Yes, Lady L—that I did."

They both entered Hamish's cab, and he started off down the road to Aberfeldy. She didn't say much until they hit the main A9 road.

"Aren't you going to ask me why I want to see Rolls Royce?"

"Must admit, Ma'am, I was a little curious."

"Then ask. What is the matter with you, lad? Open up. Well, I will tell you the truth, but if you tell anyone—especially that old gossip Thompson at Polly's—then I'll kill ye. Never forget that young man!"

Hamish laughed.

Well the "truth" turned out to be that Lady L had just had a visit from her accountant and he had warned her very seriously that expenditure was flowing out far faster than income was flowing in. If she planned to reach ninety, she would be flat, stony broke.

The dour finance man had suggested a large dose of true Scottish frugality. That, of course, was totally unacceptable to her. What other ideas did he have?

"Realize your assets, my Lady."

"Meaning?"

"Sell something."

"Like what and to whom?"

"Like that Rolls in the garage, my Lady."

"The Rolls? Are you mad? That was my late husband's last big purchase before he died. He loved that silly old car. Why would I sell the Rolls?"

"Because its value is declining 10 percent a year, and it is just sitting there. Waste of money. He spent £150,000 on that thing—maybe more. Use that money."

So that was why, she explained to Hamish, they were off to interview the nearest Rolls Royce agent. Madam planned to raise some equity, just as the accountant had suggested. And wasn't that clever?

Hamish laughed again. He had no idea that dark old house was hiding a Rolls.

"What model is it Ma'am?"

"A 1996 Silver Dawn. He bought it off some Dutchman hunter with a castle up north. How much do you think we'll get for it?"

"No idea, Ma'am. I really have not the slightest idea! Let's see what they say in Edinburgh."

The news from the dealer was not good. Vintage Rolls' were in demand, as were nearly-new ones, relatively speaking. But models ten years old or so had little value. Rich people bought new or classic. And those who normally bought old cars could not afford the repair bills or fuel consumption of the supposedly "best car in the world." At a push, to help them out, etc. etc., the dealer would offer about £22,000 subject to his scrutiny of the vehicle.

Lady L was not amused. She walked out of the dealership vowing never to buy a Rolls again. The dealer was not overly worried. Old dowagers were not a prime target market for him.

Hamish asked the dealer if he could leave his taxi on his showroom forecourt and walked the Lady down to the Dark Swan for a light lunch. The dealer just shrugged. Hamish took that to mean 'yes'.

They said little as they enjoyed a ploughman's plate each. Over coffee, Lady L seemed to brighten up a bit.

"Hamish, you are a man. You have that Internet thingy, right? Find out for me where the best place is to sell a Rolls. I need the money."

That night Hamish spent four hours Googling Rolls Royce sellers and buyers everywhere. There was no doubt Florida, California, and Monaco were the best opportunities. But those were all left-hand drive markets.

Hamish rang her up. He explained that the best markets were in the USA and on the Riviera. But they all drove on the right.

"So what?" asked the Lady.

"They would want a left-hand-drive car, my Lady."

"I told you, we bought that thing off a Dutchman. What side of the road do they drive on in Holland, Hamish, my genius?"

"The right, my lady, the right."

Lady L was exultant. "The right? The right! Hah hah! That's it. Off we go to Monaco—wherever that is. Can you drive me there, Hamish?"

"What did you say, Lady?"

"Can you drive me there? To Monaco. Soon. That would be fun."

"Drive you there? In the taxi, Ma'am?"

"Of course not, dummy. In the Rolls. We'll sell it in Monaco. Come round tomorrow and we'll discuss it. What fun. I can't wait!"

Hamish put down his phone grinning. If only he could see life more like the dowager. If only…

To Monaco? Impossible, of course. He had commitments.

Commitments, he asked himself? What commitments? His wife seemed to have technically left him. Business was slow this time of the year.

He had absolutely no commitments.

CHAPTER 6

PAZ TAKES A PLANE

Paz watched the Riviera coast glide past as the Delta airliner from New York made its final approach to Nice's compact but bustling little airport.

Natasha was still asleep next to her. Even pushing her seat back and fastening the seat belt had not fully awakened the little girl.

Now that churning feeling in her stomach returned once again. What was she doing on a plane to Europe, going to see man she hardly knew about a job she didn't understand, in a part of the world she knew nothing about? And where they neither spoke English or Spanish?

And yet, Vladimir would not leave her alone. He had called at least five more times and with ever greater insistency. She had felt her good sense slowly erode as the excitement of a new adventure mixed with an intense desire to see her occasional lover at least one more time.

Natasha had resisted. She did not want to miss school and her buddies. Plus, there was something about her memory of the gaunt Russian that alarmed her.

Despite all that, here they were. Five minutes from landing on the famous Cote d'Azur—playground of the rich and famous.

The pilot apologized for the bumpy landing (the ever-present Mistral Winds to blame) and then taxied swiftly to the far gate of Terminal Two.

She found her suitcase, nodded to the bored customs man, walked briskly through the self-opening doors—and there he was. Bronzed, happy, and handsome in a loose-fitting white shirt and khaki shorts over simple Riviera sandals. A gold chain dangled on his chest.

Paz gasped. Natasha stepped back. But Vladimir bounded forward and hugged the two as tightly as he dared.

"Paz. Natasha. So good you are here. So, so good. Was the trip OK? Did you enjoy business class? I told you my friends are rich, rich, rich."

Later, in the grey Porsche Cayenne SUV, Vladimir decided to take the coast road to Monaco. He pointed out the Promenade des Anglais in Nice, the cruise ships in Ville Franche (the Riviera's deepest harbor), the old walled city of Eze, and finally the Palace in Monaco, perched majestically on its impregnable rock.

Then they turned right and took the tunnel to Fontvieille, the newest part of the principality and mostly reclaimed from the sea.

"I have this apartment in the Monte Marina. It belongs to my boss, but he moved to a studio in Avenue Princesse Grace as he could not stand the noise of the helicopters just in front. It doesn't bother me—the view is great. The racket is manageable if you keep the windows closed."

He showed her to their room, watched her unpack, and then took her down for a coffee at the Casa del Gelato, a favorite coffee meeting place for the yachtsmen and workers of Fontvieille Harbor.

Paz told Natasha to go look for fish in the harbor water or examine the yachts and then turned to Vladimir with all the seriousness her jet-lagged brain could muster.

"All right, Vladimir—we're here. Now talk. What is this all about? The full story and no bullshit, OK?"

Vladimir finished his cappuccino, put down the croissant, sighed contentedly, and told his story.

After he had been thrown out of Mexico and his job at the Russian Embassy by the Mexico City police, he was sent to Chechnya—part in punishment for the Mexican fiasco and part to utilize his excellent analytical skills. The Kremlin desperately needed avenues into the rebel mind to try and anticipate the "terrorists'" next moves. Yeltsin's "war" was not going well. Russia had lost the battle in Afghanistan and could not afford to look weak again—especially in its own backyard.

Vladimir, divorced, with no family and no other commitments, had thrown all his energies into the job. In a reverse Mata Hari scenario, he had used his good looks to befriend and seduce some of the girls he knew had connections with the rebel leaders.

One Ukrainian girl in particular known as "Olga the Hair" for her long blondish locks, was deeply in love with him. Olga (that was not her real name—no one used their given names) was also sleeping occasionally with the leader of a smallish but still dangerous independent cell. She regarded sharing her attributes with key rebels as doing her bit to free the province of the perceived Russian yoke.

"A happy rebel is an effective rebel," she would laugh, and after a session with the leader, she would slap him on the bare shoulder and hiss, "I did my best for you; now you go out and kill them for me!"

Vladimir was not sure Olga had the slightest idea of what the rebels stood for, what they were doing, or why. She seemed to see it all as a wild game and be glad to be part of something heroic and historic, even if its aims were foggy to her.

A rebel "groupie," Vladimir said to himself.

Slowly Vladimir let Olga understand his sympathy for the rebels' aims and how he admired her for her participation. Olga lapped it up. Her ample chest would swell with pride, and she would happily tell him everything about her associations with her own Chechen rebel's darker side, but, of course, at that stage she had little to tell. The rebels may have been lusty, but they were not stupid. They revealed little to those with no need to know.

Vladimir bided his time. He led Olga to believe he was a wealthy landowner with holdings in Mexico and would soon head back. From his previous three years working in the embassy there, he could actively describe the delights of that beautiful land. Olga would rest her chin on his chest after sex, listening avidly and dreaming hopefully of one day being the wife of rich ranchero, having Mexican servants running to fulfil her every whim.

It never entered Olga's dim brain to wonder why a rich Mexican land-owner was spending days in Chechnya at that hazardous time or even to ask Vladimir's nationality or job. Of course, Vladimir had his cover story ready, but, in fact, he never needed to use it.

Some weeks later, Vladimir had the break he was looking for. During a relative lull in terrorist attacks, Muscovite entrepreneurs, floating in oil money and usually friends of Boris Yeltsin, made swift trips to Grozny (the Chechen capital), to see what they could buy up cheap.

The rebels did not want more Russian interference in their affairs, whether political or financial. They planned to lure one of these Moscow millionaires into a trap, kidnap him, and ask a formidable ransom.

The motive was dual: The money would buy more badly needed weapons from Pakistan. The kidnapping would keep other oil-rich Russians at home, especially if there was a brutal killing after collecting the money.

Olga-the-hair would be the bait. What rich oligarch could resist that chest and those golden curls? She told Vladimir, bursting with pride, that she had now been promoted to helping her country, even though HER country (the Ukraine) was hundreds of miles away.

To cut a long story short, one overconfident millionaire arrived a few weeks later interested in buying a block of only slightly damaged apartments. The estate agent tipped-off the rebels, and Olga's cell was briefed to act.

The plan was to have poor Olga sitting on the stoop of the building as the Russian arrived, in tattered (but revealing) clothes, gently crying. Of course, the Russian would stop and ask what the problem was (and he did!) even though the estate agent (a good actress) advised him repeatedly to be careful.

"She's only a poor girl who has lost her home and her family in this terrible war. What danger can she possibly be?" the Russian replied. "No one in this town knows who I am or why I am here."

Of course the estate agent knew. She was a plant. The real agent who had initially tipped off the rebels that a fat-cat Muscovite would be visiting a prospective building had suddenly disappeared!

"Disappeared" because Vladimir also knew what was happening. Last night Olga, swollen with false nationalistic pride, let out enough details to allow him to fill in the dots and arrange the estate agent swap. And "swap" in good Russian KGB code meant the original agent was probably floating facedown in some Grozny canal, whilst Vladimir's trained actress-agent took her place. The Muscovite did not seem to mind or show the slightest sense of suspicion.

Olga started to whine again…

"Please, sir, will you come see my apartment and tell me if it can be repaired? I have nowhere to live. The apartment is just down the road."

Any caution the Russian might have harbored in this essentially hostile environment was rapidly being dissolved by his raging hormones. He was already dreaming of taking this gorgeous orphan-girl back to Moscow to inhabit one of his luxury studios—rent free, of course, for which Olga would obviously show warm and active gratitude!

Olga took him by the hand. The 'replacement' estate agent pretended to look to the heavens in exasperation, and the little party moved off. The agent's cell phone rang.

She dropped back to take the call, telling the Russian she was finalizing other appointments for later that day.

As Olga and the Russian rounded the corner, the girl pointed to a semi-bombed-out building about halfway down the block.

"That's where my family lived. That's where they died. I am all alone!"

The pointing finger was the signal the six terrorists were waiting for. Olga had connected with her target. They whispered among themselves, the leaders finalizing the plan prepared the evening before.

It was not complicated. As the couple would enter the abandoned building, the man reading the newspaper across the road would cross over and walk behind them to block their escape. Two men would then jump the Russian, knock him out, and drag him to the waiting car on the other, rear side of the building. Olga would be pushed out of harm's way.

But things did not quite happen that way. Newspaper man had no sooner lowered his paper than an arm surrounded his neck cutting off sound and breath. He slumped to the ground.

From the left and the right, agents grabbed the stupid Russian and hustled him into a van, which suddenly appeared from nowhere, screeched to a halt, and then screamed off again. The two rebel operatives at the door were instantly silenced.

From the back door, two other KGB agents rushed in and opened fire, instantly killing the four other terrorists waiting inside.

Another agent shot the astonished getaway driver in the temple.

Within twenty seconds, only Olga—deep in shock—was still standing alive.

"What do we do with her?" asked one agent.

Vladimir raised his helmet and stared at her icily. Olga gasped as she slowly began to understand what had happened.

"Kill her. No one must compromise me or the estate agent."

One more shot rang out, the noise ricocheting around the empty cement walls.

She said not one more word. Blood slowly reddened that glorious golden hair that was her best feature—and a contributing cause of her untimely death.

They threw her body in the back of another van and drove off. The whole operation had taken less than ninety seconds. Vladimir was pleased.

The Russian entrepreneur was less pleased. It took him a long time to realize that it was not Chechen nationalists that had grabbed him but an elite anti-terrorist gang of the KGB—a group led to their latest killing by the KGB operative, Vladimir Koschenko.

As for Vladimir, he thanked the team, walked back to his car parked a few meters away, and drove immediately back to the KGB station where he knew the Russian would be held. He entered the interview room and closed the door. They were alone.

"You are a very stupid man, Mr. Sverdlov. Stupid to come here. Stupid not to check more carefully your contacts. Stupid to go around this town alone. And incredibly stupid to let your dick overrule your common sense. What wealthy idiot follows a pretty young girl into an empty building in this dangerous town? Don't you read the newspapers?

"Lucky for you, we were anticipating the kidnapping …."

"Kidnapping?" gasped the still shaking Sverdlov.

"Yes, kidnapping. Your ransom would have bought guns and bombs to kill more Russians. Your violent death, probably videotaped, would have discouraged others from investing in this hellhole. Now listen to me and listen well…

"You will be taken to the airport and flown back to Moscow this evening on an air force flight. You will forget your visit here. You will forget this incident. You will mention it to no one—no one. Do you understand? **No one.** Do I need to spell out to you how short your future will be if you forget what I am telling you? Death or at least Siberia—and all your millions of rubles will be of no help to you there, believe me…"

His voice trailed off. Vladimir suddenly felt tired and sick. As the adrenaline surge weakened, the image of that silly little blond-haired beauty bleeding to death was starting to kick in—a silly little beauty who had nevertheless shared his bed at least twenty times or more.

As Vladimir was starting to lose his composure, Sverdlov began to regain his.

"You knew this was going to happen, didn't you? Why didn't you warn me?"

"What, and compromise our mock real estate agent? Our objective was not primarily to save you—because what you did was beyond lunacy. It was more to rid this town and this country of a few more terrorists. Saving your sorry ass was a happy by-product—for you!"

"May I know your name?"

"Sorry—no! I have more work to do. Good luck, sir. And remember my warning. This incident never happened, right?"

"Right, I got it, sir. Here, take my card. If ever you need assistance, give me a call. It is the least I can do."

"Thank you." Vladimir pocketed the card without looking at it. He wanted—no, he needed—an ice-cold vodka, or two…

～◦◉◦～

Paz shuddered as Vladimir paused.

"God—that poor girl. Why did you have to kill her? Couldn't you just have deported her somewhere?"

43

"Maybe, but I could not take the risk…Chechnya is a very porous and very dangerous place."

"OK, but what has all that got to do with you here in Monaco?"

Vladimir finished his coffee and was about to continue his narrative when Natasha reentered the little coffee house.

"Mum, I'm tired. Can I have a sleep?"

"I guess she is jet-lagged. Maybe you are too, Paz? Perhaps it would be a good idea to have a nap and later, after dinner, I can fill in the last details?"

Paz agreed, rather happy to take a break from the increasingly creepy tales of the old Soviet Union.

CHAPTER 7

THE ART MAN OF MONTE CARLO

Mickey Prentice rubbed his sore knee and sighed deeply. In the damp April shower season, his artificial joint could act up a bit. He needed to take off those kilos his doctors kept nagging him about.

But then all those fine restaurants of Monte Carlo needed his custom—of that he was sure.

He looked at his salesroom hostess and smiled. They'd been together for fifteen years, and still he fancied those legs. In fact Mickey fancied most legs, as long as they were female and attached to a well-rounded body. That was one of the benefits of having his gallery in "downtown" Monte Carlo. Some of the most elegant ladies of Europe strode past the shop window or wandered in to take a browse and pretend they knew a little about art.

But recently sales had been rather poor. Since the new financial year, which for him started on March 1st, he'd only sold two pictures. (Always "*pictures*" to him, never "*paintings*"). A dry sales spell happened regularly in Monte Carlo. For no apparent reason, the tourists stayed away—sometimes for weeks. They always came back, but right now he was feeling a little strapped for cash, having just bid for and won three Jean Renoirs at auction.

Renoirs always sold well in this center of the "nouveau riche." The artist was well-known, a French artist to appeal to the Francophiles, and not too pricey. The flowery style also matched the needs of the many Monegasque decorators and "stylists" advising (and ripping off) the rich.

At age seventy, Mickey had been reluctant to start a website, but his young daughter had bullied him to try. It had been up a week and nothing.

He knew it. You sold art face-to-face or on the phone. How can a cold, impersonal computer describe the magic of a famous picture?

Sandy, the "hostess," let out a shriek.

"Mickey, we've got a bite on the site! This fellow in Tokyo is interested in the Renoirs."

"Which ones, Sandy?"

"Apparently all of them! He wants a reply. Shall I call him? He left his phone number."

"What time is it in Tokyo now?"

"About ten o'clock at night, I think."

"OK, call him." And Mickey Prentice dragged his sore knee from under the chair and into his little office at the rear of the gallery.

Twenty minutes later Prentice reappeared from his office-den, a silly grin on his face.

"Shit, Sandy, that Jappy fellow thinks I am an expert on Renoir and wants me to make him an offer on all three. Plus, he wants another two."

"Another two? Which two?"

"Any two. Apparently he is the chairman of Nagasaki Wall Coverings, and many of his top lines use Renoir-esque designs, which are all the rage in uptown Tokyo. So he wants some originals to run a sort of city-by-city mobile museum to support his main retail sites across Japan."

"Five Renoirs? That could total well over three million euros, Monsieur Mick!"

"I know, I know…I can feel that money already. Sandy, can you remember who's selling Renoirs these days?"

Sore knee forgotten, the art salesman swung into action. He called dealer friends he could trust in London, Paris, and Munich. He rang the auction houses. He contacted some museum agents.

Nothing seemed immediately available, and the Japanese industrialist wanted a quick reply.

"The only solution, Sandy, is to call the owners one by one. Get out the Art International list, will you? You take A to K, and I'll do L through Z.

Thus, it was that Mickey's first call found Lady Lothmere in Kenmore, Scotland.

"Is that Lady Lothmere? This is Mickey Prentice of the Galleria International. Do you have a minute?"

Lady Lothmere had a minute—even an hour. Not that many people called an old lady in the wilds of Scotland these days.

"Lady Lothmere, you are listed as owning a Jean Renoir. Is that right?"

"Why would you want to know?" she replied a little warily. She never knew if some ambitious robber was not checking her out.

"Because I have a client who wants a Renoir desperately. And you are listed as owning the so called *Three Flowers in May* picture. Am I correct?"

"So why should that interest me, young man?"

Mickey smiled. "*Young man!*" He still had the magic touch. Even with old dowagers!

"Because if you were interested in selling, now would be a very good time."

"Mr. Prender…"

"Prentice, Lady…Prentice!"

"Sorry…Mr. Prentice, I might be interested if the Rolls doesn't sell. I am about to embark on a trip to find that out. When I return, I will call you. That will be in about three weeks. Would that be acceptable?"

"No, Madam. My client needs a Renoir immediately."

Lady L sighed. She hated being hassled, especially as Hamish was coming around later that morning to finalize their trip.

"I don't know. Maybe we can pass by London on our way to Europe. In a few hours my chauffeur…"

"Madam, we are not in London. Don't talk to those London Dealers *please*. This is a very confidential deal." No way did Prentice want some West End art-shark to muscle in on his deal-of-the-decade.

"Then where are you, Mr. Prendick?"

"I am in Monte Carlo, Monaco, my lady. And please – it is PRENTICE!"

Monaco? Lady L gasped. She had always been a little superstitious. This had to be a sign.

"Lady Lothmere, are you still there?"

"I am indeed, Mr. Prent-ice (she exaggerated the last syllable). Would it be all right if we met next week? In Monte Carlo? I will have the Renoir with me. Is that all right with you?"

My God, thought Mickey Prentice, could this really be happening to me?

"Lady L, did I hear you correctly? You plan to deliver the Renoir to me here in Monaco? Next week?"

"Correct, laddie. Now give me your address. I think we will be there Tuesday."

"But, dear lady, we haven't even discussed the price!"

"If you dare to cheat an old lady your soul will rot in hell, Mr. Prent-ice. You would hate that to happen, now wouldn't you?"

Mickey laughed, happily gave her the details she needed and said goodbye. He slowly put down the phone and scratched his balding head. Then he jumped up for joy and slumped back on his chair seconds later.

"Owwwwwww, my leg. My knee…Shit, shit, shit."

Sandy ran over to help him, as usual.

Lady Lothmere also jumped for joy. Life was such fun. No matter how happy you were, there was always something happening to make you even happier.

Thank goodness she was a Solomon Grundy, who, like her, was born on a very lucky Sunday.

Then she heard the old taxi crunching up the drive.

She ran—well, at her age it was probably more like a brisk walk—to the door and couldn't wait to tell Hamish the good news.

Hamish came inside with a pad and paper. He sat down very business-like and started to go through his list.

Lady L heard him out politely but with rising impatience.

1. When would they leave? *As soon as possible.*
2. Where would they stay on the way and in Monte Carlo? *The travel agency would ring back that afternoon.*
3. How would they cross the channel? *By ferry, of course. Who needs a dreary tunnel?*
4. How would he know if the Rolls was roadworthy? *Josh at Aberfeldy Motors took it out weekly for a run and she had already called him. Everything seemed fine.*
5. How would Hamish be paid? *£250 a day plus expenses.*
6. How did she come to that figure, he wondered. *Hamish, I don't know. What do you suggest? Don't be so darn boring…*
7. Actually, £250 sounded OK… *Then put away your silly list and listen to me. Something really exciting happened today.*

Hamish listened intensely as Lady L told him about her phone call.

"Can we make Monte Carlo by Tuesday, Hamish?"

"Yes, Ma'am. But a Renoir is worth a lot of money, isn't it?"

"I hope so!"

"Then isn't that dangerous? Does it fit in the boot (trunk in American)? What will we do when we overnight?"

"Hamish, I am not dim-witted. Yes, it fits easily in the boot. At overnight stops I'll keep it my room. Do you think some dopey French hotel maid knows a Renoir when she sees it? Oh, do grow up. You are such a wet blanket. Don't you see? It's a sign. We are *destined* to go to Monaco. I am so happy!"

Hamish asked to see the Rolls, took it for a short drive, and gave it the sort of good look-through a smart taxi driver gives his own cab at the start of each day. When he got around to checking the tire pressure in the spare, he jumped. No spare. *No spare?* How could you drive one thousand miles without a spare?

Hamish ran back into the house.

"Lady L, where is the spare wheel? We can't drive all that way without it. What if we got a puncture?"

"Hamish, my husband bought those expensive run-flat things, and I think you'll find an emergency puncture kit behind the boot partition. Have a look. We used to keep the spare tire well for hiding valuables en route—you got to be careful when you go into towns with a car like a Rolls, you know."

Hamish found the puncture kit and relaxed a little. He was still a little uneasy, but then his taxi also had the run-flats, and he had never had a problem. So he put aside his misgivings, returned the Rolls to its garage, and drove moodily home.

To say Hamish was confused would be an understatement. Hamish was in panic. This was happening all too quickly. He had to think…

Lady L had read his mind.

"Stop thinking, Hamish" had been her parting words. "Be ready to leave Friday (this was Wednesday). We have to be in Monte Carlo on Tuesday, remember?"

Easy for her to say. Hamish had to worry a bit first; that was just his nature.

CHAPTER 8

VLADIMIR COMPLETES HIS STORY

With Natasha now safely asleep in her new bed, Paz turned wearily back to Vladimir.

"OK, you killed the girl. I suppose I'll just have to take your word for it that it was necessary. But I find it hard to accept…" her voice tailed off.

"Paz, it is hard for us all to accept. But sometimes taking the tough decision turns out to be the right decision."

"Well, anyway…how did all that lead you here?"

"As I just told you, the Chechnya brutality became hard—even for me—to accept, and as soon as I could, I resigned and headed back to Moscow. Resigning was not a recommended thing to do as I knew too much. But I had a medical alibi. To ingratiate myself with another cell, I pretended to have access to Afghan heroin, which the cell could trade for weapons. The army supplied the drugs, and being around the drugs so much, I was tempted to try. It sorted of eased the danger and the tension somewhat. I became more or less addicted. Drug dependents are dangerous. Unreliable. Vulnerable. So they let me go as soon as it was convenient…"

Vladimir stopped as he saw the horror on Paz's face.

"Don't worry, I never got in that deep, and they soon cleaned me up. Haven't touched a needle in months and months. Can't afford to anyway…"

Her eyes shot to his bare arms searching for telltale needle marks. "I hate drugs," said a small voice from a visibly uncomfortable Paz.

Vladimir saw her search his skin and held out his arms for inspection.

"See, not a mark! So, there I was in Moscow, a reformed druggy, an ex-anti-terrorist hit man, and dead broke. Then I remembered that card the stupid Moscow businessman gave me after the attempted kidnapping. I called him up. He welcomed me with open arms and was just too happy to help. As one of the Yeltsin boys, he had made millions off oil trading and, like many of his friends, started enjoying the French Riviera. He bought a boat and asked me to live aboard and look after it. It's just over those buildings there, in Fontvieille Harbor. I'll show you tomorrow."

Paz looked up sadly. This trip was not turning out as she expected. But then what was it exactly that she had expected? She did not know.

"He then bought this apartment but found it too noisy with the helicopters taking off just below us every twenty minutes. So he found another place—a pad on Larvotto Beach and left me to use this. Amazing—it's probably worth over eight million euros. Real estate prices here are insane! But no one wants to buy it because of those helicopters, so lucky me!"

"That is all you do? Look after a boat and an overpriced apartment?"

"No, Sverdlov (that's his name) has started investing in property all over the damn place. He has a building in Beausoleil just above Monaco where he plans to train Ukrainian boxers and stage fights down here. Crazy, but then these oil-babies are all crazy—crazy and drunk. Drunk with money and drunk with vodka. And you should see those gold diggers hanging on!"

"Gold diggers?" quizzed Paz.

"Yeah—Russian girls looking for the easy life. They'll screw an eighty-year-old paraplegic if they can get a Louis Vuitton bag out of it!"

"Vladimir, language, please…And now, how do I fit into this cozy millionaire's picture?"

"Sverdlov wanted to open a Russian restaurant, but I talked him out of it. These Monegasque cats hate Russian food—at least what they think is Russian. Only pasta and pizza Italian restaurants seem to work here. But there are scores of those.

"Then I remembered you—in fact, Paz, I never actually forgot you, but that's another story. Mexican food is gaining popularity in France, and there is only one restaurant in the region. In my opinion, it is poor—very poor! If you've ever been to Mexico, you'd know that instantly."

Paz took more interest now.

"I told Sverdlov I knew a fabulous Mexican restaurateur and suggested we let her rip, and he said, 'OK, let's do it!' It was as simple as that. The guy really trusts me. That's why I called you. I want you to open the greatest Mexican eatery from Menton to Cannes! Can you do it? Will you do it? I'll help you. Monaco bureaucracy can be really complicated. But Sverdlov has a great team of lawyers. We already have a possible site just a few meters up the harbor. I think it would be ideal. I'll show you tomorrow; I hold a two-week option. That was the urgency to get you here. If you like the place, we can get the restaurant going, and you can live here—in this apartment!"

"With you?"

"I hope so…I really hope so. But take your time. I can always return to the boat. It's forty-three meters long, for goodness' sake, with every modern convenience!"

"But Natasha…"

"I told you on the phone, she is already enrolled in the International School here. That was the most difficult task of all. There are literally hundreds of kids on the waiting list. But Sverdlov has done charity work for them, so in the end we got you a place."

Now Paz became really agitated.

"You drag me over here, expect me to open a restaurant where I know no one, speak not one word of French, disturb my life, and, above all, you have the cheek to assume I'll agree? And then you even force a school to take Natasha? Vladimir, you are something. You really are something!"

"I hope so!" and he smiled that crooked, sensual smile she had dreamt about so often.

Paz slapped her thighs in irritation, turned her back on her escort, and bade him an irritated good night.

Vladimir smiled again. He was pretty sure he had the fish on the hook. Now all he needed to do was land it. He settled down on the sofa to sleep and smiled that satisfied grin again, even as his eyes eased shut.

CHAPTER 9

ROLLING INTO MONTE

The drive down from Calais had been uneventful. The Rolls just kept on rolling, and the Old Lady dozed happily in the back. Hamish had expected her to talk more—he had even dreaded the thought. Hamish was not the world's most gifted conversationalist, and he feared he might run out of material even before they crossed the English border.

But, luckily for him, the lady had been locked in her thoughts. For all her teasing of Hamish and his set ways, the truth was that Lady Lothmere had not been "abroad" for some time. Not since her husband had died. She was, in fact, just a little more apprehensive than she pretended and at the same time nostalgic. Those trips to "the continent" with her now deceased life partner had been the highlight of her married life. On these adventures he tended to forget his business interests and started to remember her again. She had liked that.

Hamish kept suggesting she share the front seat with him; he felt a little silly driving through France with a passenger in the back. Not only that, but the necessity of devoting the boot (trunk) to the carefully packed Renoir had forced them to utilize one rear seat for the luggage.

At their dinner stops, her happier personality regained control. On the second evening, she stopped talking, looked him straight in the eyes, and whispered intensely, "Hamish, you're going to look for that girl aren't you? The one you tried to teach English? Won't be that hard to find—she'll be the only French girl speaking with a filthy Highland lilt!"

"Ach, Lady, she'll be well into her middle age now and probably drooping all over…"

"Hamish, older women do not 'droop'—they simply mature. And never you forget it!"

Hamish went red as a London bus.

"Oh so sorry, me Lady. I did'na mean no harm…"

"Away with ye, Laddie—I was only pulling yer wee leg!" But the Lady did not sound all that convincing. She firmly believed that even if she might not be all that firm anymore, you could still play a merry tune on an old fiddle.

"If I did want to find her, where would I start? I have no idea…"

"You start at the beginning. It is really not that difficult. You'll see!"

"But what if she's married?"

"Oh, Hamish, you are such a prune. Drop it. We'll work it out."

Irritably, the Lady called for 'L'addition' (the check), paid in cash, and then they retired for the night at the little French auberge, or inn, a few miles from the A7 motorway.

Hamish slept alone. Lady Lothmere slept with Jean Renoir.

The next afternoon, the Silver Dawn "wafted" (as Rolls Royce likes to call it) into Monte Carlo. It took a while to find the Columbus Hotel, but eventually they discovered the location and checked in.

In reply to Hamish's whiny query as to why they had to be reserved in this hard to find hostelry, Lady L snapped back:

"We are staying at the Columbus, Hamish, because it is owned by that racing driver Coulthard. He's a Scot. I support Scots. Don't you?"

Hamish kept his reply to himself. If it was a "Scots" hotel he hoped it did not serve "Scots food." He'd had had enough of that to fill two lifetimes.

They did not serve Scots food. In fact, Mr. Coulthard did not even seem to have that much to do with the hotel anymore. In the restaurant they mainly featured fish, and the two weary travelers shared a magnificent daurade together before retiring sleepy but happy at about ten p.m.

The next morning they had a simple breakfast together of croissants and milky coffee before Lady L called Mr. Mickey Prentice's gallery.

A girl answered in French.

"Do you speak English?"

"Oui, Madam. I speak it quite well for an English-educated lady!"

Lady Lothmere laughed.

"Can ye find me Mr. Prent-ice? Tell him Lady Lothmere is here to see him."

"Madam, it is only 9:45. Mr. Prentice is still having his morning exercise and shower. Can he call back?"

"No, you call him. I suppose he has a mobile, no? Then you tell him to dry off quickly. Lady Hermoine Lothmere is waiting at the Columbus Hotel. Good-bye, Madam."

And she rung off.

"What cheek! We drive goodness knows how many miles and he welcomes us from his bloody shower! I'll be bedeviled..."

Not five minutes later the phone rang. It was a dripping (she supposed) Mick Prentice.

"Lady Lothmere," he oozed, "welcome to Monaco. I will be over in twenty minutes, if that is all right with you."

"Fifteen would be better. We will await your arrival. Good day, Mr. Prentice."

Noticing Hamish's quizzical look, Lady L added: "You have to keep your distance with these art salesmen—not much better than used car dealers—just more expensively educated!"

In just over fifteen minutes, the phone rang again. It was reception telling them a Mr Prentice was downstairs.

"Send him up—Room 435."

"I know your room, Madam. That's how I managed to call you."

Lady Lothmere hung up. "Snooty French frog," she hissed. Hamish smiled. Lady L was getting herself mentally ready for the used car/art dealer, as if her financial future depended on it. And maybe, in fact, it did!

"Hello, Lady Lothmere. Welcome to Monaco. What a charming room…"

Lady L cut him off. "Do you want coffee or tea? Coffee? OK, Hamish please call room service."

Prentice spotted the Renoir on the bed, already unpacked and ready for inspection. His eyes greedily soaked in the Renoir magic.

"My Lady, have you had the picture valued?" he asked in his most silvery voice.

Prentice had reckoned he could sell the 'picture' on to the Japanese wallpaper magnate for about €650,000—the flower Renoirs were not as sought after as the Renoirs with people in them. If he could rip this painting off the old lady for about €250,000 he could order that new BMW 7 he had set his heart on.

He examined the painting more closely, appearing to talk to himself.

"Hmmm—not quite a full signature. That's not so good. Varnish a bit dis-colored. Frame is screwed in too tightly—hope the color underneath the frame edges is not damaged. The Japanese do like perfection."

"Well, Mr. Prentice, what will ye offer me?"

"It is difficult to be accurate. The picture is not from his best period, and there are quite a few flaws…I'd have to check…"

"Give me an idea, Mr. P."

Mick looked out of the window at the square below, avoiding her eyes.

"Well, if I had to name a price right now…" He hesitated, greed spilling all over him.

"If I had to name a price right now, and seeing as you did have the courtesy of hand-delivering the picture, I think I'd be prepared to close a deal at about €200,000…"

Mick felt a sharp pain on his sore knee. He looked down just in time to see the folded umbrella leaving his lower body.

"Mr. Prentice, do you take me for a fool? An old fool maybe? A similar painting to this sold at Christie's in New York for about half a million dollars only one year ago. This painting is worth at least the same to your hungry Japanese. You know as well as I do that Renoirs are not a dime a dozen. I'll take £400,000 and you sell it for whatever you want. Or, I'll leave it with you and you take 15 percent commission."

"Lady Lothmere, I have never been spoken to like that in all my thirty-five years…" She cut him off again.

"Ah, stop your whining. The offer I made you is very good and you know it. Do we have a deal or not? It won't take me a month of Sundays to find out who this Japanese wallpaper nut is. You've already searched most of the dealers by now, and the word will be out. Hamish, please find me Sotheby's phone number…"

"Lady, let me explain a few things about the art world where I have spent the last forty years of my life."

"Damn it, man, deal or no deal?"

"Lady, this is not a quiz show or a Turkish bazaar, you know…"

"Good-bye, Mr. Prent-ICE, and thank you for coming round so promptly…"

Mick Prentice saw the BMW fade into the sunset.

"I am taking a huge risk, but if you insist, I think I can raise my offer to about €300,000, but that has to be my final word."

"What is that in pounds, Hamish?"

"About £265,000, I think, my Lady."

"Mr. Prentice, £265,000 is not £300,000 now is it?"

Before the bewildered man could reply, the doorbell rang and the coffee arrived.

"Can we have a coffee and talk about how this art business works, Lady Lothmere?"

"You are welcome to a coffee, Mr. Prentice, but I have little interest in your world. My price is very fair, and if you are such a well-experienced art dealer, you must know that. Now, let's talk of other things. Can you find a young lady for me? Or rather for Hamish here?"

Mickey Prentice nearly dropped his cup.

"What did you say? You want me to find a young lady for this…this 'er Scots fellow? You want me to supply girls?"

"Not girls, you silly man. A girl. Mr. Macintosh fell in love many years ago with a young lassie from Toulon, and he would like to see her again. Can you help?"

"A most unusual request, dear lady, but if we can become commercial partners, I will do my best. In this business so rampant with fraud you have to get to know many private detectives."

The room fell silent.

"Find me the girl, and I'll take £280,000 for the Renoir."

Mick smiled. That was better. She was melting. In the end, he always got them one way or the other.

"Two hundred seventy-five pounds and it's a deal...girl and all."

"Get out, Mr. Prentice. Get out right this minute. I find you insulting!"

Mickey's knees started to ache again. Damn the stress of this business. He got up to go. She'll give in as I leave, he said to himself. She's bluffing. But, as he turned in the doorway to have a last word, the door slammed in his face, and he found himself very alone on the landing.

He knocked on the door again.

"Go away, Mr. Prentice. Our so-called 'commercial partnership' is over!" she said sarcastically.

Damn, he thought. He had promised to ring Tokyo before the close of their business day. He needed that darn Renoir. It was a perfect fit.

"Lady Lothmere, I accept your offer. Please open the door."

The door opened.

"The price just went up, Mr. Prentice—£285,000, plus the girl *and* dinner tonight!"

Mick smiled again. He liked this woman.

"Dinner at eight o'clock at the Café de Paris. I'll book. Would that suit? And you can give me all the details of the girl then. My assistant will deliver the contract this afternoon, and tomorrow the van will collect the picture. I presume you carry proof of ownership?"

Lady L stuck out her hand. The deal was done. The door shut. She grinned and fell into the nearest chair exhausted, elated, and financially whole again!

CHAPTER 10

BOY MEETS GIRL—AGAIN!

Lady Lothmere's Valium was just not helping Hamish. The addition of a wee dram or two of whisky was not helping either. Hamish was shaking like his grandmother's blancmange.

In ten minutes he would be meeting Mrs. Helene Latour of Menton, formerly known as Miss Helen Sortege of Toulon, Department of the Var. Toulon was well over one hundred kilometers away from Monaco. Menton was barely twenty kilometers.

Mickey Prentice's friend, the Hercule Poirot of the Riviera, took about five days to solve the missing girl puzzle. There are not that many "Sorteges" in Toulon, or even in all of France. A call to the Toulon Mairie (town hall), another to the tax and insurance "foncionaires," and a search through the wedding scrolls soon solved the mystery.

Miss Helene Sortege had fallen in love with Mr. Latour in 1985, married him in Cap d'Ail Church, moved to Menton (on the Italian border), and bred a family of two boys and one girl. Mr. Latour had a small car repair business, and his father was a fisherman working out of Menton harbor—'was' and apparently still is.

On hearing the news, Lady L lost no time. She was anxious to get on with the next problem—the selling of the Silver Dawn.

But Hamish flatly refused to pick up the phone and call Menton, and so Prentice's girl was forced to do the preliminaries.

She did them well. Helene Latour remembered. She was happy to revisit an old friendship—a young love from her youth. It had no meaning to her now, happily married in a small but comfortable Riviera house not too far from the famed Menton beach.

She would come over by train and have lunch but had to be back by four o'clock or so to welcome the kids back from school.

Hamish worried about his receding hairline and accreting waistline. He worried about communication; he spoke only a few words of French. And he doubted Mme. Latour of Menton would have had much time to continue her English lessons.

Sandy, Mick Prentice's girl with the shapely legs, was happy to play chaperone and translator. In fact, she was dying to do the job, fascinated as only an elegant French lady can be when involved in "un affaire passionel."

The threesome met at the Grill Room of the Hotel de Paris, Hamish opining that she probably had too much fish in her life, what with her fisherman father-in-law and all that.

Hamish was slow to warm up—notwithstanding the Valium, the whisky, and the lunch wine. But when Helene recounted the English lesson story with the two sisters proffering their names as Zizzi and Merde, the two French girls either side of Hamish started a fit of raucous laughter that even the scared-witless Scot could not resist.

The couple next updated each other on their life stories, and then it was time for Helene to go and collect her kids. But she insisted she would only leave if Hamish promised that he would come over to Menton to see the house, the husband, and the children.

Lovers they may never be again. But friends? That could easily become a horse of an entirely different color!

The reunion over and an apparent success, Lady L and Mr. Macintosh turned to the selling of the Rolls.

The Monaco Rolls Royce dealer had absolutely no interest unless Lady L was prepared to offer the car in part exchange for a new Phantom, priced at well over €360,000.

Lady L tried to explain that her purpose was to make money, not spend it, but the dealer would not budge. He repeated almost the exact same mantra they heard in Edinburgh—very old (vintage) and very new Rolls' sell well. Middle-aged cars have little sales appeal.

If you have money, you buy new. If you like classic cars, you buy vintage. If you can't afford either, you can't afford to run a Rolls. Just replacing that famous grill alone can cost you over €15,000.

The two Scots were shocked. Both were counting on Monaco to finally off-load the Rolls Royce. But they appeared to have driven the car down in vain.

The Rolls Royce salesman felt their acute disappointment and melted a little. He reiterated that he could not help personally, but suggested they contact a Mr. Pallazza, a Monegasque who seemed to know everyone in town and might be able to flush out someone looking for an older Rolls car.

Apparently Mr. Pallazza—faithful as an old Swiss clock—had his coffee every morning at Gerhard's harbor front German bar in Fontvieille. The Rolls dealer suggested they catch him there.

At 8:00 a.m. the next morning Hamish and Hermoine sat eagerly at the bar of the little German café waiting for Pallazza. Actually, the bar was Austrian (not German), so the coffee was excellent.

And Mr. Pallazza turned out to be very Italian. Not Monegasque. But otherwise the information was correct!

And Pallazza did think he could be of help.

CHAPTER 11

WHO IS PALLAZZA?

In every city, in every town, hamlet, and village, there is a Pallazza—a man of no fixed profession, and no fixed job, but who nevertheless seems plugged into every detail of his environment.

A man with myriad contacts but no real friends. Surrounded by acquaintances by day and sleeping alone every night. If you want to know something, you call Pallazza. If you want to get it done, you engage Pallazza. If you want to find a way around something, you confide in Pallazza. If you want to know why the project is not proceeding, you buy him lunch. Or dinner. Or a holiday in St. Moritz, depending on your urgency or your depth of despair.

Pallazza had a blotchy red face, thinly hooked nose, and two baleful eyes that sloped down and away from the nose bridge.

Not unlike "Ratso Rizzo" in *Midnight Cowboy*. Or maybe better, try imagining an Ebenezer Scrooge on steroids and with St. Vitus' dance.

Pallazza could not stand or sit still. He fidgeted. His eyes darted. He coughed in embarrassment. He avoided your eyes, turned his head away from a pretty girl. He smoked incessantly. Blew his prominent nose with a huge red hanky every ten minutes, rain or shine.

He had one simple dress code. Brown serge trousers and a dark blue wind-cheater in winter. The same trousers with a yellow T-shirt in summer. Either he never washed his uniform, or he must have once bought six changes of identical togs at Carrefour's summer sale.

Everybody said hello to Pallazza and bought him coffee. But nobody warmed to him. Like an old broom, he was useful in clearing away the debris, but do you invite a broom to your birthday party?

Surprisingly for a man of apparently limited means, he lived in a large, ground floor apartment on the French border and appeared to have been married once, although nobody could remember to whom, or ever raised the topic in his presence.

At the Grande Braderie (jumble sale), you could see him with his stall of old clothes. At the Christmas fair, he'd be selling personalized Santa Claus hats. At the January circus festival, he sold toffee apples in the intervals. In summer he entertained the rich and famous at his table at the Monte Carlo Beach Club, even though he was never seen to pick up the bill. At Grand Prix time, he'd find the last-minute desperate and dangerous a jammed balcony to perch on to get a distant glimpse of the cars for only €10,000 each.

In between, he seemed to amuse himself finding cars for people or people for cars—and taking a 10 percent commission on each transaction from each side!

Pallazza was a character all right, with no apparent power but still all-powerful. A wistful, dreary, disillusioned man you would rather not be with but just could not bear ignoring just in case he knew something you did not—which was almost invariably the case.

But this would be the man who now would be responsible for uniting the Scots, the Mexicans, and the Russians, and possibly be the role model Graham Greene had in mind when he dubbed Monaco as that "*Sunny Place for Shady People.*"

CHAPTER 12

MEETING OF THE MINDS

At a few minutes after 8:00 a.m., Mr. Pallazza walked over from the bus stop to Gerhards. Despite the hubbub Hamish recognized Pallazza immediately from the Rolls Royce dealer's accurate description and walked over to invite him to their table. Pallazza accepted the invitation as if he had been expecting it and sat down opposite Lady L., avoiding her eyes.

"Bon Jour, Madam. I think you have a car to sell, am I right?"

"Si, Monsieur—how did you know?"

"It is my business to know these things, Madam. I would like a café Americano and two croissants please."

Despite prodding, Pallazza said little until the first coffee and croissant had slipped down his eager throat.

Then he sat up straight—or as straight as his wizened frame allowed—and looked Hamish in the eye.

"It is a Rolls, right? About 1996? Called a Silver Dawn? How come that name? Most of these models were called Silver Spurs, no?"

"True," answered Hamish, "but this car was about the last in the Spur lineup before the Seraph was launched and a number were re-branded

"Dawns" for some unknown reason. It is essentially a Silver Spur three, if you like."

"Yes, I prefer. 'Spurs' are known here. 'Dawns' are not. What money do you want?"

"Sixty thousand euros, right Lady L? I think the car is easily worth it."

"We'll see. Rolls Royces are not simple to sell. They are unreliable, expensive to service, and expensive to run. You've got to find some fool who needs that ridiculous Flying Lady badge to prove he is what he would like people to think he is. That's all.

"But I have an idea. I know this Russian fellow who wants a luxury car not too expensive to go with his yacht. Can you meet me tomorrow at the Casa del Gelato just next door; the man's assistant is usually there most mornings. He is a loathsome turd, but he's also vain and stupid. These people are always good buyers of overpriced crap."

"Sure, I'll be there. Lady L, you have no need to join us." (She nodded in agreement.) "What time Mr. Pallazza?"

"Meet me at eight fifteen outside. I get 10 percent, OK? Good-bye. Thank you for coffee."

"Shall I bring the car?"

Pallazza looked at him as if he was retarded.

"That is what we are trying to sell, am I right? Or are we joining a knitting club?"

Pallazza left as sleazily as he had come.

"Disagreeable fellow," offered her Ladyship.

"You can say that again!" added her chauffeur.

———— ※《◊》※ ————

Hamish was early at Casa's. Leaning against the opposite harbor wall, he watched the early crowd assemble for their morning coffee fix—a strangely different bunch to the imbibers at Gerhards next door.

The noise inside was already deafening. Here, at least, everyone was equal—billionaires and seamen and everything in between. Class and rank meant nothing at Casa's. Providing you could pay for your espresso or cappuccino, you were welcome. There were English, Americans, Slavs, French, Germans, Dutch—everything.

The talk was normally conducted in English—the only universally understood common denominator.

This morning the topic seemed (to Hamish listening outside) less than totally intellectual. The discussion seemed to center on which nationality was the better in bed. Come to think of it, this was the major topic most mornings—that and sports cars or the damn Socialists.

Hamish was so amused listening that he did not notice Pallazza sliding up alongside him.

"Millionaires and billionaires—and all they talk about is oral sex.

Mr. Macintosh, do you know the difference between billionaires and millionaires? Billionaires show off with yachts and planes. Millionaires with cars and dames. That's why you head for the boat people. Heed my advice."

"You mean to tell me billionaires don't like girls?"

"I think they are over it. They tend to be older men, besotted with their empires. They know they can buy any broad they want, so the thrill of the hunt—or the cunt, if you like—is muted. Anyway, they also know that any bed-tested and big-chested twenty-two-year-old only wants them for their money. And holding onto their money is the main focus of their lives. Believe me. I have been dealing with these cats for years."

Hamish listened to this diatribe with equal amusement and awe, seeing Pallazza now perhaps in a newer and more philosophical light. Not only was this angry Italian obviously green with envy of the wealth around him, but he was also a shrewd observer of the 'lucky few'!

"Let's go in and see if the dumb Russian has arrived yet."

As they entered the steaming little coffee shop, conversation hushed as if it might be dangerous to let Pallazza hear too much. Most nodded in his direction. A few offered a breezy "bon jour." The loners buried their heads further into their copies of *Monaco Matin.*

The two men selected an empty table in the corner and waited. Pallazza scanned his e-mails on his iPhone, and Hamish toyed with his coffee.

They did not have too long to wait. At about eight forty-five, the door slid open violently, and there stood an impressive younger man, hoping his entry would create the stir his ego craved. It created nothing—except a call from Pallazza to join him.

"Vladimir, come over here. I want you to meet a friend."

Vladimir strutted over hoping the girl in the corner—a Tunisian bar dancer—would notice. But she was deep in conversation on one of her three cell phones.

"How's Monaco's biggest gossip?"

Pallazza smiled wearily. How many more times would he have to hear the same greeting?

"I am fine, you arrogant Cossack." Same rude greeting gets the same rude response.

Vladimir plopped down his jacket, went inside to select his croissant, and then grabbed an empty chair near Hamish.

"Who's this guy then, Pallazza?"

"He's a Scot—a Scot with a Rolls Royce for sale. I thought your boss might be interested."

"He might—if I advise him to...." Turning to Hamish the Russian added: "So you have a Rolls for sale? What color?"

"She's white, or rather Magnolia."

"She? Why *she*? Are cars 'she' in Scotland? I thought you were all machos up there, jumping around the glens and bogs. But, then again, you do wear girlie skirts. And without underpants. Right?"

Vladimir thought his little introductory speech very funny and slapped his thighs two or three times with glee.

Hamish allowed a polite grin.

"Age?"

"Forty-six."

"What the heck? The friggin' car is forty-six years old? You crazy or something?"

This time it was Hamish's turn to laugh.

"Naaa, me. I'm forty-six. The car is about nine years old with thirty-five thousand miles on the clock. Looks like new. Pampered as a baby. See—it's parked over there..."

Vladimir's eyes squinted as he followed the line of Hamish's finger.

"OK, I trust this old Italian horse thief here. If he says the car is OK, that's good enough for me. Whaddya want for it?"

"In pounds, euros…or rubles?"

"Ha, ha," answered the Russian. "In Turkish lira! Euros, of course."

"About €60,000—and no horse trading…"

"Fug me. You come in here with Monaco's biggest thief and you don't expect me to squeeze your Scottish balls a little? Forget it."

"OK then, £50,000, if you prefer. And that's a right fair price. Check it out or ask Mr. P here," turning to Pallazza. "Right? It is a fair price?"

Pallazza looked the other way.

They finished their coffees and strolled out to examine the car. Vladimir liked it.

"OK, Scotty, I'll tell my boss. Only problem is he is due back here in a week or so, and he will probably want to see it. Can you wait a while?"

"Ach—I'm not sure. I'm supposed to fly back Friday. I have a taxi business to run. Anyway, I can't afford the hotel prices here, and my Lady is leaving Monaco to go to some auction in Geneva with the art geyser who bought her Renoir a day or so ago."

It took a while for Vladimir to sort out that confusing load of information.

"Do I take it, Mr. Scotland, that you need a bed for a night or two?"

"Aye," answered Hamish a little warily.

"Don't worry about the hotel stuff. There's plenty of room in the boat for a girlie Scot like you. Be my guest. We'll have a ball."

Hamish looked shocked. But then he remembered the old Lady. 'Build your memories, Hamish. Stop thinking so much. Life is for living! Think Nike—*Just do it!*'

"OK, Mr. Vladimir. I'd like that very much."

And so started the Hamish and Vladimir show. Hamish moved on board that night and installed himself in the rear guest suite waiting for the Russian owner to return. Now *this* was living, he said to himself. This was the life all right.

Vladimir served ice cold vodkas with a squeeze of lime and heated up some terrible Russian cabbage stew. Without the vodka, even a starving

Ethiopian would have rejected that inedible slop. With a jar of vodka and a deep hunger, you could just about force it down. But it was free. That fact to a Scotsman would make even pig's manure happily edible!

Dinner over, Vladimir suggested they stroll over and see his Mexican girlfriend, Paz. Just a short walk away up the harbor on the Quai Jean Rey, to the Monte Marina, but no one was in.

"I expect she is still working in the restaurant. Let's go see."

On the way over, Vladimir related a little of his relationship with Paz. How they had met in Mexico, parted, and how he then enticed her over to Monaco.

"You know, Scotty," he concluded, "I've met and had hundreds of girls, but I can never get this one out of my mind. She is not the greatest body, nor the greatest in bed, but somehow she's different. I just want to be near her, protect her, and sleep with her—in the same bed—whether we make love or not. It's the darndest thing."

"Vladimir, my new mate, you are in trouble—and in love."

"Oh really, Sherlock Holmes. That had never occurred to me!"

They reached the little restaurant, which had previously served moules and frites for the Belgians and the Dutch, but had closed as there were obviously not enough of those around. Or, if there were, those thrifty Dutch would make their own moules on some infernal Camping Gaz cooker at the roadside.

Inside the place was ablaze with light. Carpenters were banging and sawing. Paz and her daughter Natasha ran up and down trying to control everything but in the end controlled nothing. She spied Vladimir grinning in the doorway.

"Valdimir—so glad you are here. I can't get this moron to understand that this door won't open. Talk to them in French, will you?"

Vladimir tried, but his command of the language was not good either, and the surly workmen took little notice.

Hamish made his way quietly to the bothersome door and took a quick look at the hinges.

"Mrs. Paz, there is no mystery here. These swing-shut hinges are mounted upside down. As you try and close the door, the bottom bites into the parquet. See?" And he showed her exactly what was happening.

"Well, bless my boobies, Scottie you are a genius."

That was Vladimir, and as he said it, he grabbed the foreman by the lapel and dragged him over to the hinges.

"Voila idiot—tu comprends le probleme maintenant? Allez changez les, les…" (He could not find the right word for 'hinges', so he just shoved the foremen's nose in the crack.)

Vladimir turned to Hamish again.

"You know about construction and that sort of stuff?"

"Of course. Before I had my taxi, I helped Dad around the farm and maintained all the outbuildings. Then I did the same for our neighbors. I know my way around a toolbox."

"Aha!" yelled Vladimir. "Paz, we have our solution. This Hamish fellow here, who has exactly zero to do and is living off me, will become your foreman. Scottie, earn your keep and help Paz get this restaurant open, will you? The rent is destroying my boss!"

Hamish was delighted. He loved doing-it-himself. It would be fun and a way to pay Vladimir back for his generosity in letting Hamish share the boat and the terrible Russian stew.

Beyond that, he could quickly see why Vladimir was in love. The girl had something very attractive about her. Somehow, you just felt you wanted to help her—to possess her.

And so that was what Hamish set out to do—help Paz during the day and drink vodka during the night on the yacht with her gaunt Russian boyfriend.

CHAPTER 13

MENTON BY THE SEA

With a little yelling and a little pushing, the Mexican restaurant slowly started to take shape. The architect—if you could call him that—was delighted to have some on-site help. He had bigger fish to fry than transforming a Belgian moule cafe into a Latin American eatery.

Hamish brought in some out-of-work Filipino helpers and an Italian or two who were more likely than the French to work rather than argue and grumble all day. With Hamish's eagle eye and Paz's passion, La Cantina Mexicana could now begin to think about a fixed opening date.

But Thursday would be Hamish's day off. He had things to see and do in Menton. He had promised to meet Helene in her house with her family and her husband. If everything was as rosy as he hoped, that would finally bring closure to his many years of longing.

If not—well, who knows. "Cross that bridge when we come to it," he said out loud as the train rumbled through Roquebrune Village.

Whatever happens, he had done more different things in a couple of weeks than he ever had done all those years in Killin. And strangely enough, he had never thought about his wife at all. Not once. In fact he was delighted she was not in his way. Fate has a funny way of sorting out the roadblocks.

Helene and two of her kids were at the station to meet him. It was their school lunch break, and they were curious to see Mama's old friend from "l'Ecosse."

The possibility of a former romance never entered the little ones' heads—children never seem able to imagine their parents making out with anyone or ever imagine their parents were also once kids and teens.

"Ou est son 'kilt' Maman?" said the younger one. The elder just stared as if Hamish was the first invader from Mars.

"Hameesh, so good to see you again. Welcome to Menton. We have a surprise for you. Mama is here—you remember? She used to have that little bar in Toulon where you tried to teach us Engleesh. And Albert's papa is here. He is a wonderful man and a great fisherman. I asked him to take you for a trip on his boat. He should be finished selling this morning's catch by now."

They walked down the station entrance to the town center and main shopping street, cut off to all traffic. The little group tried hard to stay together, but the bustle of the tourists and the many stalls obstructing the walkway made it complicated. Menton was the self-proclaimed lemon capital of the world, and the merchants did their best to piggyback on that image.

Lemon smells drifted through the air. Lemon everything was on sale everywhere. Lemon soap. Lemon jams. Lemon bubble baths. Lemon-colored cloths and clothes. Lemon, lemon whichever way you looked. And, of course, the occasional lime!

As they passed below the old town and back along the sea, walking became easier.

"We're going to meet in a little pizzeria, so we can eat quickly and take the little ones back to school. Then, if you are still up to it, we can have a quiet coffee back in the house. It's up in the Old Town, not far from the Cathedral. That OK with you, Mr. Hameesh?"

"Fine. I'd like that." Hamish was still somewhat uncomfortable, but Helene showed absolutely no inhibitions. They had been in love. They had made love. That was natural enough to a French lady and absolutely no reason for two old pals not to get together again. Love is part of every young life. And memories are to be cherished, and not abandoned for prurient reasoning.

To Hamish, of course, the "brief encounter" had had the impact of a famous Greek tragedy. It had not been a "natural part of growing up." It had been the seminal experience of his young manhood.

In the little restaurant, the third child—the elder son—waited with his grandfather. They were in deep debate—that was another interesting cultural observation. French children seemed to enjoy not only eating out with their parents, but actually TALKED to them.

The conversation wound down as the station arrivals took their seats. And then another shock for Hamish—the tobacco-stained older man hugged him tightly and poured him a full glass of deep red Provencal wine.

"Ah—le grand amour de son enfance. Bienvenue!"

Helene then asked for silence.

"Hameesh," she began half in French and half in English, "it is so good to see you here. You were an important part of my youth. I think the first man I loved. The last will join us for coffee soon. My son Henri has a request for you…"

"Mais non, Mama, Pas maintenant. Pas ici. Zut!" Henri looked away in embarrassment.

"Shuss, Henri. Hameesh, Henri is a leetle shy. He would like you to be his pen pal; he needs a contact in England—sorry, Scotland—to write to.|"

"Of course, Henri. I would be honored. I'll leave you my address, and I will promise to answer promptly. I will even include five euros for every letter over fifty words you send me."

Henri had a little problem following that, but after he received a crude translation, his face lit up like the Menton lighthouse after midnight.

Then the old man pulled "Hameesh" aside.

"Un petit mot monsieur. Je visite souvent a Cap d'Ail et je connais bien le Port de Fontvieille…."

He leant closer and whispered even softer.

"I undertstand you are staying on the Sverdlov boat with that Russian fellow. Please take care. I have bad feelings about him. And his boss. Bad people. Please take care."

Hamish was not too sure he quite got the full gist of the old man's warning, but Helene sped to the linguistic rescue.

"Pere does not like Russians. Especially those over-rich Russians. He wants you to take care, that's all. Pere is usually right about people. For all our sakes, please be careful."

Right then Mr. Latour (the son and husband) walked in and earlier than expected. He was grinning from ear to ear.

"Alors c'est toi!" Alors, it's you who nearly snatched my dear wife away to Scotland. Lucky for me, you did not succeed or we'd all be eating that vile British food now!"

Hamish grinned back.

"And luckily for you, Mr. Latour, I'm married or I'd try again," answered the delighted Hamish. Secretly he had dreaded meeting 'the husband.' What could they possible say to each other?

Now everyone started laughing. Helene's husband ran over and hugged him.

Hamish loved these people. He'd seen all he needed to see.

Helene was happy. The family was happy. Nobody needed rescuing. The dream was over. He was free. Helene was not to be. Not ever. Get over it, Hamish. Life must move on…

On the way back in the train, his thoughts strayed to the old man's warning. It was a bit like the old lady crying "Beware the Ides of March" to Julius Caesar on the way to the forum where he was to meet his assassins. Hamish grinned. He reckoned he could look after himself. He'd been in the British army after all.

CHAPTER 14

THE ART DEAL OF THE DECADE

The day Lady Lothmere sold the Renoir to Mick Prentice, they indeed had dinner together at the renowned Café de Paris. They got on famously, Mickey becoming more and more fascinated with the free-living, free-thinking old dowager.

After the first bottle of wine, he turned to her and whispered.

"My Lady, why did you sell the Renoir?"

"Because you called me, Mr. Prentice, remember..."

Then she added coyly, furtively glancing around in case someone was listening: "And frankly I needed the money. My husband died rather suddenly and left our affairs in a bit of mess, I'm afraid. Mostly my fault—I just loved spending money. You know how it is, Mr. Prentice. He would deny me nothing, and I never stopped to wonder whether we could afford it. Well, it turns out we couldn't really. But he loved spoiling me, and I loved spoiling him—in my own way, if you understand my meaning."

Mr. Prentice guffawed into his serviette. Then he, in turn, looked around the room and leant closer.

"Lady L, I need money too. A couple of alimonies and slack sales are cramping my style. But you know something…I have a feeling we could help each other. I have a plan I have been working on for some years that—if we carry it out correctly—could make us a few million each easily. I can't do it alone. Want to hear about it?"

Lady L wanted to say no; she smelled trouble immediately. But then trouble could also carry another, much more pungent smell—the scent of delicious, exciting danger.

Anyway, what was the harm in listening?

Prentice dragged his chair closer and talked softly. Lady Lothmere listened intently as he explained the 'big idea.'

"I need an accomplice. My plan is not strictly illegal, if we do not use other people's money. But it is shady and just a touch immoral."

"Just a touch, Mr. Prentice? A tad more than that I'll wager. But why me as your accomplice?"

"Well, I am quite sure you wouldn't cheat me. Good breeding has a way of advertising itself. But more than that, you are a well-known art buyer and collector. Your credentials are impeccable. Just add in your title, and you have the perfect fit."

"You flatter me, Mr. Prentice. But I think I like that. Are you sure this crazy plan will work?"

"I'm 98.5 percent sure, my Lady—with you aboard, that is."

The table fell silent.

"I don't know Mr. Prentice…I do have a good name to protect, but then again, what is a good name if there is no good money to back it up?"

"I'll tell you what, Lady Lothmere. Here's my suggestion. I have put an item in the Christie's auction in Geneva this next Friday. Come up with me and let's see if stage one works. The only risk is the auctioneers' commission. What do you think?"

Lady L did not think too long.

"Right. Let's do Geneva. Then I'll decide. We have to go up separately, right? I love Geneva. Mr. Prentice, I hope we at least have some good old-fashioned fun…"

Prentice considered that for a moment wondering if it could mean what he hoped it might mean. But then he dismissed the thought. Heaven's alive, the old lady must be well over seventy!

Off they went to Geneva a few days later, one by Easyjet, the other by Swiss Airlines.

As she signed in at the auction house, the receptionist smiled.

"Why, Lady Lothmere, we haven't seen you here for some time."

"I know, but I have been a little poorly, my dear. I only came here because I hear you are selling a Jacoby?"

"A what, my Lady? A Jacoby?"

"Shhhh, dear. We don't want everyone to hear. I think I am starting a Jacoby collection. But don't tell anyone."

"No, no, of course not, Madam—I mean, Lady."

As soon as the Scottish lady drifted out of sight, the receptionist grabbed her phone and called the controller.

"Jeff, are we selling a Jacoby? We are? What is that? I never heard of Jacoby. Nineteenth century junk, you say? That is not what Lady Lothmere said. Yes, she is here. I just booked her in. She told me she wanted to start a Jacoby collection for her castle in Scotland. Does that make sense? No—I thought not. She's on the level, right? Never given you any trouble ever? OK, I guess some idiot passed her a useless tip. Sorry to have troubled you…"

The receptionist turned to the next arrival and thought no more about the Jacoby or about the strange aristocrat from Scotland.

Lot 43 was announced at about 15:20 p.m. A Jacoby—a chocolate box-style landscape of Tuscany with a young couple walking side by side down some lane under a rose red sky.

Half the audience got up to stretch their legs, take a comfort break, or just rethink their strategy for the later items on the schedule.

The auctioneer said a few words about Jacoby the painter and added, "Can I start the bidding at €10,000? No? Then what about €5,000?"

Lady Lothmere slightly raised her left, lace-gloved hand. The auctioneer caught it.

"All right, I have €5,000. Can I ask for €7,000?" Prentice's number board flashed.

"And what about €10,000?"

A dark man in the back lifted his finger.

"Ten thousand it is. That's more like it buyers. Do I hear €15,000?"

Mickey's hand shot up again.

The room went silent.

"It's against you, dear Lady" offered the auctioneer.

Lady Lothmere opened her bag and read a note. She appeared unsure and just a little troubled as if she definitely had not expected this.

She raised her head and said sweetly, "Let's end this. I offer €20,000."

"Thank you, my Lady," said the surprised auctioneer. This was going far better that he had imagined. "I have €20,000. Are we all done at €20,000?" He did not expect an answer—after all, Jacoby was a serial popular artist of the late nineteenth century who had painted to order endless scenes of so-called Tuscany landscapes, even though no one could ever prove the mediocre artist had ever left his native Graz, Austria.

"Going once then at €20,000… Going twice…"

Prentice looked irritated but reluctantly raised his numbered panel. "Twenty-five thousand."

The room fell silent and buyers started to stroll back in. Lady L stood up to eye her competitor.

"Sir, I need this painting. Please desist…"

"Madam, this is an open auction," answered the auctioneer. "Please sit down. It's against you at €25,000."

Lady L looked at her notes again. Then she snorted mildly, raised her head, and barked out, "Thirty thousand—my last offer. Be gone with you, sir!" That last was intended for the art dealer in the back (Mick Prentice).

"Thirty thousand?" queried the auctioneer, not believing his ears. "Did I hear €30,000?"

"You did, sir!"

"Then €30,000 it is. I ask again, are we done here?"

Art dealers in the room now started calling their head offices wondering what the hell was going on.

"All right, €30,000 it is. Do I hear more?"

No one moved. The Lady seemed pleased with herself.

"Going once. Going twice…"

"Thirty-two thousand," said the dark man.

"Thirty-three thousand," immediately answered Prentice.

The room went very quiet again.

The auctioneer lent over his podium and almost whispered to the Lady, "Ma'am, it's against you at €33,000. Do you wish to proceed?"

Lady Lothmere stood up again and glowered angrily at the back of the room. "No, thank you. I am done."

"Then I will close it at €33,000 to the gentleman at the back."

"Thirty-five thousand," blurted out the dark man.

The auctioneer looked left and right at his colleagues as much as to say, "What the heck is this all about?" when Prentice dropped his panel and nodded his head negatively.

"All right then €35,000 it is to the gentleman in the green suit. Going once. Going twice. SOLD." The auctioneer was anxious to get this over with. True, he had generated a good commission on this sale, but the catalog had estimated from €7,000 to €10,000 maximum value. It was not good that the auction house had estimated the value so poorly.

Lady Lothmere collected her catalog and handbag and strolled imperiously out of the room, avoiding looking at the man who had beaten her.

Art Daly from the New York dealer Mosley and Maxim turned to Prentice and said, "Mick, whaddya know that I don't know?"

"I don't really know anything, Art. I am as confused as you are. I have this client in Shanghai who asked me to bid on the picture. Authorized me to go even higher, but frankly I could not in all consciousness do it. Thirty-five thousand for that piece of chocolate box cheesecake is absurd."

"The market *is* absurd, Mick. There is just too much money sloshing about. It has to crash. Thirty-five thousand for that mass producer of crap is just nuts. Mick, good luck to you. I gotta go."

"Mass art producer? You are right, Art Daly," Mick muttered to himself. "That's what it's all about, mate."

Slowly the train squealed to a halt in Lausanne Station. Lady Lothmere exited daintily and strode to the taxi rank.

"Le restaurant Chalet Lucerne, s'il vous plaît," she asked, furtively looking around to ensure no one overheard.

Seated in the back of the restaurant were three men, two of them from that morning's auction and a third stocky, swarthy foreigner from what seemed Eastern Europe somewhere.

They stood up as Lady Lothmere approached. Mickey Prentice seated her next to him, and the swarthy easterner offered her a glass of champagne.

"Lady Lothmere, meet Mordechai Mosta from Islamabad and Mr. Sverdlov from Moscow."

"Mr. Sverdlov? Why do I know that name?"

"Because, my Lady, I believe you want to sell me a Rolls Royce?"

"My God, what a small world! Are we all here to bid that old car up?" Prentice sniggered nervously.

"Lady L, please mind your language. This is a sensitive issue…"

"Are we being illegal, then, Mr. Prentice?"

"Not as long as we play with our own funds, but the ice gets thinner as we go along…you'll see."

The subject changed abruptly as the arrogant Swiss waiter approached.

"May I suggest a plate of Swiss dried meats followed by our best Kirsch Emmental fondue?" A group order would make his life a lot easier.

"No. You may not suggest anything, thank you," Sverdlov stared icily at the stunned waiter.

"Lady Lothmere, I have eaten here before. May I suggest either the Zander filet—a great lake fish gently fried in olive oil—or the veal steak fried in butter."

"The fish would suit me just fine, Mr. Sverdlov."

Orders over and the waiter safely out of earshot, the four heads huddled closer.

"Group," started Mickey, "that went rather better than I expected. Today we set a new benchmark for those worthless Jacobys. And I don't think the auction house suspected a thing, thanks to our Shakespearian actor here. Lady L, you were magnificent. The real English dowager…"

"*Scottish*, Mr. Prentice. Not the same thing," shot back the only woman at the table.

"Sorry. So to continue, I think we started well. Lady L, to bring you fully into the loop here, Mr. Sverdlov entered that Jacoby through a St. Petersburg art dealer. Mordechai, our pet Pakistani here, bought it and it will go back into stock. All of us will share paying the commission (about 20 percent) as I explained, and then we move to stage two."

"Art Daly from New York also edits *Art Dealer and Auction House* monthly, and that's why I sat next to him. He is bound to mention this auction in his next issue. Everyone in the business reads that rag. Jacoby owners will start to take notice, I hope.

"But we have to be patient. As far as I know, this mass producer and so-called artist painted about 157 almost similar pictures in his worthless life. Some one hundred or so still exist. Sverdlov here has amassed for me over the last four years, anonymously, about sixty."

"Fifty-two to be exact, Mr. Prentice."

Mickey nodded and continued.

"OK, fifty-two it is. Most bought at an average of about €8,000—about €400,000 worth. At today's rate, those crappy pictures are worth close to two million. And the hype has just begun. I think we could well clear five million by the time we are finished."

"Lady L, we need you in this business. No one would suspect you of anything other than being a dotty old collector."

"'Old' maybe, Mr. Prentice. 'Dotty'? Watch your young tongue…"

Everyone laughed heartily. Sverdlov refilled the glasses and offered a toast to dottiness. Even the old Lady smiled.

Micket Prentice took up his tale again.

"Lady L, since it was my original idea, I have 40 percent of this syndicate and have funded most of the capital. My two partners in crime here own 30 percent each. Our idea is to offer you 20 percent—10 percent from me and 5 percent each from my partners here—in return for your Renoir.

In five years or less, that money I offered you for the Renoir could easily be worth triple or more."

"And Lady Lothmere, I will buy that Rolls for €150,000 sight unseen, which must be about what you originally paid for it, no? But that will be a little side negotiation we can discuss later. I have a good reason to be so generous, believe me."

He broke off and started to laugh. "This evening is beginning to sound like one of those Ginza Knife commercials. "Buy sixteen thousand knives now, and we'll throw in a year's supply of onions and a box of MacDonald's Happy Meals!"

This particularly amused the Pakistani who almost choked on his Swiss Bundnerfleisch.

"Anyway, what I was going to add, Lady L, is that you can drive the car back to Scotland and bring it down again when we all meet in a few months—after the London auction."

"My, Mr. Sverdlov," cooed the Lady. "Why so generous? My husband always said, 'If it sounds too good to be true, maybe it is.'"

"It is a true offer, believe me," snapped back the Russian. "As I said, I have my reasons…"

The group chatted on with Mick Prentice describing in detail the plot to further hike the benchmark Jacoby prices at the forthcoming London Auction.

Ostentatiously and again unsuccessfully, Lady L would try once more to add to her collection and land another Jacoby, plus hopefully generate some news and gossip.

"I can see the headline now—'*Lady Lothmere tries again to win her Jacoby and explains why she likes them so much.*' By the way, Lady Lothmere, our Russian Bear here will send you one of the less objectionable Jacobys to hang up in your castle in case anyone wants to test your alibi!"

"Why? I don't even like that artist."

"Why? Who's ever heard of a famous collector who has nothing in her collection? You see, dear Lady, we think of everything!"

"Correct, Mr. Prentice. Everything—perhaps even a bit too much!"

CHAPTER 15

PREPARING TO ROLL THE ROLLER HOME

"You sold the car, Lady? Already? To Vladimir's boss? But you haven't even met him yet?"

"Hamish, the world moves in strange ways! I met him by chance in Geneva, and I did the deal."

"But Ma'am, you may have met him, but has he seen the car?" continued an incredulous chauffeur.

Lady Lothmere just shrugged and smiled.

"Prepare the car, please; we leave on Sunday."

"What car, me Lady?"

"The Rolls, of course, Hamish." Lady Lothmere was enjoying his confusion and discomfort.

"I thought you told me you sold it?" Hamish was getting a little peeved.

"I did sell it, but Mr. Sverdlov does not need the car for some months, so we can drive the Rolls home and later drive it back!"

"Back? Drive it back? Back where?"

"Hamish, you are being tiresome. Yes, drive it back. *Back* means here. Here means Monaco because that is where we are right now. Are you up to the job, or do I find another driver?"

Lady L was really having fun now.

"Drive it back when? Why? I never heard of such a thing."

"Hamish, listen. I sold the car for a great price. Mr. Sverdlov does not need it now. I asked him if we could drive it back as I hate aircraft. I promised to drive it back down when he wants it as I thought both you and I were becoming rather attached to Monaco. Or am I wrong?"

"But you'll have to fly back eventually?" Hamish was still confused.

"So…that is then. This is now. OH, and by the way, Sverdlov will supply us a spare tire." And she walked into her hotel.

Hamish did not move. He used to admire his erratic passenger. Now he was beginning to think she had gone from interesting to totally wacky. *Spare tire? How did this new owner who had never even seen the car know about the lack of a spare? Why did he even care?*

Hamish had to have a beer—and a think.

He had the drink at the little Mexican restaurant, now beginning to look like what a Frenchman might imagine a Mexican cantina to be like. Little white tables dotted the small space, with red chairs and green table cloths. A honeysuckle was already beginning to climb the rear wall separating the kitchen from the dining area.

Paz sat at one of the tables checking her invoices. She looked up as Hamish entered and gave him a big grin.

"How are you, Hamish? I needed you this morning. That damn French plumber still can't get the hot water in the toilet sink to flow smoothly. Can you check it out?"

"Actually, he's a Pole! And I've told him ten times to extract the limiter in the tap (faucet)—it's so damn easy. I'll do it. But first, have you got a Corona on ice yet?"

"Sure, help yourself. I don't know what I would do without you!" She smiled sweetly and he melted. Since writing Helene out of his dreams, he had become more and more attracted to this cute Mexican girl. Again, he feared, he was doomed to disappointment. She was Vladimir's and that was that. What a pity. Hamish felt he would have loved to run that little establishment with her and share her life—and maybe even her love.

He pulled himself together. "You're dreaming on the rebound!" he told himself as he opened the fridge and helped himself to a cold beer. He sighed and strode purposely into the little toilet area to attack the reluctant hot water outlet.

Faucet fixed, he grabbed a seat at the other end of the table Paz was working on.

"Paz, we have to leave this Sunday. The old Lady wants to go back. She sold the Rolls, but we can keep it for a while. Then she wants to come back down here again in the Rolls and deliver it. Don't you think that's odd?"

"Odd? Why? If that's the way it is, then that's the way it is; stop worrying about it. You worry about everything. Natasha will miss you. And so shall I…"

She looked down at her papers as she said the last phrase.

Hamish felt his heart beating like crazy. He wanted to repeat his own feelings of sorrow at their parting, but something was holding him back—as usual. So all he said was, "And I'll miss hanging out here and helping you guys. When is the grand opening now?"

In about two months, when Mr. Sverdlov is here for a longer stay. I am more or less ready, but he wants to cut the ribbon and all that stuff. Pity you can't be here. You helped so much. How can we ever thank you?"

Hamish said nothing. His heart was breaking. Killin, the cold moors, the soulless taxi service, the mists, the loneliness, the problems with his wife (or ex-wife) all came flooding back. A tear welled in the corner of one eye.

Paz caught it. She stood up, walked over to his side of the table, and hugged his head to her bosom.

Hamish sobbed softly as she held him tightly.

"Hamish, you will always have your friends here. Come back whenever you want. We'll be here to welcome you."

CHAPTER 16

WEST READING SERVICE AREA

Three days later, Hamish drove the car out of the hotel garage and gave it the once over. They had planned to leave early the next day. As he was peering in the coolant reservoir checking the water level, a shadow blocked his view. It was Pallazza.

"Good morning, Mr. Macintosh. Mr. Sverdlov asked me to bring over a spare tire for your Rolls. Seems he bought your car, but it does not have a spare wheel. I find that strange. Apparently Sverdlov did too!"

"It is not strange. The car has these run-flat tires, if that is any of your business."

"Well, you're right. It is none of my business. But Mr. Sverdlov wants the car to have a spare, and it is in the back of my car. Can I give it to you?"

Hamish sighed deeply and opened the trunk allowing Pallazza to bring over the tire and drop it in the spare wheel bay.

"Take care, Mr. Macintosh. The wheel may still be a little wet. I could only find a blue RR wheel and had my friend at Pneu Azure respray it to match. It should be completely dry in a few hours."

"One other thing, Mr. Macintosh. Since you presumably sold the car, there is something left over that *is* my business. My 10 percent. You were not planning on forgetting that were you?"

"Mr. Pallazza, I had nothing to do with the final sale. That was handled entirely between Lady L and this Sverdlov fellow. They met somewhere. I don't even have any idea of the price. All I know is the car seems to be sold but Mr. Sverdlov only needs it later, so he is allowing us to drive it back to Scotland and then back down again sometime in the future. OK?"

"But I need my 10 percent. I introduced you to Sverdlov through Vladimir, and please don't you forget it."

"Wait, Mr. Pallazza. I'll call Lady L on the mobile…Hello? Lady L? I have Mr. Pallazza here…Yes, he delivered the spare wheel. What? You want me to show Mr. Sverdlov the wheel? Why? It's the right model—I checked that. All right, all right—I'll go over to his apartment after lunch. But I am calling you because Mr. Pallazza wants his 10 percent."

Hamish listened to the voice for a few minutes and hung up.

"My Lady says the car is sold but that she has not received any money yet. Either you wait until Mr. Sverdlov pays when we are back, or she'll offer you €6,000 now. She assumes Sverdlov will pay what she asked, but she is unsure…"

Pallazza thought it over for a few moments and then answered.

"OK, tell her I'll take the €6,000 now. And thank you!"

After lunch, Hamish drove the Rolls over to Sverdlov's apartment only to discover he was at the yacht. Hamish then parked as near the ship as he could and strolled over. Sverdlov saw him from afar and bounded down the gangway to meet him.

"How are you, Hamish? Welcome. I heard a lot about you. I hope you enjoyed staying with Vlad on the boat. Did you bring the tire? Good. I was expecting it. Please wheel it up the gangway will you? I need to have it checked out. Must be sure it's a genuine Rolls spare wheel, you know. I'll call you in a few hours, and you can collect it. Must give it back to you tonight as I am off to Moscow in the morning. I'll be back for the grand opening in a few weeks, though—hope you'll be there." And he hurried back inside the ship without waiting for an answer or acknowledgement.

Hamish was now absolutely sure he was dealing with a playbill full of total idiots. The guy Sverdlov buys a Rolls without looking at it, then buys a spare they don't need and insists on examining it for three hours to see if it is genuine. And then he sends Hamish and the Lady home in the car he's just bought. It made no sense. Nothing in this principality made any sense. Maybe it was better they go back to sane Scotland as fast as possible.

Two days later, they actually did leave Monaco. The new spare tire was well stowed in its space. Sverdlov had indeed kept it for a few hours to "examine it," and Hamish had collected it again at about seven the evening before they departed. Hamish decided there was no more value in continuing to worry about the spare wheel, and anyway, he now was far more focussed on the trip home and ensuring the Jacoby painting Mr. Prentice had delivered was safely stowed behind the driver's seat.

The run to the French Channel coast had been uneventful enough—motorway all the way. They stopped at an Autogrill for lunch and reached the Paris area at about dinner time.

For most of the trip, Lady Lothmere was locked in thought. She had agreed to join the syndicate and signed her Renoir over to Prentice for 20 percent of the Jacoby stock. She had no contract or paperwork to prove it—Mick explained there could be no paper trail. That had bothered her a bit, but then she convinced herself that maybe Prentice might be tempted to cheat her, but there was no way he'd mess with Sverdlov or even the Pakistani, who she really never got to know very well as he spoke so little. But he did not seem a pushover either, those fierce dark eyes boring deeply into the soul.

From her Michelin Guide book, they found a little Inn in St. Cloud with a lock-up garage, dined together, and then retired wearily to their beds.

The next morning they shared a quick breakfast and were rolling again by nine thirty. Two thirty saw the ferry dock at Dover and by four thirty they had hit the M4, just missing the rush-hour traffic on the M25 London Ring Road. Customs had stopped them—not that many Rolls Royces pass by on the average morning. But the inspector had been more interested in the car than their luggage. He lifted the Jacoby, examined the sale invoice from Prentice, and placed it back. He'd never heard of a Jacoby, and since its owner had been Russian, he assumed it was just another piece of the Old Soviet Union sold off for Western cash. Anyway, customs was much more concerned with art *leaving* Britain, rather than with any entering it!

As they turned into the M4, just after Heathrow airport, Lady Lothmere grabbed her cell phone and called. Hamish could not hear the conversation, but it was not long.

Twenty minutes or so later, as they passed the first Reading exit, Lady Lothmere leaned forward and whispered, "Hamish, stop at the next service area will you? It should be called Reading West."

The fuel gauge said half full, so Hamish assumed the Lady needed a 'comfort break.'

They entered the Service Area, but as Hamish prepared to pull into the restaurant parking spaces, she motioned him to continue on past to practically the end of the parking area near its wooded border.

Lady L jumped out of the car and examined the back rear tire then surreptitiously removed the valve cap and let air escape until the tire was significantly flatter than the three others.

She searched in her bag for the cell phone again and reconnected with the last number.

"Yes, we are at the far end of the Reading Service Area going west. One tire is almost flat, and the chauffeur complains of swerving as we drive. OK—five minutes is fine."

She put down the phone and approached her totally confused "chauffeur."

"Lady L, what the heck is going on?"

"Hamish, I'll tell you after we leave. Please do not make a fuss now; there are cameras here everywhere. Just follow my lead or we will both be in very serious trouble. Now remove the luggage in the boot and please extract the spare wheel."

"Lady L," said the tired and exasperated Scot, "we do not need another tire. We do not need to move all the luggage and get out the spare. There is nothing wrong with that tire—you just let out the air!" Hamish was almost screaming by now.

"Hamish, shut up and do as I tell you. Remove the spare. Place it next to the wheel on the car with the puncture."

Just then a tow truck drew alongside. Out jumped a thirtyish, unkempt West Indian man in oil-stained jeans.

"What's the problem, lady?"

"Slow leak, I think. Can you fix it?"

"Let's take a look...Sure, no problem...but I'll have to take this tire back to the shop. Look, see it's torn on the sidewall," and he pointed very obviously to the sidewall.

"There is absolutely no tear on that tire," answered Hamish angrily. "It's almost brand new. Are you all stark-raving mad?"

Lady L and the West Indian stared icily at Hamish. Lady L clearly but silently mouthed the words "Shut the f—k up!"

Hamish walked away sullen and disgusted. "What the hell is going on, he kept whispering to himself. They all have tires on the brain!"

But what happened next really tested the poor Scot's sanity. The crazy West Indian jacked up the car, removed the wheel, compared it with the spare, whirled them both around like a break dance routine, and then filled the flat tire with air from his truck.

He then twirled both tires again, one in each hand and replaced the *same tire he had just removed.* The other tire (the spare supplied by Pallazza) he threw theatrically into the back of the tow truck. With a great show of bureaucratic efficiency, he gave her his business card and a receipt. Loudly he told the Lady he would call when the tire was fixed and send it to Scotland by UPS. She handed him a fifty-pound bill and with a courtly wave of her hand suggested he keep any change.

The West Indian drove off. Hamish walked back to the car enraged.

"Lady Lothmere, what the hell? We could have had that tire fixed in Killin, but it wasn't punctured and..." She cut him off.

"Hamish, kick the tire. Check that it's well-filled. Isn't that what chauffeurs do?"

By now totally bemused, Hamish was surprised that he actually did as he was told. Lady L grinned with amusement as he walloped the black rubber with an almighty soccer-style kick.

Giggling, she got back in the rear seat, whilst he slipped behind the steering wheel, grumbling to himself and slamming the door in deep irritation.

Once safely back on the M4 to Bath, she leaned forward again.

"Hamish, me boy, you are €15,000 richer today. I received €150,000 from Sverdlov for this car in return for delivering that spare tire. That's about three times or so more what this old crock is worth. In that spare tire was something that black fellow really wanted. Cocaine, I guess. Who cares..."

Hamish swerved first right and then left; cars blared their horns.

"Jesus, Lady L! That's as illegal as hell. You could have gotten me ten years."

"Naw, never. You are just a dumb chauffeur. You knew nothing. Maybe eighteen months max. But cool off. Everything is fine. We have our money. Sverdlov will get his receipt for the tire in the mail proving the spare was delivered, and I will give you €15,000 in cash when we get home. Not bad, eh?"

"That tire was full of...full of Cocaine?" Hamish could not believe his ears. "And we are carrying €150,000 in cash?"

"Yes, I think so. It's in the Carrefour cooler bag in the rear; the customs man actually moved it to look at the Jacoby! No, of course not, silly boy. Sverdlov will transfer the funds to my account. But, as I said, this old hearse is worth €50,000 max. Remember what that crook at Rolls Royce Perth told us? But the good thing about a Rolls is everyone always thinks they are worth far more than they actually are. When my bank manager gets a €150,000 transfer for the sale of the Rolls, he won't question it! You have to be careful with all this money laundering nonsense, you know."

"Lady Lothmere, first of all, never ever do that to me again. Secondly, I am shocked that you'd be involved such a thing."

"Aw, shocked, schmocked. We both need the money. If some dumb ass Jamaicans want to shoot crap into their veins, more fool them. Anyway, I am only assuming that is what was in the tire. Relax...it could have been Russian pickled pigs' feet for all I know!"

They drove the last 350 miles home in total silence, Hamish in cold fury, Lady L fast asleep!

As he deposited her at her house and switched her car for his, she said softly, "Hamish, you will be taking me back down in a few months, won't you?"

"I don't think so. Lady L, I have this strange habit—I try not break the law. I'll see if I can get you another driver."

"Pompous ass," she said more to herself than to him.

"What did you say, Lady L?"

"Nothing. Have a good life if I never see you again."

But, of course, they did meet again.

PART TWO

CHAPTER 17

THE GRAND OPENING

With Hamish gone, the workers in the Mexican cantina started to slacken off again. Paz realized once more, although she probably never forgot it, that it is a good thing for a woman to have a man around. She had one, of course—the ever-present sexual predator, Vladimir. But he was as useful in checking a French gas fitter as a dead whore.

Vladimir hovered around her like a vulture over his prey, waiting for the moment to pounce. She sensed it and also knew that if she allowed proximity, her body would probably succumb.

But she had to think of Natasha on the one hand and the memory of her ex-husband Peter on the other. His role in her life could not be sullied by a mismatched or misjudged affair.

Of course she remained courteous and even grateful; after all, Vladimir had provided the basic idea for the restaurant and provided (through Sverdlov) the real estate and the financial backing.

But he was useless at detail. If she went to him with a problem, he just shrugged.

But now two events loomed requiring some brave decisions. First, Sverdlov was intending to take his boat out on an extended cruise. Vladimir was not invited. His job was (and would continue to be) looking after the Russian's properties, staff, and business ventures in and around Monaco, including, of course, the new Cantina Mexicana.

The only place he could live, with the boat out to sea, was the apartment overlooking the Heliport—Paz's apartment. Could she handle that? Or should she just give in and do what her heart really wanted her to do, i.e. welcome him actively to her bed and let Natasha just get used to it. A new partner had to happen sometime, somewhere. Why not let it be the only man—faults and all—who had ever really aroused her?

Secondly, the cantina was nearing inauguration day. It was one thing to plan and physically open a restaurant. It was quite another to market and promote it, especially in a place with a well-known and ingrained prejudice towards Italian eateries.

She decided to invite him over to dinner at the apartment, have a meeting and then see what happened.

"Vladimir," she started after enchiladas, "we have to plan our opening and our marketing strategy."

"What strategy?" asked a sleepy Vladimir already imagining an active late-night workout.

"Well, I think everything will be ready within three weeks or so, but you can't just open your doors and cry "*Hallelujah*." We have to make a stir. Have a grand opening. Get some of the beautiful people to come try us—that sort of thing."

Vladimir immediately slipped into his delegation mode. He searched his mind for someone or something to take the problem off his hands.

"Ooh," he sighed, "let's use our brains here, Paz. Who do we know who can help us? We need someone who knows publicity and someone who knows the celebrities. Any ideas?"

"Well, you remember our little escapade in Mexico? Anthony Ashdown is the best publicist I ever met. You recall how he made me a national idol and cult figure in just a few months. Then I thought about my ex-husband's two daughters. One has a husband who is a real captain of industry; the other is a brilliant marketing brain."

Vladimir cut her off. "They are all miles from here. Ashdown married one sister and fled to Argentina or somewhere, and the other sister is in the USA, no?"

"No, she is in London."

"So what's *your* plan then?" Vladimir was getting bored. He was having trouble controlling his groin; the more the wine flowed the more he needed this woman. Gawd, how could he get her off this dreary subject?

"I thought we'd have a grand reunion here. Invite them all over soon and pick their brains. What do you think?"

Vladimir thought the idea stupid, but he wanted the subject closed.

"Great plan, Paz, my dear. Let's do it."

"Good. Will you help me organize things please tomorrow?"

"Of course, of course. Now can we move on?"

And with that he jumped from his seat, scooped her up, and almost rushed her into her bedroom.

"Vladimir, Natasha might..."

"She's asleep. Paz, don't deny me anymore. I told you one hundred times. I need you. Right now...and always."

He almost threw her on the bed and practically ripped the clothes off her. Paz did not resist. Regardless of her doubts, it was so satisfying to be wanted so intensely and so flattering to find a man absolutely determined to have her and possess her.

He undressed in a few seconds, and as she watched his magnificent torso unfold, memories of those sweaty nights in Mexico and Florida came flooding back. She sensed her heart pounding again, both physically and emotionally.

Paz needed no preliminaries. She was ready—as ready as he was. They swayed and sweated for about four minutes, and then it was all over in one perfectly timed and orchestrated crescendo.

He turned off her as she snuggled into his shoulder, exhausted.

He dozed off—comatose with a somewhat demented grin on his face.

She watched him for about fifteen minutes, debating with herself whether to break the affair off then and there or let what must be, be. It had to be one thing or the other. There could be no middle way with this passionate man. Caution was not an option.

She sighed deeply. She deserved some happiness. Slowly, she reached down and started coaching him back to life, marveling once more at his strength and slender majesty. Vladimir responded slowly to her caress, opened one eye, and then the other. The grin widened into a hopeful smile.

Looking at her straight in the eyes, he nodded toward his stomach.

She smiled back. She understood and slowly moved her head down to where her hand had just been. Instantly he was fully prepared again. She grabbed him with one hand, kissed him softy, and slowly dropped over him.

Normally Paz was not too fond of 'going down' on a man. She had obliged her husband from time to time because she had loved him and because she knew he liked it. It was more of a duty than a pleasure.

It wasn't because she had a hang-up or found oral sex distasteful but more because she considered God had intended the ultimate coupling between a man and a woman to be otherwise.

But with Vladimir, Paz felt different. She loved the power this position gave her to please and yet be in charge. Now *she* was at the controls, as it were. Instead of hoping as before that her man would climax quickly, she deliberately backed off when she felt him twitching and rising to a boil— anything to prolong the agony before the ultimate release.

Vladimir moaned and pleaded for closure. She smiled as much as circumstances allowed and refused. But after the next teasing 'intermission,' he acted.

As he felt her lips gently glide over him again, he grabbed her head with both hands and thrust himself up as far as he could go—again and again.

To gag would have meant losing this little love battle. She fought the urge as much as she could, even when he finally and triumphantly reached the closure he so desperately wanted.

Feeling him subside, she released him slowly, exited the bed, moved to the bathroom, and filled herself a glass of cold water.

Sitting on the closed toilet seat for a few minutes, she chortled happily to herself as she sipped the last tastes of her lover away. He had ended the oral tussle with brute force, it had to be admitted.

But Paz had left him no alternative. It was she, Paz, who had ultimately dictated and dominated the agenda. Something inside her felt that this had been an important point to make. With her husband, such feelings never arose. He was a gentle and loving human. Domination never entered his head.

Vladimir was another breed entirely. He was a warrior: dominate or be dominated. That was the difference.

Returning, she found Vladimir exactly as she had left him. Prone on his back. Spent. Satisfied. Amazed.

She moved in alongside him. Slowly he turned his head toward her and growled hoarsely, "Paz, that was truly incredible. You are my woman. Will you be my wife? Please?"

"Yes, I will" she answered, startled at the speed and audacity of her instant reply. But again she sensed equivocation could be seen as weakness. Vladimir must never see her as weak—of that, she was absolutely certain!

Anyway, she reasoned, so far this was the only man who had fully brought out the woman in her. What reason was there to hesitate? Or think? Thinking would only complicate matters.

Vladimir simply responded with one word. "Good!" And he went to sleep again with his hand firmly lodged between her very Mexican legs.

CHAPTER 18

RETURN TO MONACO

Hamish sat stiffly by his desk, reading light illuminating the letter in his right hand. He had read it many times already that day. He felt he should feel sad. In fact, he actually felt oddly relieved.

"I have decided not to come home. I am happy here. Happier than I have been for years. Our daughter is a great support, and I love Hamish Junior. Australia suits me—the sun and the simple life suits me. In fact, I have found a new friend, and we would like to get closer together. It is nothing against you, Hamish. We had many good times over the years, but something just went out of our lives. The light faded. I only realized how dull our life had become when I met Andy.

I would therefore like a divorce. Mr. Maitland can arrange it. I have already phoned him. Whatever is reasonable I will agree to. I suggested 50 percent of our savings (about £36,000 it was when I left). You keep the house— you have to have somewhere to live. But if you sell it, I hope you will be the gentleman you always were and give me half the proceeds."

The letter went on for a few more paragraphs about their past life and the baby and her new happiness in Brisbane.

Hamish started to read the letter again for the fifth time when the doorbell rang.

"Who could that be at this hour?" he said to himself. It was 8:45 p.m.

He opened the door a crack and saw the Rolls Royce dripping wet in the pouring rain. Then he saw her, sheltering under the portico roof.

"Hamish, can I come in? It's very wet out here."

He opened the door to allow her entry.

"Lady Lothmere, I thought you could not drive. Your poor eyes and all..."

"I thought so too, but here I am, and I missed every tree along the way!"

"What can I do for you, Lady L?"

"A cup of tea would be a good start. It's damp as heck out there!"

"Would that really be such a good idea, my Lady?"

"Yes, Hamish, it would. Now please just do it. I will wait for you in the study since that is where the only light seems to be shining."

Seven minutes later, Hamish brought in two cups of stewing Yorkshire Extra Strength tea and placed one on the side table next to her.

"Hamish, Mr. Maitland told me the news. About the divorce, I mean. I don't know whether to be sad for ye or not. But I guessed you may be feeling little down at heart..."

Hamish said nothing.

"Well, I mean, divorce is divorce, and no matter how it happens, it still is disrupting, wouldn't you say?

Hamish remained silent.

Lady Lothmere sipped the tea.

"Well, Hamish have ye lost yer tongue as well as your wife?"

That did it. Hamish rose to his feet, eyes blazing in fury.

"My personal affairs are none of your darn business, and I will kindly ask you to leave!"

"All right, boil in your own misery. But read this letter first before you sleep, and come and see me tomorrow for breakfast."

"I doubt that I will be doing that, my Lady."

"Oh, I think you will, laddie. A good night to you. Wish me luck missing all those trees again!"

Hamish watched the closed front door for a minute or two in black anger at the infuriating old lady who could always unsettle him and make him feel he should be doing something when all he wanted was to sit and wallow in self-pity.

He was equally angry with himself. Was he really irritated at a silly remark from the Lady or because he was simply taking out his frustration of his aimless life on someone else?

He shuffled back to his study and finished both cups of tea, staring at the electric heater, as if that orange glowing relic might somehow give him inspiration.

"Aaach, shit," he finally said. "Where is that frigging letter?"

He opened the second letter of the evening. It appeared to be from Paz in Monaco and included two expensively printed cards.

The cards were duplicate invitations to a "simple wedding ceremony" in about two months' time at the church in Fontvieille and the Mairie (town hall). Paz would be marrying Vladimir.

"Jesus Christ…marrying? I never thought it would get to that. I never thought they would marry. Damn, damn, damn it…"

He then opened the handwritten note.

Most of it told of the impending grand opening of the restaurant and how Natasha was doing at school. Then this:

"I do miss Hamish. He was such a help to me. I always felt so comfortable having him around. I lost his address. Please hand him a copy of the invitation and make sure he comes. Make sure both of you come. No excuses now! I promise you as many free enchiladas as you can eat!"

The letter ended with this comment:

"Lady Lothmere, I do hope you think I am doing the right thing. I feel I need someone at my side. I know Vladimir has his strange side, probably a result of what his country asked him to do. But woman to woman, you can understand that he just affects me as no man ever has before. I have decided to risk it all—wish me luck."

Hamish reread those two passages again and again. "*Hamish ...makes me feel comfortable!*" and "*Vladimir—affects me as no man has done before.*"

"I could kill that stupid Russian fuck-head. Why, Paz, why? He is not good enough for you...F–k me. He's simply a dud Cossack stud."

Angry, confused, and disappointed as he was, he swallowed his pride and drove over to Lady Lothmere's house for breakfast.

"Good day to ye, Hamish. As you will have noticed, the table is set for two. Welcome!" And she smiled deliciously.

After a feast of scones and strong tea, Lady L tidied up and grabbed her pad and pen (stolen from the Geneva hotel).

"So we go down for the grand opening and we stay for the wedding? Is that agreed? And you further agree to stop looking down yer nose at an old lady. And you will never ever scowl again. And you will make all the arrangements. And you will accept your part of the, let's call it, *special delivery spare tire* payment. Agreed?"

"I guess so..."

"And Hamish, you'll undo your breeches and try and get Paz out of that loathsome Russian's bed and into your own. Right?"

"What did you say?"

"You heard, Hamish, you heard. Now, good day to you. We'll meet again in a few days. I have work to do on my 'Jacoby collection.'"

"What did you mean, Lady?"

"About the Jacoby collection?"

"No, about Paz."

"Think about it as you drive home, Hamish. Good-bye, dear boy!"

CHAPTER 19

GRAND OPENING

A few days after Paz said yes to marrying Vladimir, they sat down to plan. Not the wedding, she had that in hand. But the grand opening was still an open issue. Paz had already contacted her ex-husband's two daughters. Marsha, who lived in Argentina with her American advertising executive husband, decided they just could not pop over to help, but she would try and make the wedding. No promises; it was so far away and her kids were still so young. But she did e-mail some marketing thoughts.

The younger sister, Elsie, married to Jack the British business tycoon, was more responsive. They would arrive in their private jet over the next weekend and spend a few days enjoying the Hotel de Paris and seeing how they could be of assistance.

"Wow," said Vladimir "That sounds like a good start. What did Marsha write?"

"She had a number of good points. Let me read some I underlined.

1. "Make sure the opening is an event the movers and shakers want to attend. Make sure 'the beautiful people' come and talk

about you. Avoid too much advertising. Let them discover you and pass on the good word. Monaco is a small village. Word will spread.

2. Personalize the chef. Make sure he is good and get him talked about.

3. Be ready for the six-week slump when the opening fades in the memory and the glitterati go back to the tried and true. Plan promotions; that means knowing who the first clients were, so get their names and addresses.

4. Make your suppliers work for you. If they want your business, make them pay for your menus, or banners, or whatever.

5. Get the Latino embassies, etc., to support you.

6. Keep on good terms with paparazzi. In return for tip-offs when the rich and famous eat, make sure they mention 'seen at the Mexican Cantina' in the credit."

They went through the full list of twenty or so items and finalized their ideas to discuss with the Londoners when they arrived a few days later. Paz was getting excited. Vladimir was bored. His solution to everything was a simple "Ah, just give them a free vodka every now and then! That's all you need!"

Jack and Elsie arrived lavishly and loudly in a hired stretch limousine. They immediately invited Paz and Vladimir to join them for lunch at the famed Hotel de Paris, suggesting they meet first in the hotel's American Bar where a beer can cost more than the most expensive item on Paz's menu!

"Paz, how are you?" shouted Jack, his Armani suit glistening in the light pouring through the hotel bar window. "How can you afford to live here? Never paid a year's salary for a glass of champagne before! Here, I want you to meet Eugenio who, I am reliably told, is the best event organizer in the area."

Eugenio, camel-haired coat slung over his broad shoulders Italian-style, stood up and bowed deeply.

"Vladimir, congratulations!" said Elsie looking more English than her native American in a pink chiffon dress and white Ascot hat. "I am so happy for you both. Come sit here beside me and tell me all about the romance and your wedding plans."

Pleasantries over, Jack took over the meeting as was his habit.

"Look, Paz, this is what we have been able to arrange so far. One of my companies does some business with the principality. They make here a frothy beer product that we distribute throughout the Old Commonwealth. I've met the Prince once, and I hope we can entice him to at least make an entry at your opening. He always tries to help a new venture, but he is a very busy man. If he can make it, you will have to work with the authorities on security. In fact, that could be one of your jobs, OK, Vladdie boy?"

Vladimir nodded a bit sullenly. He was not too happy at this round-bellied, perfumed Brit throwing his weight around and issuing orders to him, the dominant Russian male. But he said nothing.

Jack raced on.

"You will remember from our Mexican adventure that I have close ties with Norteno Breweries of Monterrey—the makers of Negro Noche and other Mexican brews. They will send you enough free beer to keep you afloat for at least six months and will arrange for the Mexican consul from Marseille to be here, **and**, and, and—listen to this, Vladdie-Laddie—they will try and see that Gloria Adora—Norteno's spokeslady and the Mexican TV star—sings if you like. I think the Prince knows her and likes her."

"Who?" asked Vladimir with a touch of aggression.

"Gloria Adora. Paz will know who she is. Remember 'La Rosa Rosa'?"

Paz nodded excitedly.

Jack marched on for another full five minutes, snapping out directives and ideas until a thought struck Paz.

"Hold it, Jack. You haven't even seen the restaurant yet!"

"Of course I have. Eugenio took all these pictures and already has some preliminary thoughts."

"Thoughts? What thoughts?" asked Vladimir peevishly.

"Well, for example, the inside area of the cantina is too small for a big inaugural party, so Eugenio has already asked the authorities for permission to place a tent over the car park space for the opening. He has excellent relations with the chief of police..."

As he talked, Jack opened his briefcase to extract a huge stack of drawings.

Vladimir grew more and more restive.

"I guess all *we* have to do is wash the dishes!" he snapped.

"How's that?" asked Jack, who was totally immune to any form of sarcasm.

Paz stared at Vladimir.

"Look, I thought I was supposed to be in charge of the opening. You guys seem determined to take over."

"Well, Vladimir, if you have your own plans, maybe you should share them. Time is not on our side here," replied a somewhat stunned Jack

"Yes," added Paz. "I apologize if you were working on something. Vladimir, you never told me…"

They all looked over at Vladimir. He said nothing for a minute and then cleared his throat somewhat dramatically.

"I had thought of inviting Jenny, or 'Scotty' Lafer over."

"Scotty—the underwear girl?" asked Eugenio dumbfounded. "How would she fit in?"

"She would create the stir we should be looking for," countered Vladimir, a little embarrassed.

That 'Scotty' Lafer could create a stir would be instantly confirmed by any regular night owl in the principality. 'Scotty' always caused a 'stir' wherever she went. She was born Jennifer, or Jenny. But everyone knew her as Scotty.

How Jenny earned the nickname 'Scotty' is a famous Monaco cocktail tale, especially among the younger men.

Jenny used to hang out at Mosser's Restaurant and Nightclub. Her passion was backgammon, and she was expert. In the evening before the club became too raucous to concentrate, she'd sit at her corner table and challenge any brave enough to try and beat her. Young lads and mature men hopeful of a dance invariably tried. They rarely won. Either her skill, or her long blond hair, or the short silver skirt defeated them. Nine evenings out of ten, the challengers lost and paid for their temerity by settling her bar bill.

Markos Marios, a Greek ship owner and another so-called backgammon pro, was constantly prompted to challenge her. He usually declined; he knew Scotty would not be an easy conquest.

But one famous evening, she seemed out of sorts. Markos watched her lose to a young man who, on a good day, would have been mangled in her dust.

Markos sensed the time had come to add fame to his fortune. He challenged Scotty, but his challenge contained a twist. If he won, Scotty was to do a strip dance for him and his party.

Scotty smiled. Hustling was not her game. Markos persisted. Eventually she stood up and faced him angrily.

"All right, all right. I'll play you for a look at my body if you play me for your Ferrari. Is that a deal? Or not?"

The barroom howled with delight. Every man there had often fantasized on the personal charms of the beautiful English girl with the golden locks and the endless cleavage.

"Do it, do it, do it!" they screamed. Markos could not back down now without risking a massive loss of face. He had challenged—and he was challenged in return.

He had to accept or be laughed at. Ridicule was the one thing a proud Greek could never tolerate. Eventually, he accepted.

The area was cleared, and a table and two chairs were set up in the middle of the dining room. Jenny sat facing the bar, Markos opposite her. The challenge was the best of five games.

Scotty won the first easily, trapping the Greek by closing off his entry quarter. Markos eventually grabbed the second. After two hours, the score stood at two games each. Game five would be the decider.

Scotty smiled. The gods would be with her. She could feel the red Ferrari wheel between her hands already. Markos imagined himself staring at her bare thighs.

It was a close game, and then the doubles started to reward every other throw of the Greek's wrist. He won. Everyone screamed with delight. Scotty swept the game off the table and motioned the band to start playing. If she had to lose, she would lose graciously.

As the band played "Celebration," she jumped on the table and started swaying her hips and arms with total abandon. Voices hushed. The males drew closer. The girls wondered what they could learn from this amazing display of pure feminine sensuality.

Eventually the little white blouse was unbuttoned and slipped off to reveal a perfect pair of unsupported breasts, provoking intense and sweaty desire in every pair of trousers standing by.

Two minutes later the lower zipper was eased down, and the silver skirt finally revealed the apex of male lust under a thin, sheer, transparent red G-string.

Scotty swung her hips nearer and nearer the nose of the fascinated Greek. Suddenly, the crowded started chanting again.

"*Take it off. Take it off. Take it off.*"

Markos was being challenged once more. He stood up and with one beautifully timed swoop of his hand, ripped the little slip right off her hips. The crowd went wild. Scotty went even wilder jumping up and down, exposing then hiding her most secret and very smoothly shaved private parts.

Suddenly, the manager stopped the band. Enough was enough. Scotty, a look of wild triumph on her face, scooped up her skirt and blouse and bounced off to the ladies' room. The torn G-string remained on the table—and stayed there all night, no one apparently daring to disturb it.

Ever since that famous night, rumor had it that Scotty never put on underwear again. The rumor became a fable and the fable a folkloric fact. The nickname 'Scotty,' of course, referred to the fact that the Scots were reputed to wear little under their kilts.

Paparazzi did their best to prove or disprove the story. As Scotty exited her chauffeur-driven car, they would be ready, cameras poised to "catch the bare snatch" (as one so inelegantly put it).

This was the 'Scotty' Vladimir wanted to feature at the Cantina ceremony.

"So that is what I had in mind," finished Vladimir with a flourish of both arms.

"Everyone wants to know if Scotty wears briefs or not. I'll ask her to reveal all on opening night. We open. She opens. She'll lift her skirt for all to see once and for all! I know she'll do it. That's the sort of girl she is.

"And to get the ball rolling, I thought we'd ask Hamish to lift his silly kilt and moon the crowd, and after Scotty we'd ask any girl who also wanted to reveal all to join the fun.

"Guests could bet €1,000 to challenge any lady to see if she was wearing undies or not. If they guess right, they win a magnum bottle of champagne. Lose and the €1,000 goes to charity.

"As a climax, and to complete the festivities, the last girl to show all would be Lena, a Brazilian transvestite I know. Imagine the hilarity when she lifts her skirt and bingo, *she* becomes a HE. It will be a real gas, believe me."

Vladimir sat down in triumph. He had won he felt sure. Who could top that big idea? Nobody said anything. No one dared look at each other.

Finally, Eugenio found the courage to say what they were all thinking.

"Vladimir, I don't think we can do this with the Consul and maybe the Prince in attendance. It wouldn't be right."

"Well, then cancel the frigging Consul. Who needs him? We need to create fun and excitement."

"Sorry," added Jack, the brewer. "He's already invited and he's accepted. Let's try your ideas at a later date, OK?"

Vladimir had enough. He threw back his chair and stood, hands on the table, glowering at the three others.

"Fuck the lot of you. Why don't you all just piss off and let people who know the area do what's best. If you can't recognize a great plan when you see it, then fuck you all. Do what you want. I'm out of here." Vladimir stalked out.

Paz's eyes followed his exit. No one said anything for a few more minutes.

"You sure he is OK?" asked Jack of Paz. "We are only trying to help, you know."

"He'll be all right, don't worry. I guess this was all a bit overwhelming for him. Please continue."

They did continue, but a bit of the initial enthusiasm had eroded away.

<hr>

Lady Lothmere was busy on her own preparations. Mick Prentice had rung frequently and once again professed himself delighted with how things were going.

He'd seen the note in *Art Dealer and Auction House* magazine placed by his friend Daly remarking on the new interest in Jacobys, and he'd even found one small editorial in the *Herald Tribune's* Saturday Culture section wondering where the next big collecting craze might land, mentioning the recent interest in painters like Jacoby.

"But, Lady, we must not rush things or we could create suspicion. As we agreed in Lausanne, I plan to place via St. Pete's one more Jacoby in an auction in London next week. I hope you can be there doing the same thing you did in Geneva. Tell everyone you are still searching for your second Jacoby and show exasperation when you lose out—again. I will be telephone bidding against you through a pal in Devon. If all goes well, we'll plan a special Jacoby auction here in Monaco next month, maybe somehow associated with the cantina opening. I don't know yet...I have to think it through. You'll be here then, isn't that correct? For the grand opening of your friend's restaurant? Good, good. Best of good fortune to you in London. Call me when it's over—on the landline, of course. Cells are so easy to trace."

Actually, the London auction followed almost exactly the Prentice script.

Not only did the 'planted' Jacoby fetch over £60,000 ($100,000) before Lady L emotionally gave up again, but another late-entry Jacoby from Russia even surpassed that amount without Lady L or Prentice's stooges doing a thing.

Art Dealer and Auction House magazine's reporter followed a sad Lady L out onto the auction house balcony overlooking Park Lane.

"Lady Lothmere, could we have a word?"

"Who are you, girl?"

"I represent *Art Dealer and Auction House* magazine and was sent here by Mr. Daly. I noticed you were after another Jacoby. Mr. Daly saw you, I think, in Geneva some weeks ago, is that right?"

"Yes, I was there. Very disappointing. Very disappointing."

"Why are you so interested in this comparatively minor artist?"

Lady L was not sure this was just a curious reporter following an emotional bidder or whether she (or Daly) smelled a rat and were quietly digging.

"Come join me for a coffee, will you? In fact here's five pounds. Please get the coffees from the counter, and I'll be sitting over there. Getting a little old, you know! My bunions are acting up."

The girl, somewhat taken aback, did as she was asked.

"How old are you, lassie?" Lady Lothmere asked when the girl returned with the two steaming cups. "I would guess about twenty-six to thirty? If I am correct, you are entering the finest decade for a woman. Enjoy it. I am about three times your age.

"Now to answer your question as to my interest in the rather mediocre Mr. Jacoby and his works: it has all to do with my husband. I was married for many years to a man who adored me and gave me everything I needed—emotionally and financially.

"Then he died suddenly...died a few weeks, in fact, before we were about to make a trip around Europe. Do you know why we had planned that holiday? In my dining room is one lone Jacoby we bought in Italy many years ago. My husband loved that corny Tuscan vineyard scene.

"For some reason I will never quite understand, Scots men like to hang their pictures in pairs. Two views of the highlands. Two hunting scenes. Two sailing boats on a Loch. Two portraits of ancestors. You know the sort of thing?"

The reporter smiled. She warmed to this dear old lady.

"The lone Jacoby in the dining room bothered him. Only a second, somewhat matching, Jacoby would balance the room in his mind. I wanted to find the twin Jacoby he always craved. I thought it would cost me no more than £10,000—only paid about £5,000 for the first one, I think. But suddenly these Jacoby prices have gone insane."

Lady Lothmere now leant over and grabbed the girl's arm.

"I can't afford £60,000. I dare say you know your way around this crazy art world. Do you think you can find me one before these art pigs price me completely out of the market?"

The girl smiled and evaded the question.

"Could I take a picture of you, Lady Lothmere?"

"Why?"

"I'd like to do a little piece on you. Maybe that will unlock a Jacoby in some attic somewhere!"

"Thank you, child. Do what you like, but I am sure you could find me one. I did buy you a coffee, remember?"

The reporter laughed out loud as she took the picture.

"I'll try, Lady Lothmere. I really will try!"

"What is your name, dear?"

"Janet Jameson, Lady."

"Well Janet, it was a pleasure to chat with you. Here's my card. If you find that Jacoby, give me a call. There's another coffee in it for you!"

Janet smiled again and said her farewells.

When she left, Lady Lothmere called Mickey Prentice and recounted quickly what had just happened.

"What is the reporter's name?"

"Janet Jameson, like the whisky. I think your pal Daly sent her…"

"Be careful, Lady L. I know her column. She's a bit of a muckraker. Loves a seamy expose. Take care."

"Don't worry, I charmed the thongs off her firm, young bottom…"

They said their good-byes.

Lady Lothmere was right. Janet Jameson had been enthralled. She rang Daly as soon as New York opened.

"Art, I got those pics on the Constables they'll be offering next month. And I had a coffee with that old Lady Jacoby collector. She's as pure as Highland spring water. There's no story there—except one of a dear old lady trying to fulfil her husband's last wishes. I got the story. Makes a nice emotional filler for next month's "Collectors Profiles" column. Tell you about it later. See you, Art…"

Daly trusted his prize snoop, Jameson. He drew a line through 'Jacoby Manipulation' on his to-do list and substituted 'Find Jacobys to sell.'

Janet Jameson's plane was late. As usual. She sat in the British Airways business lounge staring out of the window bored and irritated.

"Should have flown Virgin," she grumbled. "But then I am not much of a Virgin." She grinned as thoughts of her last affair floated through her mind. That macho Argentinean thought she would be an 'easy lay.' Boy, she made him really work for his orgasm. She got a great kick out of exhausting arrogant men in her bed. The Argentinean never called her back, but then she didn't want him to.

"Where the hell are the real men, these days? The keepers?"

This well-worn lament of the successful thirty-something city girl caused her mind to drift back to the Scottish Lady and the Jacobys.

"Married for yonks years, loved and looked after, and still she carries a torch for her old man—dead or not. You don't see that too often these days."

The old lady had asked to help find a twin Jacoby, and frankly she had had absolutely no intention of obliging—far too busy, etc.

And maybe, she thought, that was HER problem—always far too busy to take a deep breath and do something just for the good of it. Not for money. Not for fame. Just to be...good.

She opened her laptop and booted up. She would see if she could find that old dear her dream.

After a ten minute search, she discovered that a Mr. Sverdlov had purchased a number of Jacobys three or four years earlier, mainly in Vienna. Mr. Sverdlov was now listed as living both in Moscow and in Monaco.

Janet knew nobody in Moscow, but she had a warm spot for that old rogue in Monaco called Mickey Prentice. He was always trying to get her to puff up some 'picture' or other he was currently trying to off-load.

"Hello, Mickey boy? This is Janet Jameson. How are you?"

Oops—bad idea. Asking Mickey how he was would expose a person to hours of his medical miseries. Mr. Gloom, she called him.

Janet cut him off.

"Mick, I am about to get on a plane. I have a request of you. Do you know a Russian called Sverdlov? He seems to be resident in Monaco. Rich guy. Probably one of these oil barons. Collects art like you and I collect hotel shampoos."

Mick froze. This was Janet Jameson, the *Art Dealer and Auction House* investigative reporter. Was she smelling a rat?

"Sverdlov? Name rings a bell. What do you want him for?"

"Apparently he collects Jacobys. Bought a bunch some years ago. I am wondering where those went and if he still has them."

Mick was doubly frightened now. She was on to them. Hell and damnation.

"Janet, I'll see if I can locate him. You still have the same mobile number?"

"Yes, I do. Mickey, the reason I want to contact him is because you may have noticed the price of Jacobys has skyrocketed lately to absurd levels, in my view. But who am I to judge?"

Prentice grabbed his bottle of 'emergency crisis' Grappa and poured himself a stiff slug.

"The thing is, I met this old Scottish Lady who has been trying to buy a Jacoby lately and is being outbid every time. It made me think..."

Prentice poured another slug.

"I wonder if this Sverdlov guy might want to part with one of his Jacobys at a decent price so this old dear can have her second Jacoby and die peacefully."

Prentice put down the glass of Grappa and began to breathe again and ever more calmly as Janet told him the full story of her suspicions of a price-rigging cartel and then meeting the old lady and how she had been asked to help find a Jacoby for her.

Mick's mood now swung 180 degrees from terror to triumph.

"Janet, I'll see what I can do. Yes, I saw that old lady in Geneva when I was bidding myself for a Japanese client. What is it about these damn Jacobys lately? They really seem to me to be selling over the top. Insane prices."

"I know, Mickey, these crazes happen. For a while my boss Art suspected a bunch of shills operating a benchmark sting. But it is not that;

it is just that Jacoby has become New York and London cocktail chic. It happens. You know that."

"Janet, I'll get back to you as soon as possible." Mick replaced the phone and started to jump in the air until a spasm in his back reminded him that his two perforated discs and artificial knee did not appreciate such exuberance.

He plopped back in his chair and sat pondering life for a few minutes before grabbing the phone.

"Mr. Sverdlov, please. Yes, it is urgent. Please tell him Mickey Prentice is on the line. Hello? Serge? Listen, we have had an almighty lucky break. Have a pencil handy? I will be e-mailing you shortly, and here is exactly how I want you to respond to me."

Prentice dictated the reply, replaced the phone, and then opened his laptop to send this e-mail.

To Serge Sverdlov,

I think we have met. Anyway, I am trying to locate some Jacobys. I need one for a contact at Art Dealer and Auction House *magazine who has always been very supportive of this gallery. She wants to pass it on to some old lady in Scotland who is down on her luck or something. I know you bought a bunch of Jacobys some years ago.*

Regards, Mick Prentice

Serge Sverdlov read the message, smiled, and e-mailed back exactly what Prentice had dictated over the phone.

Reply to Mr. Prentice

Yes, Mr. Prentice, we do know each other. You tried to sell me a somewhat overpriced Renoir! Yes, I own a bunch of Jacobys. I bought them mainly in Vienna as a gift for Boris Yeltsin's dacha outside Moscow. It was thanks to him we all did so well. The idea was to hang them in his entry corridor; Jacobys are all almost identical, and Yeltsin liked symmetry. He had absolutely no taste! I never got around to giving them to him; some other grateful oil trader beat me to it! I might sell you one—what are they worth?

Prentice replied as soon as the e-mail came in, blind-copying the entire correspondence to Janet Jameson.

Thanks for your reply. Great news, Serge. I guess you paid about €5,000 each for them. Would you be able to sell me one for €10,000 - €15,000?

To which Sverdlov replied:

What are they worth now, Mr. Prentice?

Prentice:

Sell me the one for €15,000, and I'll tell you. It is for a very worthy cause.

Sverdlov:

OK, you have a Jacoby for €15,000. You pay all transport, etc., costs. Send me the details. You have my bank account, no?

Prentice:

Thank you so much. The good news is Jacobys have been selling lately for over €50,000. So your other Jacobys could easily net hundreds of thousands more. Nobody understands it. As you say, if Boris Yeltsin liked them, they must be crap!

Sverdlov:

You conned me. I take back my acceptance of €15,000.

Prentice:

Come on, you agreed. Anyway, it is for a good cause. I have an idea. If you don't want the other Jacobys, why don't we try and sell them here for you in Monaco? I won't charge you full commission. OK?

Sverdlov:

I'll think about it. You are an old carpet salesman…

Prentice:

No, I am an astute art dealer.

Prentice reread the e-mail exchange, copied it again to Janet Jameson at *Art Dealer and Auction House* to make sure she received it, and smiled. He had, thanks to her inquiry, not only done her a personal favor, for which she should be eternally grateful, but the woman he feared most had offered the cartel the most obvious excuse to hold a Jacoby sale in his gallery. Probably she would write about it, vain as she was, revealing, probably, how her shrewd talk with a dear old lady had unearthed lost art, answered the old lady's dream, and would possibly make a fortune for a collector who had no idea of the value of works he no longer needed and had parked in his garage somewhere in Russia.

Prentice was right. That was exactly how the article was written in the August edition of *Art Dealer and Auction House*. It even suggested that Jacoby owners should sell their collections now, whilst prices were so high.

Could there be any higher irony?

The feared investigative reporter—the revealer of fakes, manipulations, and cons—is beautifully conned herself. Wonderful!

Prentice immediately started planning the big Jacoby art sale where at least six of the syndicate's Jacobys would be sold. In Monaco. In his Gallery. At absurdly high prices. Nosy Janet Jameson would be cordially invited!

He rang up BMW and confirmed his order for a white 7 Series, nicely loaded.

Then he e-mailed *Art Dealer and Auction House* one last time as a letter to the editor:

Reference Miss Jameson's article on finding a Jacoby for the Scottish collector and her desire to fulfil her husband's dying wish, isn't it great in this greedy day that a good deed carried out for a frustrated collector actually leads to another owner realizing the new worth of art he no longer wants or needs?

For your information, Monaco Galleria Internationale will be offering part of the Sverdlov Jacoby collection Miss Jameson wrote about and other Jacobys for sale in October in Monaco. Probably never before have so many Jacobys been offered at one time. And it is all thanks to a chance meeting in an auction house café and with one dedicated reporter's wish to do a good deed for a dear lady.

Game, set, and match. *Art Dealer and Auction House* was now directly linked to what would one day be known as the art con of the century.

CHAPTER 20

AN UGLY RUSSIAN BEAR

When Paz returned home from the opening ceremony meeting with Jack and Elsie, Vladimir was not there. He was, in fact, at Jimmz's Disco with some dubious Russian friends and enjoying—if that is the right word—rather more vodka than was good for him.

At about three in the morning he banged and bumped his way into the apartment and woke both Paz and her daughter Natasha.

"Vladimir, what the hell happened to you? Natasha get back to bed. I'll handle this!"

"Fuck you, woman. Mexican whore."

"What did you say?"

"MEXICAN FUCKING BITCH-FACED WHORE!"

"What the hell did you say that for?"

"Because, bitch-face, you listened to those dumb dicks from England and pushed me—me, your man, your soon-to-be-husband who got you everything—you pushed me aside like some old used toilet paper. Vladimir does not LIKE THAT."

"Well, I don't like drunks. I've seen too many in my family. Go sleep it off, and we'll talk about whatever is bothering you in the morning."

"Pushing me away again, bitch-face? I will sleep in your bed and you will put your bitch-face over my great Russian cock…"

At that Paz slammed her bedroom door closed and locked it.

She didn't go back to bed until she could hear the deep snore of the very drunk Russian.

In the morning, Vladimir was still sound asleep. She quietly made Natasha her breakfast, and they both carefully evaded the comatose body as Paz took her daughter to school.

When she returned about forty minutes later, she heard Vladimir in the shower. She sat down at the dining room table until he appeared with a towel wrapped around his middle.

"Would you like some coffee?" she asked him tentatively.

"OK," he replied as he sat down opposite her.

Coffee served, Paz waited until the caffeine had somewhat circulated through his bloodstream before she spoke.

"What was all that about last night, Vladimir? You know Natasha probably heard much of your ranting. Whatever was bothering you?"

Vladimir did not reply.

She asked him again.

"Why did you attack me last night? What did I do? Speak to me, Vladimir. You owe me that…"

Vladimir put down his cup, his fine black hair still dripping from the shower.

"Paz, I owe you nothing. You owe *me* everything. I brought you here. I got you space for your lousy Cantina. My boss financed you. I even offered to marry you…"

He stopped.

"And?"

"And you, Paz…You piss in my face. You treat me like I don't exist. First, you do all the planning with that slimy Scottish jerk who shared MY boat. I even got his old hag's car sold. Then you ask me to arrange your opening. And then you do it all with Jack the jackass from London. Watch it, lady—Russians don't like being pushed around. If you didn't know that before, KNOW IT NOW! Treat me with respect or…"

"Or what, Vladimir?"

"Or go back to the Mexico City barrios where I found you."

"You 'found' me in the 'barrios' of Mexico did you? I thought you came after me in Florida. I seem to remember being begged to join you. Maybe I should have stayed there."

"Yes, maybe you should have."

He finished his coffee and went back into the bathroom. Paz grabbed her handbag and left for the restaurant.

"Jesus," she said softly to herself. "Why are the most attractive men so damn complicated?" For sure she'd have to be more careful in future—if Vladimir and Paz indeed even had a future.

But that decision could wait a while. For now there was work to do.

CHAPTER 21

ASHDOWN RESURFACES

"Paz!" It was Jack's very English voice on the phone.

"Paz, we have the most wonderful news. There is so much to tell you. Can you come over to the hotel today. Maybe even now?"

Paz wondered if she should find Vladimir and take him along, but she thought better of it. Vladimir's reaction could not be guaranteed anymore. Paz decided at this stage is would be wiser to go alone, and she joined Jack at the hotel about 12:00 p.m.

Jack and Elsie and Eugenio were sitting at the boardroom table of their suite. Papers were strewn all over the surface between them.

"Paz, Eugenio has come up with some fantastic new ideas. Here—sit by me. Wait till you here all this. Eugenio, spout the good spout, will you?"

The suave Franco-Italian brushed back his hair with his palms,

allowing the jacket sloped over his shoulders to slip back over his chair-back, and then dramatically cleared his fine Italian tenor.

"Miss Orteno, let me start by saying that none of us here really understood or knew your true background. Mr. Jack here has told me all about your adventures in Mexico when you became the face of the opposition, the talk of the country, and how you rallied Mexican womanhood to insist on its rights. Miss "Brown Power" they called you. And you named the women you championed Brown Diamonds. I liked that. Jack showed me some of the video and pictures—very, very impressive.

(Eugenio was referring, of course, to the mad Mexican adventure so fully chronicled in the book *The Litt;e Brown Dioamond.*)

"I let the palace know surreptitiously who they had here lurking in their midst, and even the Prince's staff are dying to meet with you. I will arrange the meeting through Captain Carpentier, the Prince's aide de camp. Of course interviews with State TV and the other local media will follow. Within a week you and this restaurant will be as well-known as the Casino or the Palace.

"The Minister of State, Mr. Jouster, also wants to know who planned the Mexican thing, and we let him know all about Ashdown. They want to meet him too and—well, you tell her Mr. Jack."

"Paz, I have sent the Learjet to Argentina to get him; he'll be here in two or three days. Isn't that fantastic? Ashdown at first said no, but the lure of that jet finally broke him."

Eugenio took the imaginary microphone again.

"The Prince will come to the opening for sure now, so all the glitterati and hangers-on will follow. Mr. Carpentier will even give us his list of the most important opinion leaders in town.

"Next, you may have heard that there is to be a major art sale and show here sponsored by Monaco Galleria Internationale—Mr. Prentice's place. They will be selling part of some Russian billionaire's collection of Jacobys, which seem to have recently become very fashionable. The Russian collector happens to be your sponsor—Mr. Sverdlov. Small world isn't it?"

Paz followed speechless. This was going too fast, like a car rolling down the hill without brakes, but she said nothing.

"Well, Sverdlov agreed to donate one of these Jacobys to the restaurant in return for getting some publicity going both for you and his own art sale. We will auction the painting and send the proceeds of the sale to the Mexican abused women charities you supported. To your Brown Diamonds!

"This means the Mexican Ambassador—not the Consul from Marseille—the **Ambassador** from Paris will be flying down to attend. Because he is coming, the Prince will try and find the time to participate in the auction, but we promised we will arrange that he is outbid. No more room in the palace for anymore paintings!"

Eugenio paused and grinned in immense self-satisfaction.

"And," added Jack again, "we'll still have this Adora broad willing to sing; she remembers you well from those crazy days in Mexico. And we were right, the Prince knows her. So all the pieces for the grandest grand opening ol' Monaco has ever seen are bang in place. Just leave it to the men!"

Paz started to speak, and then she thought of Vladimir and the crazed look in his eyes. She rose slowly from her seat, tried to say something, and then gently collapsed as a blow-up doll might after losing its air.

The three men brought her around soon enough with some water and brandy. Jack offered the opinion that she had probably been working too hard. Paz slowly rose to her feet.

"Thank you all so much, gentlemen. Your ideas are fantastic. Please excuse me for now—I don't feel too well. Can we meet again tomorrow?"

And she walked out.

The three men were quiet for a moment and then turned back to their work. These were men of action, and there was not much time to spare—and so much still to do.

CHAPTER 22

HAMISH WALKS IN

Hamish had accepted the briefcase with the €15,000 a little sheepishly but accept it he did. He decided to bring the money with him and deposit it in a bank in Monaco—far from the prying eyes of a divorce lawyer.

The morning they left Scotland, Hamish did, however, give the car a good going-over. He was determined that the Lady L would not stash another freight load of illicit drugs under his nose. When he opened the spare wheel space, he found it empty.

He rushed into the kitchen.

"Lady L, did the West Indian ever return that spare tire from Monaco? It is not in the car."

"No, I guess he stole it. Can't trust anyone these days. Anyway, Hamish, you always said we don't need a spare, right?"

"No Lady L, it was always *you* who insisted we don't need one, remember?"

"Whatever, Hamish—let's get on and pack the baggage. I like using that spare tire space for valuables anyway."

Hamish shrugged. The subject of spare wheels drove him insane.

"OK, Lady L, But Sverdlov will be pissed. He ordered that spare especially for this car."

"Hamish, that spare wheel had a job to do and it did it as you now well know. It is no longer our affair. Forget it!"

The next day saw the car (well packed and polished) start its second trip down to the Riviera Coast.

The ride across France was uneventful. They traversed the channel by car ferry from Dover and overnighted just south of Lyon. Eventually, they reached the Marriott Hotel in Cap d'Ail late the next evening.

The Marriott was somewhat cheaper than the Columbus and since they planned to stay through the wedding, offered a more economical solution. Yet the hotel was no more than a ten-minute walk from Fontvieille Harbor where the Cantina was nearing its opening day.

After a late breakfast and getting the Rolls washed for its new owner, Hamish hurried over to the little restaurant. It was about eleven thirty by the time he got there.

He nearly missed the Cantina from all the commotion and construction going on. A huge tent was being erected over the restaurant 'terrasse' and the car parking places opposite. Traffic was rerouted out of that part of the harbor and was diverted through the nearby car park tunnel. That was a first—annoying to the residents, but since the orders had come from the very top, no one said much.

Inside the shadow of the tent had darkened the main dining room. Hamish saw no one inside, even though all the doors were open. He was about to leave again, when he thought he heard a faint sobbing noise coming from the kitchen. He walked over.

Paz was sitting at the food preparation table, head in hands, sobbing softly. Hamish felt his stomach turn. He now knew it—he loved this woman. The old Scottish Lady had been right. She knew it long before he did. Paz was his to lose, if he would allow it!

"Paz, what's going on? Why are you crying?"

At the sound of the Scottish lilt, she looked up, sighed, and rushed over to greet him. She hugged Hamish as tightly as she could and started sobbing again.

"Paz, stop your crying will ye? Whatever is the matter?"

"Nothing and everything is the matter, Hamish. But it is so very good to see you. I am so sorry I greeted you like this. Where are my manners—would you like a coffee or a beer or something?"

"I'll try one of those weak Mexican brews of yours, thank ye!"

She moved to the fridge and handed him a cold bottle of Norteno's best, flown in only the day before from Monterey, Mexico.

The two sat down at one of the small dining tables.

"OK, girl, now tell me all. What is going on here?"

She told him. How she re-fell in love with Vladimir. How she had wanted him to help her plan the opening. How they had hit on the plan to ask the old Mexican gang for help. How Jack and Elsie had taken over and prepared the most amazing launch she could imagine. How the palace wanted to meet her—she told him everything.

"So what the sodding hell is the matter with all that, you daft lassie?" insisted a puzzled Hamish.

"The trouble is Vladimir. He went nuts the other night. He can't stand the competition. He feels he started this whole Mexican café thing—which is true—and now he feels he is losing control of the venture. And of me!"

"Of ye?"

"Yes, he stormed out of a meeting we had with Jack and then got drunk somewhere. He came raging into the apartment hurling abuse at me. In front of Natasha he called me a 'bitch-faced whore.' Oh, Hamish, why do my projects always end up in chaos?"

Hamish was silent, stunned, and simmering inside with cold rage.

"He called you what? *A bitch-faced whore?* I'll beat the living shit out of the bugger…"

"No, Hamish, he was drunk. Please don't make things worse. Anyway he is a dangerous, trained killer; do not go near him.

The problem I have is this. If he went berserk over the rather modest initial grand opening plans, he is going to go even more crazy when he hears what the team is cooking up now. The Prince, TV interviews, press, ambassadors, singers, auctions—you name it—all done in days without any input from him or me! He'll go nuts again. What do I do?"

Hamish went silent again, but his brain was racing. He kept remembering his earlier self-advice: Paz is yours to lose—yours to lose. The thought provoked a twisted plan to slowly form in his mind.

He told Paz he planned to have 'a few' drinks with Vladimir that night and cool him off. He promised he'd be careful and calm, but nonetheless, he cautioned her to lock her doors and not let him in until Hamish had delved to the bottom of Vladimir's hang-ups. Paz agreed, relieved to have been able to confide in someone.

Hamish called Vladimir on his cell and arranged to meet that evening at the English pub The Ship and Castle very near the Monte Marina apartment building.

Vladimir was not in a good mood.

"What brings you back here, Macintosh?"

"The Rolls, remember? We promised to drive it back. And attend the grand opening. And you invited us to your wedding—or did you forget?"

Hamish said it with a smile, but his eyes were cold.

"*She* invited you to the wedding, not me. You don't have to stay for that—if there *is* going to be a wedding at all."

Hamish feigned surprise.

"What? No wedding? Why ever not…"

"'Cos the bitch shows me no respect."

"Shit, man," answered Hamish, "she's marrying you. What more respect do you want?"

"I want her to send all those perfumed English advisers out of here. I have—or at least I *had*—everything planned and under control."

"You mean you arranged the meeting with the Prince?

"What meeting?"

Hamish explained in withering detail.

"And what a coup to get that art auction at the opening and the ambassador coming from Paris. Brilliant planning, I'd say…Good work, Vladimir."

Bleary-eyed, Vladimir gazed back at him icily.

"What are you talking about? What ambassador? What auction?"

Hamish explained more and again in excruciating detail.

"And the TV interviews with Ashdown—whoever he is. Didn't you arrange all those things, Vladimir? I thought you said you were in charge of the grand opening."

"Ashdown? Coming here? Who invited that asshole over?"

Vladimir was now standing, or rather swaying, his eyes not thirty centimeters from those of his torturer.

"Why, Vladimir, didn't *you* invite him? I thought you were the big grand opening guy? I thought you said you had it all under your control."

Vladimir slugged down the last of his vodka and raged out of the pub, knocking over seats as he lurched into the night.

Hamish left a one hundred euro note on the bar and then followed at a safe distance.

As he watched Vladimir storm into the Monte Marina building, he quietly dialed 17—the Monegasque Police number.

They arrived just as Vladimir was angrily trying to kick in the locked door of Paz's apartment.

Enraged even further by the sight of the two police agents, he picked up an umbrella from the stand just outside the door and slammed it onto the head of the leading cop.

That is something you just do not do in sleepy, well-ordered Monaco. Vladimir was instantly overwhelmed by both officers and carted off to the local jail perched high on Monaco rock.

Hamish smiled. Round one to Scotland.

He then called Paz on the mobile and asked her to let him into the apartment. He found her petrified, hugging her daughter protectively, both shivering with cold or fright or both.

"Paz, I am so sorry. I tried to stop him, but you are right. Something has snapped in that fellow. He is paranoiac about the grand opening and his lack of involvement. Luckily I called the police in time. Watch him Paz. Keep away from him. Are you all right now?"

At the sight of the reassuring Scot, the woman and daughter calmed down, had a pot of tea with Hamish, and then went back to bed. Paz cried herself back to sleep.

When Sverdlov heard the full story about his protégé, he was furious. Russians in the principality try to maintain a low profile until they feel they are more accepted, so many nouveau super-rich having flooded the small nation recently. He decided no bail. Let Vladimir sweat out the grand opening behind bars. Let him cool off. Keep him out of the way. They would worry about his release later.

That decision certainly was expedient, but it did not mellow the mood of the angry Russian. Far from him cooling off, his rage intensified with each passing hour. Now he was certain 'they' were conspiring together to keep him out of it—out of everything. '*They*,' he reminded himself, would be sorry about that—'*they*' obviously were forgetting who '*they*' were dealing with here. A mistake he vowed '*they*' would all deeply regret.

There is little to compare with the fury and frustration of a caged bear—especially a Russian bear with extensive KGB training!

CHAPTER 23

ASHDOWN AND PAZ GO TO THE PALACE

Anthony Ashdown, former Latin American head of the world's largest global advertising agency, *Donnelli*, watched the Maritime Alps give way to the villas and hotels of the Cote d'Azure. He had not been here for years, not since he was based in Paris and spent weekends chasing clients, prospects, and Riviera cuties during the August holiday month in France. He smiled at the memory of those bare eighteen-year-old breasts bouncing happily on the beach of the Grey D'Albion Hotel in Cannes.

He could almost taste the fried sardines of Marseille, or the bouilla-baisse at that well-hidden beach eatery, Chez Camille, near Saint Tropez. He longed for a cold bottle of Provencal Rose, which goes down so well with a Mediterranean sunburn and a basket of crudités (raw vegetables).

He forgot all he had hated so much about France—the snobbery, the rudeness, the arrogance. Only the happy summer days and the hot summer nights fueled his nostalgia now.

The tires screeched as the landing gear touched tarmac and the Learjet used reverse-thrust violently to drop quickly to taxi-speed.

"Mr. Ashdown, we have landed in Nice. Our agents will meet the plane and take you through immigration and on to Heliair Monaco for the short ride to Monaco. They are telling me a helicopter is standing by for you. Have a great stay here on the Riviera."

Jack and Elsie were waiting for him as the Heliair chopper gently touched down at Monaco's famous Heliport, one of the world's busiest helicopter terminals.

Jack's chauffeur grabbed the suitcase, as the three hugged and grinned the happy smiles of renewed acquaintance.

"Tony, sorry to do this to you, but the palace is anxious to meet you. The Prince's equerry has a slot open at about sixteen hundred hours."

"Jack, sixteen hundred hours? You back in the British marines? Don't you mean four o'clock in the afternoon?"

"OK, four for a backward American isolationist. Get with the future will you? Anyway, four o'clock or sixteen hundred hours, that's when he is free. Can you do it? You're not too jet-lagged?"

"Jack, if you can stay awake, so can I. Let's go for it. And then let's go look at some Riviera cuties at Jimmz's tonight, OK?"

"Tony, you are married to my sister, cool it," laughed Elsie.

"Geez, Elsie, I said *look*—since when is looking a crime?"

"It's a crime when looking leads to letching."

"Elsie, really!"

The car was now entering the Metropole Hotel entry lane.

"You are checked in already. Here's the key. Go straight upstairs. We'll take a coffee in the lobby; you shave, shit, and do the shirt-change thing. We'll wait for you. You should leave for the palace in about twenty minutes. OK, Tony?"

Anthony Ashdown was ready as the government Mercedes rolled slowly into the Metropole entrance.

"Good luck, Tony. Paz is already there being interviewed and photographed as the famous Mexican Brown Diamond. The government thinks you were the mastermind behind all that stuff."

"Well I was, Jack. Remember?"

"No you weren't. Your clever wife—my clever sister—was," answered Elsie. "You only did the selling, *remember* Tony?" mocked Elsie as she kissed him good-bye on both cheeks.

The second the limousine entered the palace gates he saw her—Paz in her Brown Diamond uniform draped over one banister of the sweeping palace courtyard stairs.

Ashdown exited the car quietly and watched. She preened for the cameras, and as she moved over to the interview chair, she spotted him.

"Tony!" she shrieked. "Tony, how great to see you. How are you? How's Marsha? The ranch? The kids?"

"Hold it, lady—one question at a time. But first let me look at you. As beautiful as ever. Tight buttocks. Slim waist. Firm breasts…"

"*Tony*, please. We are in the palace courtyard. Shut up!"

"OK, I'll shut up if you agree to sleep with me tonight. You never did grace my bed in all that time in Mexico."

"Tony, you never change. You are a married man and a *father*. Grow up!" But Paz was probably more flattered than irritated.

"Sir, Monsieur Carpentier is ready for you now."

Ashdown kissed Paz good-bye and followed the assistant into the inner sanctum of the Grimaldi empire.

He was shown into a modest study full of pictures of the Prince with stars and sports personalities. The bookcase was similarly full of trinkets and souvenirs. It looked more like the study of a football coach than the nerve center of a thriving little economy.

The Prince's private assistant, or equerry, entered with his ear to a mobile phone. The back of his loose shirt was riding out over his belt, but the pants were creased razor-sharp, and the neat brown shoes shone the shine of an army-trained polish.

"Bon. OK. Bon, Bon. D'Accord. OK. Do it. Ciao."

He silenced the IPhone and turned around to face his guest.

"Mr. Ashford, how nice to see you. Did you have a good flight over?"

"Ashdown, sir. Not Ashford."

"Sorry, but welcome anyway."

"Can we get straight down to business? Please give me some open advice—we are alone, and no one is taking notes. Mr. Ashdown, the Prince was very impressed when I showed him how you based a whole political turnaround in Mexico on galvanizing national pride—that whole Brown Power thing and all those incredible rallies—very impressive. You turned a whole political process on its head. And you did it all in weeks. I talked this morning to Miss Orteno, who was your focal lady. I had no idea she was even here, in our own backyard.

"My Prince is very dedicated to his program, but is finding it irritatingly difficult to get all his people behind at the speed he would like, which in his case means tomorrow, if not earlier!"

"Sir, your Prince sounds very American to me. I had expected something else. "

"Something else? Old European, maybe? Remember, Mr. Ashdown, the Prince had an American mother and was partly educated there.

"Mr. Ashdown, I e-mailed how I see the problem. The Prince's father was known as the 'Builder Prince.' He really took this sleepy place apart and rebuilt it."

"With the help of the Philadelphia mafia, right?"

"I suppose that's true, but then I wasn't here at that time. The present Prince wants to be known as the first European ruler to take the environment really seriously and do something about it—to set an example, as it were. You see, he argues that we are small here, which means it should be easy to experiment—to get ideas off and running—make Monaco a test market for exciting and far-reaching possibilities, if you will. It does not take a large expenditure to ensure that our whole principality follows and tries a progressive idea. And if it works here, there is then little excuse for larger countries to keep prevaricating. At present, idea after idea is simply kicked into some useless committee. The Prince does not have time for that. He was mightily impressed by how much you achieved in Mexico in those few months and thinks maybe we can learn from you how to move things along at higher speed.

"For example, we have many influential men here who share the Prince's vision and are experimenting with better garbage disposal, reducing the carbon imprint, the fabrication of electrics cars, and even reducing the cost of public transport. But these are all initiatives of the few. Where is the participation of the many? Where is the project that grabs the headlines and galvanizes our ordinary citizens to join in—to jump on the bus—to feel an active engagement in this environmental 'jihad'?"

With the word 'jihad,' the equerry was on his feet gesticulating wildly, eyes burning with determination. Then he sat down again, but this time right next to Ashdown on the sofa. He turned to him and, looking at him directly in the eye, softly added, "Mr. Ashdown, can you help us?"

Ashdown liked this man. He thought he'd find the usual effete Peter Pan Playboy courtier. He actually had a frustrated crusader before him—or at least the apostle of one.

"Mr. Carpentier, I got your e-mail and I admire your zeal—I really do. The trouble with humans is this: good causes are always someone else's job. Me—I am too busy, or too poor, or too insignificant to help. I love polar bears, but they are far away. My broken car battery and my nagging wife are here now!

"Environmental utopia is not their religion; only their wallets inspire their devotion. You've got to get at them via that wallet. It's the key. Better environment may be the goal—the Holy Grail if you wish. But materialism and self-interest are the keys! The road to the pussy is through the purse, as the hooker might say. Right, Mr. Carpentier?"

"A bit cynical, Mr. Ashdown, but I suppose essentially accurate!"

"Tell you what, sir; I do have a little presentation prepared for you. But I need a full hour of your time—relaxed time. When would you have a peaceful moment?"

The equerry called his secretary.

"Marie, cancel my next appointment…"

"But sir, it's the new Spanish Ambassador. You are supposed to take him to present his credentials to the Prince?"

"Marie, you take him."

"I can't do that, sir."

"Yes, you can. If the Prince wonders where I am, tell him that I'll explain later."

"But, sir…"

"Marie, do it. Just do it," and Carpentier turned to smile at Ashdown. "You have thirty minutes. Will that do?"

"Of course—if we are not interrupted!"

Ashdown opened his computer, and the two men watched it slowly boot up.

Ashdown pressed Power Point, and he was off as usual. Back in business again. Let the cattle on his ranch roam free for a few days. It would be fun to taste the sweet smell of selling again—of getting a big client to buy a great idea!

"Monsieur, I have one request. If you like what you see, present it to your Prince *today*. Unedited. Un-censored. Un-diluted. Speed derails the bureaucrats every time."

"OK, Mr. Ashdown, you have a deal. Now show me what you've got. The clock is running."

CHAPTER 24

THE GRAND GRAND OPENING

The media reacted well to Paz and her Brown Diamond story. A few days earlier, Monaco had known her (if they recognized her at all) as a hard-working little Mexican trying to open a new Cantina. Now the principality saw her as a celebrity: the Mexican Brown Power girl who wowed and captivated every man and woman in her home country and nearly overturned the whole national political process, until she and her whole entourage suddenly and mysteriously disappeared…And then they turned up just as mysteriously here in Monaco.

The palace spokesman even said a few words on-screen and hinted the Prince himself may visit the cantina opening. That hint alone was more than enough to garner over 80 percent acceptance to the many invitations sent out to all the 'beautiful people' whose patronage can make or break any new eating establishment.

Mickey Prentice provided the Jacoby promised by Sverdlov, and, of course, handed out flyers signaling the "Art Sale of the Century" the next week when over eight Jacobys would be offered on auction in his gallery.

The Cantina was officially opened by the Mexican Ambassador whose promised few words actually morphed to far too many words until the band and Gloria Adora finally shut him up by singing the Mexican and Monegasque national anthems.

The Prince did make an entry just as the national anthems ended.

Immediately and predictably all the ladies milled around trying to catch the eye of the most approachable Prince in Europe. The Prince, as usual, suffered the uninvited attention in good humor.

As soon as he saw the Prince, Prentice grabbed the microphone, introduced the auction, and confirmed that 'most' of the proceeds would go to a Mexican women's charity suggested by the Ambassador. Of course he also added a reminder of his own auction a week or so later.

The bidding started at €30,000, and with the prince actively involved, soon soared to €60,000. The prince now smiled sweetly at one of the British billionaires. The man quickly got the message. The price climbed to €80,000. The prince then glanced over at another successful industrialist.

The price now hovered around €95,000.

The auctioneer turned back to the first British billionaire bidder.

"Mr. Gold, it's against you…"

"OK, let's draw this to a close—€120,000 and a big hug from Miss Brown Power here. Do I have a deal?"

"You do have a deal, Mr. Gold—at least from me!" crooned the auctioneer. "Miss Orteno? Are you game?"

Paz stood up and walked over to Mr. Gold. She placed a long, wet kiss on his startled lips. Everyone cheered.

"Mr. Gold, I think you got a bigger dose of Brown Power than you bargained for?" giggled the auctioneer.

"Make it €125,000, not €120,000—that kiss was well worth another €5,000."

The auctioneer asked if there were any other bids—which, of course, there were none—and closed the deal saying, "Miss Orteno, I hope you come to my next auction. Your kiss is worth more than a thousand words from me!"

Everyone laughed. The Prince and the Ambassador shook the new owner's hand, waved a friendly good-bye to everyone, and strolled back into the Monaco evening.

The restaurant was now well and truly launched. Paz was a celebrity. Mick Prentice had a remarkable new benchmark price for the Jacobys. And many of the 'beautiful people' had promised to attend the "world's biggest Jacoby auction" the next week at the world-famous Hotel de Paris, just opposite the Casino.

Sverdlov was even happier. His restaurant was already proving a huge success, and he had high hopes of getting rid of many of the syndicate's ugly Jacobys at really silly prices.

Only Lady Lothmere was a little bothered. It was hot in that tent. She hated 'spicy' food. And she was worried about Hamish. There was a fiery new look in his eyes she had never seen before.

And Vladimir? He was still in jail. That did not augur well for the future. No matter what the media said, the Cantina Mexicana really had been his idea! But no one was giving him any credit—or much respect.

That rankled. That would be a mistake.

CHAPTER 25

ASHDOWN PRESENTS TO THE PALACE

Ashdown placed the little travel laptop on the equerry's desk and dragged two chairs as near as he could to give them both a better view.

"OK, sir, this is what I got.

(The PowerPoint file was by now fully booted up.)

"Hang on to your knickers, Mr. Monaco. Here we go. I suggest we attack the issue in distinct and measured stages.

1. **Stage 1 – Get the show on the road**
    "The first thing we have to do is get the whole issue of the environment out of the intellectual leader pages of the 'quality press' and into the consciousness of Mr. Average—the man, remember, who is preoccupied with the ass of his secretary and whether or not he should pick the boil on his nose. Boring Mr. Nobody.

"I suggest we give the subject some fresh air, remove it from the stuffy backroom, and get the damn show on the road—create a little pop-culture attention.

"How might we do that?

"Mexico taught me that men like to *look* at girls, and women like to *listen* to girls. I invented the Brown Diamond girls to create attention there. I offer you the Green Emeralds here. See, here they are. *(Ashdown showed the uniform of a sexy young beauty in white bottom-hugging Tropeziene shorts and tight green T-shirt. Across the chest lay, diagonally, a banner with the words 'Be clean – think Green'.)* These babes will be our ambassadors. Like them?"

The aide *loved* them.

"Well, they—the guys—will love them too. And take notice. And the ladies will listen because these girls may be sexy, but they will be briefed as well. They are there to get the message across. They will look smart and talk smart."

Stage 2 – Lamps

"Lamps?" asked the aide.

"Yes, lamps. 'Ampoules' in the Gallic tongue!"

"I do not follow…"

"You will. Give me a minute. The Green Emerald girls will create the buzz—the selling atmosphere. But what are they selling? Well, remember, we said that to get Mr. Arse watcher to buy, we must get him off his arse-watching and set him up in a mood to listen. The only way we can do that is to provide the attention device (the girls).

"Now that he is in the mood, we hit him with an offer he can't refuse. The girls will be selling something that Mr. Arse-Watcher wants. That costs him little. And gives him something.

"Some offer that is also something small and manageable— that will not create huge administrative and political waves. Start small, but make sure what you start will succeed."

"And that small thing is an ampoule? asked the equerry quizzically.

"Right, the lowly little ampoule. A product we scarcely think about but that collectively burns up a lot of energy and eats a lot of ozone."

"Mr. Carpentier, let me ask you another question. What is the easiest contribution we can all make to energy saving?"

"Ampoules?" ventured the equerry again.

"Right, energy-saving bulbs. What I want you to do is replace every single-filament bulb in this kingdom! Every last one of them. In a few months not one will be glowing anywhere. Now, I know you will be thinking that quite a lot of countries are encouraging the move to energy-saving lighting—even offering incentives or considering legislation. And even now I would guess 60 percent or more of replacement sales are already energy-saving.

"But not one country in the whole stinking, energy-wasting world will be able to claim for years a total ban and a total replacement of ALL their old lamps. But we will. And we can show them all how really easy it is. Your kingdom will be the undisputed leader…"

"Principality, not kingdom."

"Sorry. We are going to replace every single bulb in this *principality* by the end of the next few months—new bulbs for old. I calculated 300,000 to 500,000 bulbs will be needed. Mass ordered from China, they will cost you no more than one million euros. Can you imagine the impact? Every single person living here will be impacted and feel involved. Plus, I repeat, from next year, Monaco will be the *only* country on earth entirely free of energy-wasting ampoules.

"Giving the bulbs away free allows you to pass a law forbidding the sale or possession of anything other than agreed-upon energy-saving bulbs. Now that is LEADERSHIP—and leadership that every one of your citizens and residents will endorse because it costs them NOTHING to support the program. They are getting new bulbs for zip. Free! They can even cheat and buy the old-style bulbs in Italy and trade them in. The new ones cost at least twice as much. But in the end, the whole program is peanuts to a rich country like yours!

"Possibly, it could cost the state nothing as well. I haven't examined the sponsorship issue, but I am sure you can lean on a few outfits and billionaires to help supply free bulbs?"

"Mr. Ashdown, I like your ideas, so I am keeping my part of the bargain. I intend to brief the Prince today. In fact, I'll go see the Prince right now. Can you stand by?"

Of course, but first give me five minutes to take you through stage three. Stage three I call 'Toyota'."

"Toyota? The car company?"

"None other. It doesn't have to be Toyota, it could be Honda or VW or even Peugeot. Any brand that has a mayor presence here, and offers hybrids. But Toyota is the big prize – they are the largest in the world, no?"

Stage 3 - Toyota

"When our 'Green is Clean' and the free energy-saving lightbulb deal is over, we start the next program so quickly that once more the enemies of progress will still be scratching their balls wondering how to stop the first initiative.

"Consider your principality. How do its residents show their status?"

"With Toyotas?" queried the aide de campe.

"You are close—with cars. Flashy cars. What other country in the world has more cars than residents—about thirty-two thousand residents and over thirty-three thousand cars? Answer—none.

"Monaco is cars. Stupid rich cars. Stupid show-off cars. Now we can't really ban the gas-guzzling Ferraris and Bentleys—the tourists would be very disappointed. But only the visitors and millionaire residents have these dumb-fuck machines. The Monegasque *citizens* by and large do not. They don't need that kind of flash.

"Now I want at least 20 percent of your citizens (not residents) to be driving hybrids by the end of the next few years. All Toyotas. All painted green. How are we going to do it? Aha, I thought you'd never ask!"

The equerry was beginning to enjoy himself. This man Ashdown was action—all action—a refreshing change from the bureaucrats he had to deal with daily.

"Here is how we do it: We get Toyota to sponsor the 'Car of the Month Club.' Look—they have three hybrid models: the Prius, the RX, and something else. Let's take the Prius as an example. They offer us ninety cars at a discount—that is to say, without interest on partial payment. Say they cost €30,000 each tax paid. We select ninety citizens and offer them a chance to get a Prius now cheap. They must agree to pay €1,000 a month for thirty months. There you have the €30,000 purchase price.

"Now here is the trick. Each month you hold a competition. Good PR. Three lucky people get a new Prius for €1,000. This happens every month. Your risk as a participant in the club is that you get the car now, or in next month's draw, or—if you are extremely unlucky—at the end of the thirtieth month. But interest-free, in any case. Isn't that a great idea? I stole it from Volkswagen Mexico! Every month at least three new hybrids will grace Monaco streets—thirty-six by the end of the year. If we can persuade Toyota to also offer three RXs and three of the other model, that makes nine hybrids a month—270 in a year and about nine hundred by the end of the program. And by the end of the third year, 10 percent, at the least, of your car population will be hybrid. No other country can match or offer that either.

"Will people participate? Of course—it's a helluva a deal for them. Will Toyota cooperate? Why not—what does it cost them? They never sell their cars at full price anyway. For this promotion they will. And think of the worldwide publicity for them and for us, refreshed regularly by the monthly lottery draw. How much does it cost your treasury? Almost zip—and that's the real beauty of this idea."

"Shit," said the aide. "Holy shit. This is brilliant. More than that, it's fun. And stage four?"

Stage 4 – Polluting Bikes

"Next, we attack those polluting two-stroke bikes and scooters that besmirch your streets. Your license people know exactly who owns these horrors. We mail them all a Golden Key: the first fifty who trade in the smelly, polluting two-strokes for a four-stroke or electric scooter and can prove it with an invoice from a Monegasque dealer, gets a chance to drive up to the palace and try and open one of fifty boxes. In each box will be a small emerald on a lapel badge signifying they are a Green Warrior and a certificate. Depending on the box they select, they can get from 5 percent to 100 percent rebate on the price they paid."

"Why not have just a few high awards and forget about the 5 percent awards? Wouldn't that be more motivating?"

"No sir, not at all. People hate to lose in public. If you have just a few top prizes that means most people open a box and get no rebate. They will hate that. They won't expose themselves to the risk. In the best promotions, everyone wins at least something!"

"Damn it, Mr. Ashdown, you thought of everything!"

"Everything except those mother-fugger-truckers. I haven't quite thought that through yet, but I'm flirting with the idea of flirts. These macho drivers love scantily clad girls. Somehow I want to use our Emerald Girls to shame these fuggers into having their engines checked for pollutants. But whatever we finally come up with, the main point is this:

"We have constant action—constant focus on the environment. Yet, every move seems to be very consumer-friendly. You are doing well by getting good, if you follow my drift!

"No meetings, no conferences with do-nothings. Just action, simple activity no one will refute."

Ashdown sat down.

The equerry slowly rose, excused himself, and walked out to talk with his Prince in the throne room still chatting to the new Spanish Ambassador.

The Prince made his excuses, and followed his equerry to his study, where he excitedly outlined in French what he had heard from Ashdown. The Prince asked a few questions and then walked to the open door and nodded to Ashdown.

In fluent English he simply said, "Thank you for coming. You have some interesting ideas. How long are you here, Mr. Ashdown? In Monaco, I mean? A week or so? Good! I'll have my people contact you as soon as possible. Maybe you can spare me a little more of your time. I'd like to get to know you better."

And that was that!

<hr />

The next morning, Mr. Carpentier called in Enrico Palhiero, a key figure in the cabinet, and outlined the Ashdown plan.

"But, Monsieur, a plan with such radical elements must be discussed with the…"

"Enrico, please just get it done! The Prince wants you to do it."

"But, Monsieur, what about the…"

"Enrico, let me say it one more time and for the last time. 'Just do it!' OK?"

What Enrico 'just did' was to call Pallazza, the man who had arranged the sale of Lady Lothmere's Rolls. Enrico held two car franchises through a Virgin Islands company. Pallazza was one of his prime sales channels to off-load the used cars he took in part exchange. Pallazza was not amused at what he heard.

"Enrico, this will totally screw many of our sales programs. Toyota will have a huge advantage. They are already a major threat. Enrico, our sales are already down about 12 percent in both your dealerships. They'll go down even more. And those arrogant Japs have always refused to do business with me—with us…"

"Lightbulbs? Who cares? Most people have switched to the new bulbs already. As for the leftover stock, Carrefour and the rest of them will simply send their unsold conventional bulbs from here somewhere else. Lightbulbs are a tiny part of their business anyway. They won't be hurt. But cars? Forget it. We'll be killed. Those interfering bureaucrats on the rock have to be stopped."

"What about my Yamaha interests, Pallazza?"

"You'll be fucked, Enrico. Most bikes you sell here are two-strokes. The dealers are as stuffed full of them in inventory as you are. What are you going to do if only four-strokes and electrics sell?

"Enrico, we can't accept any more of this nonsense. Where did the palace get all this crap from? Who? Anthony Ashdown? Who is that? Friend of the Mexican whore from that Cantina restaurant? You know Enrico, it is time we did something about that bitch and her interfering pals—high time. We must talk soon. They are all getting on my nerves. Meanwhile, can you stall the 'rock'? I know it will be difficult, but just try."

Enrico put down the phone and sighed deeply. It was not easy, he decided, to be a good bureaucrat and a good businessman at the same time!

CHAPTER 26

JACOBYS GALORE!

The grand opening with its Jacoby auction generated a sufficient tailwind that Prentice's later Jacoby "sale of the century" became the most eagerly anticipated art event of the autumn—to the amazement of the thirty or so other galleries and art showrooms in the principality. It did not, of course, hurt that many auction magazines and art reviews continued to debate the causes and fashions that had precipitated this growing and inexplicable new Jacoby mania.

The "syndicate" laced together by Mick Prentice provided eight or so Jacobys funded by the shareholders: Sverdlov, Prentice, Mosta (the Pakistani), and Lady Lothmere.

The auction, or sale, was held at the Salle Empire of the Hotel de Paris. The event started off with a short video of the artist's life and work and a not-so-short speech by Art Daly of Mosley and Maxim (art dealers in New York) on the phenomenon that was fueling the new Jacoby craze.

By the time the first Jacoby came under the hammer, the champagne-oiled crowd of nouveau-art connoisseurs were in high excitement.

As one commentator later wrote, it reminded him of the Tanzanite craze. This deep blue stone from Tanzania had been hyped by the world's fashion jewelers as the best possible stone investment since the raw diamond because the major mine producing the best examples had collapsed and would 'never be reopened.' That was essentially true. That mine did stop production. But before it did, tons of these stones had flooded the market, many of very poor quality.

The eight Jacoby paintings—each almost an exact replica of the others—sold for an average of €87,000 each. This was not as high as Prentice had hoped but much better than the syndicate had imagined when they had plotted together in the little restaurant in Lausanne, Switzerland.

The final total was just under €700,000, and the syndicate still had scores of hoarded Jacobys left in stock!

Four days after the sale, the four conspirators met again in a little pizzeria between the old station and the casino in San Remo called Club 64.

The four elegantly dressed émigrés from the golden squares of Monaco made an odd contrast to the Italian workers and families enjoying a simple Friday night meal out.

After ordering, Mick brought out the accounts.

Proceeds just under €696,000. Sale room expenses, video, and drinks, canapés, etc.: €16,000. Monaco Galleria International commission (22 percent): €153,000. Net proceeds to be divided: €527,000 or roughly €175,000 each.

"Mick, what is this gallery commission of 22 percent?" asked Sverdlov.

"That's the commission—a quite normal commission—my gallery charges for selling the pictures."

"But you own the gallery; you are part of the syndicate. You can't get your 25 percent share plus 22 percent commission. That's nuts!"

"Of course it is not 'nuts' as you so inelegantly put it. I am an investor like you are. But the gallery handled the sale. If it had been another gallery, you would have been charged the same commission—maybe more. The fact that I own the gallery has nothing to do with it. Surely that is logical?"

"Doesn't sound logical to me. You charged us all the sale expenses—even the lousy, stale peanuts you handed out," snapped Sverdlov.

"Sounds like sharp practice to me!" added Lady Lothmere. "I remember nothing about 'commissions' in my agreement. By your so called 'logic,' Mr. Prentice, all *my* expenses and time forcing faux-bidding are thus also deductible?"

"No, of course not; otherwise, I'd have to charge my out-of-pockets as well," answered the visibly irritated art dealer.

"Then you'd get paid *three* ways?" added Sverdlov sarcastically.

"No, no, no. You don't understand..." But Sverdlov cut him off.

"Oh, I think I understand, and I think Lady L gets it as well. Mick, I suggest you revise these figures tomorrow and eliminate the commission. In fact, it is more than a suggestion—it is a strong recommendation. Lady L, I think I have had enough pizza—and enough bullshit for one night. Would you allow me to drive you home?"

"Thank you, Mr. Sverdlov. I do think that not just the wine was a little sour here tonight."

Mick tried to stop them leaving, but Sverdlov pulled back Lady L's chair and politely escorted her out and to his gray Porsche SUV, leaving a silent Mosta and an agitated Prentice to pay the bill.

The two said little as they followed the coast road back to Menton, France. But once past the self-appointed lemon capital of the Riviera, Lady L opened the dialogue.

"Mr. Sverdlov, do you think there is a genuine 'mal entendu' (misunderstanding) or that Mr. Prentice is trying to put one over on us?"

"The latter, dear Lady. I can smell a sleazebag a block away. He is deliberately trying to shortchange us."

"What will you do if he does not give way?"

"Lady, you don't want to know. We Russians can play rough."

"Mr. Sverdlov, why play rough when maybe we could play smart?"

Sverdlov stopped the car in a lay-by. He turned off the engine and asked, "What had you in mind, dear Lady?"

"Mr. Sverdlov, a number of those sold Jacobys are going abroad are they not?"

"I think most are! Lady, I don't follow you...."

"Mr. Sverdlov, shame on you. Are you really allowing an old lady to outthink you? Here is my suggestion. Prentice pays us the full amount, and nothing happens. Or he keeps the commission, and we liquidate the syndicate and divvy up the remaining Jacobys we collectively own and Prentice holds. In his greed he will probably accept the latter because I am sure he thinks he can make more selling his share of the remaining Jacobys than we can. And I also know he thinks the Jacoby craze, self-generated as we all know it is, will soon blow out. The artist is such a loser that in the end common sense must prevail, and the value will sink back to about €10,000 a painting. Even that is too high in my opinion..."

"Yes, that makes sense..." said Sverdlov. "But then what?"

"Mr. Sverdlov, do you remember asking me to make a little delivery for you to Reading a few months back? Well, I suppose you are still in that business, and I suppose you would not be averse to ensuring that one of those crated Jacobys going abroad includes a little bonus package?"

Sverdlov tapped his ring finger on the steering wheel for a few minutes.

"Interesting, dear Lady, very interesting. OK, that's what we'll do. I love it, dear Lady, I love it! We will fuck Prentice as he planned to fuck us."

"MR. SVERDLOV! Language, please..."

Sverdlov looked her in the eye and smiled. "Sorry, dear Lady, but I have a feeling you are a lot more street savvy that you appear!"

"The only thing we have to figure out, Mr. Sverdlov, is how to deliver that "bonus" package into its crate. But I will leave that up to you. Now, Mr. Sverdlov, please drive me home to my hotel. I do feel a little tired."

CHAPTER 27

THE CAGE OPENS

After the official meeting in the palace 'on the rock,' Ashdown had time the next day to sit down and really catch up with the old Mexican gang. Paz had steamed up some tacos and a tortilla soup, with a good jug of Sangria to help push the mood along. It was about eleven forty-five—early 'dejeuner' before the regular lunchers arrived and Paz would have no time to chatter.

Ashdown gave them all a rough outline of his recommendations to the palace, and they all then congratulated themselves on how well the grand opening had gone. Ashdown laughed as he remembered the idiot department store billionaire bidding well over €120,000—the highest ever recorded payment for a Jacoby.

"But it's an ill wind that doesn't blow someone some good. Did you see how well Prentices's Jacoby monster sale went the next week?"

That was Elsie, Jack's wife from London.

Lady Lothmere, sitting at an adjoining table, squirmed a little at the memory and even more as she recalled the meeting earlier that week where Prentice had flatly refused to pay back the commission or even break up the syndicate and distribute the remaining Jacobys in his possession.

"Now, Paz," asked Ashdown, "tell us what the heck is going on with that boyfriend of yours? Is the wedding on or off? Has that crazy Soviet cooled off?"

"Tony, I wish I knew. I went to see him in jail a few times, but he hardly talked to me. He is all roiled up at the fact that no one is giving him credit for the restaurant. And...." (she dropped her voice) "he seems to resent my getting advice or even talking with you guys. I don't really understand..."

Hamish looked away.

"Jack, put down that damn *Financial Times* and tell us what you think," snapped Elsie, his wife.

"What I think? I think, Paz, that you give this guy a miss. If he acts crazy now, he'll act crazier later. And drunks are always dangerous!"

"But, you know," wailed Paz, "he never was like this before and...and he does—or did—mean so much to me."

"An old whore with no teeth can give you great head, but you're not going to marry her. Keep him as your lover but not as your mate."

"Jack, what kind of twisted advice is that?!" screamed Elsie.

"If you don't want my opinion, dearest, then let me read the paper will you? Iceland Breweries is in play."

"I want him out of jail so we can talk this through; then I'll decide," added Paz softly.

"Is that a good idea?" asked Hamish. "Are you sure he has come to his senses yet?"

"Who knows? But I have to decide; the wedding date is only a few weeks away."

"I'll handle it. I think maybe I can spring him out the hoosegow," said Ashdown.

And he did. That evening he called the Mr. Carpentier on his private cell, and the next morning Vladimir was sniffing the early Riviera air. It was Sunday and few people were about. The Russian smiled at the bright southern sun, strolled down the hill from the jail in Monaco Town, and walked over to Monte Marina where Paz was still very much asleep.

He undressed and quietly slipped into the bed next to her. He lifted up her gown, and she spread herself immediately and without question to welcome her lover home. When it was over, she kept him inside her and held him tight. She wanted more of this man. Paz listened to his heavy breathing as he dozed off. Still trying to hold his now calming manhood, she lay back and wondered why was she so involved with this obviously unstable Russian. She had been married for six years to a man she loved deeply—loved because he had rescued her from a difficult life. Because he had provided for her. Because he was the father of her daughter. Because he was a good man who loved her to distraction.

Here she welcomed without question a man who had called her a bitch and a whore and who was determined to control her. A man who had tried to break down her door. A drunk who could not control his temper.

The difference was that for Peter (her late husband) her satisfaction came from *his* satisfaction. With Vladimir, it was different. He satisfied her in a way a girl dreams of being satisfied—totally, completely, and uncontrollably. Their bodies melted into one. The physical release was total and coordinated.

She sighed deeply and whispered to herself: "Goofy guy, great sex. Great guy, dreary sex. Why, oh why, does life have to be so very complicated…"

※

The next day Monaco was all abuzz with a new set of rumors.

The story was that the health authorities had raided the Cantina Mexicana and demanded a full review of the fire and sanitary arrangements.

They insisted on the placement of three more fire extinguishers, a reduction of four tables to allow greater separation, and the reinstallation of automatic spray extinguishers over the stove. New regulations, they claimed, required powder extinguishers, not water. Water does not extinguish an oil flame.

"But, sirs, you passed this establishment for opening only a few weeks ago—even the Prince was here," yelled Paz in acute frustration.

"Yes, that maybe true, but things change. There have been complaints. We expect compliance within two weeks or we must close you down."

"Close me down? Are you people mad? I only just opened!"

"Sorry, lady. That's the way it has to be."

Pallazza watched the episode with satisfaction from the other side of the street. Enrico and he felt good; they were protecting the government from its own folly. And Monegasque business from, well, outside interference! Over the years scores of people had thought they could manipulate Monaco to their will—from Onassis to this group of shady Mexican-American con men. They had all failed. And always would fail. Thanks to the Pallazzas of this world.

"Excellent," he said softly to himself. "We'll soon have that bitch and her stupid friends out of here. When will these foreigners learn to stop trying to change things in Monaco? You operate here at our pleasure, and Mrs. Mexican whore, you do not please us!"

His thoughts were disturbed by a noise from the back of the restaurant. Vladimir was yelling at Paz, eyes blazing with fury.

"I told you to leave the opening and the organization to me. Instead you listened to these morons from the West. And now look what happened."

"Vladimir, what the hell is the matter with you? I thought your stay in prison had cooled you off. Stop yelling at me."

"You think you can just sleep with me and then everything is OK? This damn restaurant is my idea. You insist on listening to these people who know nothing about how you do things here, and now the locals are going to close us down. LET ME HANDLE THINGS IN THE FUTURE, OK?"

"Vladimir, we both agreed to call those people in, and they did exactly what we hoped. This restaurant is on the map. Off and running. Full every night. If it was all your idea, why aren't you happy?"

"Because, you silly bitch, they are going to close you down. Didn't you hear that fellow? Are you deaf?"

Pallazza squirmed with delight on the harbor wall as he listened. This was all going better than he had hoped.

Paz turned away saying over her shoulder, "Vladimir, you are either drunk again or stupid. I have no time for this…I need people to help me solve problems, not create more!"

"No time for me? Are you crazy? You have time for me until I tell you don't. You are supposed to become my wife. So you listen to me."

Paz did not break her stride.

Vladimir jumped up and grabbed her by the hair, shaking with fury.

"Let her go, Vladimir. NOW!" said Hamish, who had been sitting quietly in the corner nursing a Corona.

"Piss off home, you stupid Scottish loser! Put on your girlie skirt and go play the bagpipes or something. This is man's business."

"Let go, Vladimir. I mean it."

Vladimir let go and whirled around to face Hamish.

"You mean *what*, you worthless old hag driver? When you have £10 to your name, maybe I'll listen to you. Right now, get out of my way."

Years of frustration and of feeling second-rate welled up inside the Scot. He realized if he was to teach this man a lesson he'd have to hit first and hit hard. He tried to remember his army training.

He reached up and grabbed the Russian's head, pulling him hard down and toward his chest. At the same time his other fist erupted into Vladimir's midriff with a force that completely winded the man.

Then his knee came up to split the Russian's lip.

The Russian coughed and spluttered and gasped for breath. When he had recovered somewhat, he stared at his aggressor with cold hatred and reached quickly for the knife Paz had been using to cut chilies.

Hamish was ready. As the enraged Vladimir turned to lunge at him, a thick Scottish boot kicked him hard in the groin. The knife dropped and skidded across the floor.

Pallazza rubbed his hands in pleasure as he called the police on his mobile.

His pal Remy was the first cop to arrive on his motorbike. Remy rushed inside, just in time to see the Russian reach for a pistol from an ankle holder.

"Arretez imediatement, imediatement!" screamed the officer as he drew his own weapon on Vladimir.

Now two more police stormed in, guns drawn. One ordered both to raise their arms. Vladimir complied and dropped the pistol.

Once both men were cuffed, the police re-holstered their guns. Remy turned to his friend Pallazza and asked him if he knew what was going on?

Pallazza knew all right, and realizing that none of the others (Paz, Vladimir, or Hamish) understood French, richly embellished the event. The Scot didn't really appear such a threat to Pallazza and his Monegasque cronies. So he focused the blame on the Russian; Vladimir had started the row that lead to the trouble. It was not a difficult sell to Police Sergeant Remy, as it was Vladimir who had wielded the weapon.

Remy smiled at Pallazza. He didn't like foreigners either. From base he was informed that the Russian had only just been released from jail for exactly the same charge: being drunk and disorderly.

"This time even God won't get him out of jail, Mr. Pallazza. You can be sure of that!"

"Good," said Pallazza to himself. Now it's time for a little Russian tea with that Sverdlov fellow. Pallazza was feeling very pleased.

CHAPTER 28

MENTON

Hamish drove slowly down the coast road to Menton from Monaco called the Bas Corniche. It wends and weaves its way through villages and peninsulas until it straightens out at Roquebrune Beach, which eventually merges into Menton Beach.

Menton is the last French outpost before French baguettes give way to Ligurian pasta and the road crosses the Italian border to Ventimiglia.

Hamish was spending more time lately with his old flame and her family in Menton, including helping her father land and sell his daily fish catch. Hamish kept his room in the Marriott Cap d'Ail, but he only overnighted there. After the Vladimir fiasco, he dared not enter Monaco.

The court had believed Pallazza's version of the fight with Vladimir and decided to be lenient with the Scot. Hamish would be let off provided he agreed never to set foot in Monaco again.

Vladimir, on the other hand, was back in jail, bail denied, and a court date set way into the future. It was doubtful he would be free for his own wedding date.

Hamish would have liked to go home now, back to the Highlands, but Lady Lothmere seemed loath to leave until her "affairs were in order." This meant until the dispute with Mick the art dealer was finally resolved.

So the Scot passed the lazy days in Menton hanging out with Helene and her old fisherman father. The two men seemed to find warmth and comfort in each other's company. They did not talk much, as language problems made communication difficult.

But the dour man from the Highland taxi service and the "old man from the sea" shared similar values: silence, closeness to nature, and the common sharing of introspection that a solitary occupation brings.

Hamish would go down to the pier, watch the boat chug in, help unload the catch, and then they'd both walk over to Café Arletto for beer and (sometimes) a glass or two of red wine.

At midday, Hamish would often wait to see Helene and help her prepare the kids' lunch time, finding peace and contentment in the harmony of the domestic routine of a well-balanced family.

Then he would drive the Rolls slowly back to the Marriott, wondering, as he did every day, when Sverdlov would finally take ownership of the car he purchased so many weeks ago.

Hamish tried not to think of Paz, Vladimir, or the restaurant. He wanted to forget. Forget the fight. Forget his longing for the girl. Forget the worries of her life. Just shut it all out as a closed chapter and head home.

Sooner or later he would be back driving among the moors and glens, and the Monaco adventure would dissolve into nothing more than a pub evening story.

But today, as Hamish entered the hotel garage to collect the Rolls, it seemed to have a problem. It leant crazily to the left. Damn—another flat tire. But this time it was not staged by a crazy dowager. It was real.

Hamish cursed and returned to his hotel room. He tried to remember the name of the tire service where Pallazza had repainted the spare wheel— aha, there it was in the phone book: *Pneu Azure.*

He called. They came. The tire was repaired, and Hamish made his regular trip to Menton, if a few hours later than usual.

CHAPTER 29

PALLAZZA MEETS SVERDLOV

Sverdlov answered Pallazza's urgent call and agreed to meet him at the Casa de Gelato once voted the second best place in Monaco to have a cappuccino. Pallazza sat under the TV monitor showing an Italian soccer match. The soccer crowd noises, he reckoned, would drown out their conversation from any prying ears.

"Mr. Pallazza, I am a rather busy man. What is so 'urgent' that it simply couldn't wait?"

"Mr. Sverdlov, please sit down. Would you like a coffee? No? Something else? OK, (to Claudio the Italian waiter) Claudio, *due San Pelligrino, grazie.*"

Sverdlov sat down opposite the man he had heard from gossip was odious but well-connected.

"Mr. Sverdlov, I have a message for you and it comes from the top. Almost the very top. Whatever you decide after our conversation, I must have your word that this rendezvous never happened and that we never met or talked. Is that agreed?"

"If you insist, I agree, but I am a little too old for 'cops and robbers' games."

Pallazza grinned. He liked men—men who acted like men.

"I think you realize that this little principality is a small village. There are only some seven thousand Monegasque citizens, and the rest of the residents are from most of Europe—about twenty-five thousand of them. The locals know they need the foreigners' money spent here to stay rich, but they are basically suspicious of them. Most of these immigrants are very well-oiled and successful millionaires or billionaires here to escape tax. But they obviously have the financial ability to take anything over they want. Such is the power of unbridled wealth. It is a power that bothers us.

"We watch them and tolerate them if they pay and if they mind their own business. We get agitated if they appear to meddle in what we regard *as our business.*"

As Pallazza uttered this last phrase, his fist pounded his chest. Sverdlov noted the gesture and raised his eyebrows as much as to say, "Son, you don't scare me!"

"Do you—and your 'friends'—believe I am not minding my own business, Mr. Pallazza? Every endeavor I have here has been sanctioned and endorsed by your authorities. Are you suggesting otherwise?"

"Mr. Sverdlov, on the official level, I am sure you are 100 percent covered. But in other, shall we say *less* official spheres, you are generating some concern—concern with people who can make life difficult. You probably noted that your little Mexican restaurant is threatened with closure?"

Sverdlov cut him off.

"Mr. Pallazza, hear me well. I have lived through more wars, rebellions, political upheavals, and financial turmoil than you have had espressos. Please do not attempt to threaten me—officially or unofficially. I do not like it. I have a feeling this meeting is over."

Sverdlov got up, searched in his pocket for money, and contemptuously threw a ten-euro note on the table to pay for the mineral waters.

"Wait. Wait, Mr. Sverdlov. Please hear me out. Just five minutes more, please. I am here to deliver some information I am sure you will appreciate."

Curiosity got the better of the Russian. He sat down again.

"Five minutes only. Not one second more. Go ahead, Mr. Pallazza. I'm listening."

"Mr. Sverdlov, there are people on the 'rock' (Monaco town where the palace and government offices are located) who are annoyed that your friend from Argentina is advising the palace on matters that are none of his business, like giving preferential treatment to Toyotas and selling four-stroke or electric bikes. The people in those trades do not object to this advice if our eco-friendly prince wants some new ideas. But they do object to being cut out of the deal, especially by people like your Argentinian friend who does not understand the delicate balance of trade here."

Sverdlov started to laugh.

"Delicate balance of trade? What a joke. You mean you and your friends do not have any energy-efficient cars to offer and you are scared of losing a dollar or two? Anyway, your eco-minded government (as you so derisively call them) actually asked for that advice, did you know that?"

"Please hear me out, Mr. Sverdlov. My five minutes are not over. You have probably noticed that most foreign businessmen like me who succeed here do so with local partners. It is much easier in the end."

"Get to the point, Pallazza. I am getting irritated."

"The point is simply this: work with us or we will work against you. And we will win. We always do."

"Pallazza, your brain is right up your arse. For a start, it is the Monegasque government that wants Monaco to be a shining light in the fight to save the environment. Frankly, I thank them for it. But that policy has nothing to do with me. If you don't like their policy, go fight them. Stop wasting my time. You are not even a Monegasque yourself for Christ's sake—you're a frigging Italian. So I could say to you mind your own damn business. Go back to Rome or wherever the hell you are from. What the government decides here is none of your business. Or mine."

"It does have something to do with you, Sverdlov," retorted a visibly agitated Pallazza. "Your Cantina and that Mexican whore brought those Madison Avenue wonkers here and put all those crazy ideas into the palace's heads. The rubbish you bring into a house you take out. Now do you understand? Get your foreigner buddies out of here. Do you get the message now?"

"And should MY message to you and your cronies be 'f–k off,' just what will you and your pals do about it?"

"Run you out of town. Close down your businesses, as we are closing down that Mexican bughouse of yours. Within the year you will be back in Russia, or somewhere else. For sure, you will not be here."

"You will run *me* out of town? Ha—bloody likely. You are nothing but a sleazy secondhand car salesman. And not a very good one at that…" Sverdlov started to leave again.

Pallazza flushed with anger.

"Sit down, Sverdlov. Maybe it's time to take the gloves off. This *sleazy car salesman* is already well on the way to screw you, you arrogant and uncouth Soviet barbarian. Sit down and listen."

Sverdlov sat down, curiosity getting the better of him once more.

"Car salesmen watch people, know people. I have been watching you. I have had many talks with your stupid Russian servant, that lout Vladimir something-or-other."

"Vladimir Koschenko, to you Mr. Pallazza."

Pallazza ignored the remark and carried on.

"Whatever his name, you all think he's boozed out on vodka. And he does drink, I know that. But Russians like him can drink liters without getting out of control. Vladimir has repeatedly run out of control recently. And I know why. It's cocaine. I saw him snort the terrible stuff—on your boat.

"Now I wondered where he could have found that here in Monte Carlo? True, it is available, but you need lots of money. You do not pay him that well, I know; a friend supplied me with his bank account. And yours too, by the way. Lots of cash moving in and out. The money-laundering experts in France might be interested in that.

"But let's get back to the cocaine trail. I started to watch you all a little closer. I saw this strange friendship bloom between you, Lady-whatever from Scotland, and her weird chauffeur.

"The clincher was that Rolls. The one I advised Vladimir to get you to buy off that Lady. You did buy it; I saw the papers. But then you let the two Scots drive it home. Strange that, I thought.

"Until I remembered the spare. Your dumb ass Vladimir asked me where he could buy a spare tire for a Rolls at a good price. I called this Englishman, James Crombie, who deals in cars and parts. He got his contacts in the UK to find one. In the time available, he could only locate a dark blue wheel, and I had it sprayed white at Pneu Azure—or off-white as I think that Rolls was sort of ivory-colored."

"Magnolia, actually Pallazza."

Pallazza ignored the correction and plowed on …

"Then the Rolls and the two tricky Scots appear here again within a few months. And still you do not take possession. That made me even more interested.

"A few days ago I entered the Marriott garage and pushed my trusty Swiss army knife into your rear tire. The chauffeur came down, noticed the flat, and called the tire service. The Italian who runs it is also a pal of mine. He told me the Rolls did not have a spare—curious considering the extremes you entertained to ensure that car always carried a spare wheel."

"Not at all, you nosy but very stupid idiot," blurted out a visibly agitated Sverdlov.

"The lady came down here originally without a spare as she needed the space for luggage. She was delivering a Renoir, if you know what that is. I did not want her to drive back without a spare, so we got her one. On the way back down again, she left the spare back in Scotland. She needed the space to hide her valuables. Big mystery indeed, Mr. Pallazza! No wonder your Italian police are such amateurs!"

"Oh come on, Sverdlov—what nonsense. The car has run-flat tires. It does not need a spare. But more than that, I hear you ordered yet another spare from Rolls Royce Cannes a few days ago."

"Correct, Sherlock. Mrs. Lothmere might trust run-flats. I do not. So I ordered another spare wheel. Is there a law against that, Mr. Pallazza?"

"Why on earth would you, a very wealthy Russian businessman get so involved in a little problem of a spare tire? It made no sense. Until I started to add two and two together. I suspect the Rolls went back to the UK with the spare I supplied not full of air but of something a lot more valuable? Am I right, Mr. Sverdlov? Quite clever I must say. Who would suspect a Scottish noble Lady and her chauffeur? My guess is the Rolls spare and its contents are now gracing the crack houses of East London or the USA? The new spare from Cannes is probably also about to be loaded with some lucrative substance—a substance that Vladimir is also using from time to time. How say you, Sverdlov? Am I getting close?"

"Just what are you insinuating, Pallazza?"

"That you and your pals are transshipping cocaine around the world in any conveyance you can, including spare wheels. Quite clever, I repeat. The only problem is you employ buffoons like that Vladimir idiot, who I hear also happens to have had a drug problem back in cocaine-snowy Moscow. And that explains his odd behavior now. Mr. Sverdlov, it all fits together. Shall I inform my friends in La Condamine (police headquarters) of my suspicions?"

Pallazza sat back with intense satisfaction. He was well-pleased with himself.

Sverdlov scratched his leg and eventually addressed the grinning car salesman.

"And you want in on this supposed drug dealing arrangement? Is that it?"

"No, I don't do drugs. But neither do I care what you do. If people are stupid enough to take cocaine, more fool them. Here is what I *suggest*, not what I *want*.

"First, ditch the Mexican whore and her daughter. My ex-wife can run that place; all the hard work has been done. Give me 40 percent of the shares. Then keep that dangerous fool Vladimir out of Monaco forever."

"He's in jail, Pallazza. Got into another fight with the chauffeur for some reason."

"Mr. Sverdlov, that is a detail. I know he is in jail—again. And I can get him out—again. Just as soon as I have an understanding with you! Getting him out of jail and out of here is not the issue. The point is can you *keep* the dumb fool out of here? Keep him mining coal in Gdansk or somewhere."

"Gdansk is in Poland, Pallazza…and it's a port, not a mining town."

"Who gives a shit—just keep stupid fucker out of here." Pallazza's lip snarled as he answered the suave Russian.

Sverdlov stared the angry Italian in the eyes and answered very slowly.

"The answer is yes. I can do what I want with him. That will not be a problem. I own him."

"Good," responded Pallazza. "That's one thing out of the way. My next request to you is do not let any of the so-called Mexican gang (the Argentinean bullshitter or the English Brewery guy, etc.) come back either. If the palace writes and asks for their advice, tell them to say they are busy, or sick, or dead. I don't give a damn. Just keep them all out of our business. Out of Monaco—forever."

Pallazza stopped to take a breath.

"There, those are my demands and they are not that hard to swallow are they, Sverdlov? Sounds like rank good sense. Win-win for everyone, as the Yanks say."

For the next two minutes or more, Sverdlov said nothing. He just sat clutching his glass of water with both hands. Pallazza avoided his eyes by watching the glass and wondering if it might crack under the pressure of Sverdlov's obvious anger.

Finally, Sverdlov smiled a crooked smile and seemed to reach some inner conclusion. He grabbed Pallazza's arm lying on the table opposite him.

"Pallazza, you've added two and two together all right, but you reached five. You think too much. Take a tranquilizer and get some sleep. We are manipulating art, not dope. So, Sherlock, back off and cool off. Mrs. Orteno's advisers are already out of here; they were asked to help and they did. What your government does with their ideas is, as I told you, your affair, not mine. They won't be back. They don't make money farting about with your lightbulbs and scooters. They could not give a damn. Believe me, they have bigger fish to fry than your little country.

"But I like your working-together idea. It costs me about €8,000 a month just to house the Mexican girl and her kid and another €5,000 or more in salary. That is a lot.

"Furthermore, I will be spending more time in Moscow soon and could do with a local agent or partner. And who cares about Vladimir? If you are right and he's into drugs, more fool him. Drugees are dangerous; they need money and talk too much.

"Now, as my new partner, and one who apparently knows how to get things done here, I need a favor. I no longer like Mr. Prentice, Mr. Pallazza. He is not a man of his word. Close him down for me, will you? Let me tell about an idea Lady L and I had and see if you can help us."

The two men talked on for another ten minutes as Sverdlov explained Lady L's plan to trap Prentice. Could Pallazza interfere with a crated export?

"No problem!" replied a happy Pallazza.

Then they both left. New partners? Maybe. New friends? Unlikely!

As they parted company, Pallazza hissed more to himself than to Sverdlov: "Two and two equals five, eh? Art not dope? You are the dope if you think I believe that. You want me to stuff a package into one of McCleary's crates? And that package does not contain drugs? Come on, give me a break."

———————

A few days later, yet another rumor spread through the principality. Prentice had been arrested and his gallery shuttered. Apparently, a bag of cocaine had been found in a boxed painting headed for Bulgaria. The crate contained one of the Jacobys from the recent 'sale of the century.'

Prentice furiously defended his innocence and because of his past many years of good behavior was let out on €500,000 bail, but his passport was removed and his movement restricted to his house or the gallery only.

A morning before this new rumor appeared, Pallazza received a visit at home. It was Etienne, head of a freight forwarding company that handled most of Prentice's work. Just coincidentally, Etienne also just happened to be Pallazza's cousin.

"Cousin Pallazza, how are you? Can I come in for a coffee?"

He followed Pallazza into the kitchen and sat down at the rickety white table whilst the ageing espresso machine raised enough steam to force a few drops of superheated water through the coffee powder—just enough to cover the bottom of a thimble-sized cup with treacly strong brew—exactly as the Italians love it.

Coffee down, Etienne started to talk. But slowly and very deliberately as was his wont.

"Cousin, when I let you into our warehouse the other evening, were you looking for a crate going to Bulgaria?"

"Could be, Etienne."

Pause.

"Did that crate contain a painting?"

"Could be, Etienne."

"From Prentice's shop?"

"It's possible, Etienne."

"Did you open the crate up and drop a bag in it?"

"What makes you think that, Etienne?"

"'Cos you had a crowbar with you."

Pause.

"And a canvas bag in your other hand…"

Pallazza did not answer.

Etienne watched him and then the serious face broke into a grimy grin.

"Yeah, thought so. Thought it probably was you who did Prentice in."

Pallazza said nothing.

"You are a good regazzo, cousin. I never liked that Irish arty-farty man. Always late paying. Hate that. Really hate that. Looks like you got him good, cousin Pallazza. Why?"

"Best you don't know, OK?"

"OK. Whatever you say. Bye, cousin. See you soon."

"Wait, cousin, how did the police get to know about the…the…well… stuff in the crate?"

"Dogs."

"Dogs?"

"My dogs. They don't like the smell."

"The smell?"

"Yeah—the smell of dope. They kept barking so I opened the crate and called the cops. Where did you get that shit, cousin? Ahhhh, I remember. Best I don't know! You do your business, I do mine. That way we stay friends, right cousin Pallazza? Bye, cousin."

Pallazza saw Etienne out and called Sverdlov, but Sverdlov did not answer, so he left him a message.

"Package delivered. Sometimes it is good to have partners. Agree, Mr. Sverdlov?"

CHAPTER 30

FORCE MAJEURE

Sverdlov did not answer the phone because he was deep inside the Casino Square garage, hiding in the one corner where he knew the cameras were not focused, but also where he could see Prentice's BMW Estate car.

At about 6:00 p.m., Prentice strode toward the car and pushed the remote key release. Sverdlov followed him onto the backseat.

"Drive out naturally and do not try anything funny," spat out Sverdlov. From the driving seat, Prentice slowly turned his head.

"You don't scare me, Sverdlov. What are you planning to do? Beat me up in front of one hundred fifty Monaco police and four hundred street cameras? This car and I cannot leave the principality, you know that. I am under house arrest, remember? By the way, someone placed cocaine in that Jacoby crate I sent to Bulgaria. I wonder who tried to stitch me up and who tipped off the customs? Eh, Sverdlov? Don't you think the Monaco police—sleepy as they maybe—will sooner or later work out who stuffed crap in my picture? Enjoy our jail food, Sverdlov—it's still better than Borsch in Smolensk."

Mickey Prentice guffawed loudly.

"And if you think your childish antics will make me release your money or your pictures, think again. You and your gang of morons are such stupid amateurs."

Sverdlov let the art man ramble on, but when he had heard enough he slapped him hard on the back of the head.

"Drive and shut up, Prentice. You'll soon see just what amateurs we are."

"So, where are we going my Keystone Cop?" sneered Prentice, turning around again and staring icily at the Russian.

"You played hardball, Sverdlov, and you lost. You could have made a fortune with me, but you wanted to cheat me out of my gallery's rightful commission. So now you have nothing. There is not one shred of paper linking you or that stupid Scottish Lady to the Jacobys—all of them I hold here. They are in my possession now. Play silly buggers all you like. It alters nothing. You lost."

"Drive to Fontvieille. Make a false move and you'll regret it."

"Oooh, Sverdlov, I am so frightened. Scary, scary."

But Prentice did as he was told. Russians can be dangerous.

Once through the tunnel to Fontvieille, Sverdlov gave him new directions.

"OK, now take the port road and stop in the car park at the end by the Beef Bar."

Once there, Prentice carefully placed the car in an empty parking space and again turned to face his aggressor in the backseat, a sneer still smeared contemptuously all over his face.

"Now what, Sverdlov? Is the KGB coming to help you?"

"Prentice shut your stupid mouth and listen. You are already in deep shit because of that 'substance' in the crate you sent. You will probably get out of that, I know. You have no previous convictions. But it will take time, and meanwhile who is going to buy a 'picture' off you? No one!"

"But the crate incident, so easily executed, should make you consider a little more who you are dealing with. The 'substance placement' is only the opening act. This letter and the article attached is the finale. Why don't you read them? Then we'll talk."

Mick Prentice grabbed the two documents, the sneer still firmly in place.

The letter, on the gallery's own letterhead, was addressed to Janet Jameson of *Art Dealer and Auction House Magazine*. A copy was sent to Art Daley, the famous New York art dealer and self-appointed art fraud investigator. It offered the article attached for publication.

The article was entitled: *"See how easy it is to manipulate today's art market…The Jacoby Auction Story. By Mickey Prentice."*

Prentice was quiet now as he read every detail of the benchmark price manipulation over the last months and the phony auctions culminating in the giant auction in Monaco of a few weeks earlier.

When he had finished reading, he turned to Sverdlov. "You go down, I go down. We were in this together."

"Mickey, you yourself reminded us frequently that we had no contracts, no agreements. Nothing—nothing to link you to me other than the fact that you offered to sell my paintings. You on the other hand collected those monstrous paintings for years, and you abused the old Lady sending her hither and thither bidding up prices. I have many pictures of you and her together in your gallery; her chauffeur liked to record all their trips and visits.

"Finally, as you know, it is illegal to manipulate markets in the name of third parties. I can so easily prove the origin of the paintings I gave you at any time. They were mine to sell. You did the manipulation. Give up, Mick – you're done."

"No so fast, Sverdlov. Lady Lothmere will bear me out; she's my friend. She'll say I was acting for you both as agent. The invoices of our settlement will prove it." Mickey Prentice did not sound quite so cocky now.

"Invoices? What invoices? The only paper I hold confirms you received a number of Jacobys from me. As for Lady Lothmere, do you really think she'll help you? That's a good joke, Prentice. Do you know who wrote that article? She did. She is an ex-journalist and a pretty good one, don't you think? *My* English is nowhere near good enough to pull that off! Lady Lothmere help you? You must be mad, Mick. She *hates* you.

"In fact, she has already prepared a letter to the editor bewailing how she was duped into swapping her Renoir for a Jacoby. Remember you exchanged it for her share of our syndicate? That exchange is recorded on paper! One Renoir for one Jacoby—my Jacoby as it so happens. Boy, will that look good to a third party. And all she was looking for was a twin Jacoby in memory of her dear dead husband. Jameson will corroborate that. She thinks you arranged a cheap sale for Lady L. Wait till she sees that all you apparently did was arrange a swap of a €400,000 Renoir for a worthless Jacoby. I'd love to read that article in Art Dealer and Whatever magazine!

"Read the letter. Very touching it is too! It will bring tears to even your jaded eyes."

The car went very silent. Prentice read the letter and then said slowly and softly, "What do you want, you bastard? Are you trying to ruin me? And if so, why? We had such a good thing going…"

"Ruin you? No, not yet. Maybe later, depending on how you cooperate. Why am I doing this? Because I cannot do business with you. You are a cheap cheat. I can't trust you.

"As to what I want, it's simple. I want a check covering my and Lady Lothmere's share of the Jacoby sale proceeds, no commission withheld. I know you have your checkbook with you. Greedy bums like you always do.

"Then I want our share of the Jacobys back—the ones you still hold and won't release unless I twist your arm. I want all you owe us plus one more from *your* stock as interest and to punish you for being an asshole.

"Then you will give me another Jacoby for Lady L to compensate for the poor old Lady's stress. You will give me those paintings now, tonight, from your storeroom here in Fontvieille."

"Sverdlov, you are an ignorant Russian buffoon. You won't give Lady Lothmere one Russian kopeck. You'll keep the money yourself, filthy pig that you are."

Furious, Sverdlov slapped the art man across the face starting a considerable nosebleed. Feeling the blood starting to pour, Prentice reached for his handkerchief, unbelieving. Things like that were not supposed to happen in the gentile atmosphere of the tidy principality.

"Prentice, you can ask Lady L in a moment if I plan to cheat her. Meanwhile start the car and drive to the storeroom. Any nonsense and I will kill you. Now go."

Mickey Prentice growled under his breath but started the car and drove to the vault behind the Pastor Building. He rummaged in the glove compartment until he found the keys to his locked area and one by one brought the required Jacobys to the car. The security guard knew Prentice, of course, and was not surprised to see him so late in the afternoon. Prentice regularly brought pictures in and out of the security rooms after hours to change or update his gallery display.

Big as the Estate's baggage area was, it was still tricky fitting all the paintings in. In the end, Sverdlov was virtually hemmed in by the look-alike Jacobys. He even had to hold one of the smaller ones on his lap.

"Now what, Sverdlov?" asked Prentice testily. "Are we going to deliver those pictures to your boat in the full view of everyone?"

"No. Drive to the car park at the end of Plage Marquet, Cap D'Ail, where you will find Lady L waiting in the Rolls Royce. We'll take it from there."

"I told you, neither I nor my car can leave the principality. I am under house arrest."

"There are no cameras there," answered Sverdlov. "It will only take a minute. Drive."

They drove slowly down the little backstreet to the car park of the famous beach where princesses and paupers enjoyed the waters together. At this time of the year, and at this time of the evening, nothing was in sight—except the magnolia Rolls Royce with its engine quietly purring, allowing the climate control to keep things comfortable for the old Lady sitting primly in the back.

"Park your car alongside the Rolls, Prentice."

He did as he was told. Immediately Hamish jumped out and helped Sverdlov transfer the paintings. Although the Rolls was not a Break, or Station Wagon, its cavernous interior swallowed the load more easily than the Bimmer.

"Did you like the article I wrote, Mr. Prentice?" asked Lady L sweetly.

He did not reply.

"Did you sign the covering letter to the magazine, Mr. Prentice?" she insisted.

"F—k you, you phony. You are no Lady. You are…"

Prentice got no further. Both Hamish and Sverdlov grabbed him and spun him around.

"Don't you swear at my Lady, Prentice." That was Hamish.

"And listen to the Lady." Added Sverdlov. "She wants the letter signed. So sign it, or never sign anything ever again."

He signed.

"Now the two checks. One to me. One to Lady L. Both made out to 'Cash' please. Exactly to the full amount due us. And tell me now, who is the cheat?"

Prentice did not move. Sverdlov slowly walked up to the gallery owner and kicked him sharply in his artificial knee. Prentice yelped and winced, eyes tearing in pain. He hobbled over to his briefcase and extracted the checkbook. He wrote the two checks on the roof of the Rolls. He handed them over.

"Sverdlov, tell me one thing. How did you get that cocaine in my shipment?"

"None of your damned business. By the way, you remind me—whilst you were finding our Jacobys in your vault, I sprinkled a few specks of that white stuff all over the back of your car. It is of the exact same type and origin as was found in the crate. You wouldn't want anyone to find that, now would you, Prentice? Cocaine dust is very hard to remove. Better we stay friends, Mick. Better you don't even think of stopping those checks."

"If that stuff is so hard to erase, your flat or damn boat must also be full of it. Stalemate, Sverdlov."

"Stalemate? Really? Mr. Pallazza just informed me a few hours ago that the police found another two little sacks hidden behind two pictures in your gallery. Pity you have prostate trouble, Prentice. You spend too much time in your WC. And Sandy is too stupid to wonder why that customer you had this morning spent so much time looking so closely at your showings. Give it up, Mick. We are miles ahead of you. Let's just stop getting in each other's way and finish this as friends."

"Sverdlov, one day I will get you. I swear it!"

"Not if I get to you first, Mickey, me boy!" Sverdlov laughed heartily. What a delicious night's work, he thought.

No more business to attend to, Sverdlov jumped into the front of the Rolls. He rolled down his window:

"Hey Mick, fancy a drink at the Marriott?"

"F–K YOU!"

CHAPTER 31

VLADIMIR AGAIN...

"Your Honor, my client admits he entered into a common brawl with the Scotsman who was here on vacation. He admits he was wrong. In the deposition before you, you can read the sworn testimony on the reasons for that brawl, which corroborates broadly with what the other protagonist stated and with what eye witnesses saw."

The lawyer blabbed on for another ten minutes but ended with this plea:

"Therefore, we find it unfair that my client is denied even bail whilst the court saw fit to offer the other protagonist conditional discharge on the basis of promising never to enter our principality again. Surely, my client deserves equal status?"

The judge considered what he heard for a moment and then replied:

"Your client was granted a pardon from a similar and previous offense and abused that concession. Also, he was the only one to carry and threaten with a concealed weapon. That is quite a different affair.

"However, we do understand your client was severely provoked in his own mind. If he is also prepared to leave the principality and also agrees never to return, I think the court can save itself time as in the end he effected no severe bodily harm."

The judge turned his head to the public gallery, found Pallazza, and winked. Pallazza smiled back.

The lawyer conferred with his client, agreed to the conditions, and only a few hours later Vladimir Koschenko was on his way to Nice airport in one of Pallazza's cars.

The accompanying detective asked him to sign some release papers, unlocked the cuffs, and saluted in a twisted sense of courtesy as Vladimir boarded the plane for Paris, Charles de Gaulle airport.

Once in Paris, Vladimir never actually made it to the gate for the flight to Moscow. Instead, he took a bus to Orly airport, had lunch at the airport buffet, and then took the next Navette (shuttle flight) straight back down to the Riviera.

Arriving at Nice airport again a few hours later, he wanted to hire a car, but the Monegasque authorities had not returned his credit card or driving license, and all the spare cash Pallazza had given him he had used to pay for the Air France flight to Nice.

So he took the bus back to Monaco and got off in the Port Hercule area of La Condamine.

There he waited in the Rascasse Harbor bar until the International school a few hundred meters away exited for the day.

He saw Natasha long before she saw him. He hailed her as she walked past and told her that her mother had asked him to pick her up and take her to the cantina.

"But, Vladimir, I have violin lessons this afternoon. Did Mamma forget?"

"They are canceled for today. Sorry."

Natasha called out to her friend who had intended to accompany her to music class.

"Hey, Gloria, did you know music is canceled today?"

"No, no one told me. Are you sure Natasha? Sure it's canceled?"

"My Momma sent a message, so I suppose it's true."

Natasha accepted Vladimir's offer of a Coke and sat down at the Russian's table. Vladimir excused himself to visit the WC, where he called the Cantina.

Paz answered the call. The message was short and sharp. Meet at the Rascasse immediately and plan to return with Vladimir to Moscow or never see Natasha again.

"Vladimir, when did they let you out of jail? I heard they were thinking of pardoning you, but I did not think it would happen so soon."

"I was released this morning. I have a good lawyer. As I told you, Paz, I know my way around these parts. It is time you listened to me—and listen to me now. See me here in the next fifteen minutes at the Rascasse or Natasha will be in trouble. And if you are tempted to call the police or anyone else, don't."

Paz slowly put the phone back in its base and sat down at the Cantina's little welcome counter. She poured herself a tequila. Strangely, she wasn't nervous or that concerned. Somehow deep down she knew Vladimir would never harm her daughter. He was obviously trying to scare her and force some sort of submission on her part.

Slowly a plan formulated in her head. She called Vladimir back.

"Vladimir, we can't talk in the Rascasse bar with hundreds of people around. Come to the Cantina. I'll meet you there."

"Listen, woman, you do what I tell you for once."

Paz cut him off...

"No, Vladimir, you listen to me. I have had enough of these tantrums and shenanigans. Do as *I say* or I will call the police.

"We need to have a serious talk. I am worried about us. About you. About the Cantina. I need your help. Damn it, man, we are supposed to be married in a few weeks...Help me, don't fight me!"

Vladimir smiled. "Help me" is what he had waited so long to hear. Finally this cow realized that she needed him.

"OK, Paz, it's your last chance. Let's meet at the restaurant. I'll be there in ten minutes. Don't worry about Natasha."

"Vladimir, I know you would never harm her. But come around to the back of the restaurant. Some lunchtime eaters are still around, and we are short-staffed."

Vladimir thought about that for a minute wondering if he was facing some sort of plot. Those who have worked for any secret service for any time tend to sense danger anywhere and everywhere.

"Paz, I have a better idea. Meet me at the ship—Sverdlov's boat—on the rear deck. You can see and watch the restaurant from there, yet we will be able to talk in private. Be there in ten minutes."

Paz replaced the phone again and let out a relieved sigh. Then she placed one more quick call, warned her head waiter she'd be out for a while, and walked slowly to the Sverdlov boat about seventy meters down the harbor from her thriving little restaurant.

By the time she got there, she saw Vladimir already nursing a vodka on the afterdeck.

"Where's Natasha?" demanded Paz as she carefully negotiated the narrow gangway on board.

"In music school. I just told her I had misunderstood you about picking her up. You wanted to talk, so let's talk."

"I think you are the one with the most explaining to do," answered Paz, "so why don't you start? I thought you were supposed to be back in Moscow waiting for me?"

Vladimir thought about that for a moment.

"OK, you are right. I owe you an explanation. First, I do not like being told where to go and when. F–k the Monaco Police. Second, you are living in my apartment, the restaurant was my idea, marrying you was my idea, and you finally admitted you need me, so that is why we are meeting and why I am back."

"Vladimir, get real. The apartment belongs to your boss. Yes, the restaurant was your idea, but Sverdlov's money made it happen, and the Mexico gang you so hate made it an instant success. As for marrying you, that depends on what happens today, here on this boat. I am not getting hitched to some vodka-soaked macho who thinks women are possessions. I had enough of that in my youth. I fought against that in Mexico. I won't accept it here now from you or anyone else."

"NOT MARRY ME? Are you crazy? It is all agreed. Maybe we now can't marry here 'cos of my tussle with that idiot Scot friend of yours, but you are my woman, and you will be my wife and you will shut up."

"Vladimir, I will not shut up nor will I let you walk over me. Get used to it, or it's over—all over."

Vladimir looked at her over the rim of his glass of vodka as he sipped noisily. He calmed down a little and replied softly, "You said you needed me, bitch."

"Yes, I needed you to find out why the authorities are trying to close us down. Someone obviously hates our success. We have to get to the bottom of it. But if you won't help, well, I'll get someone else to help."

"Like who? The stupid Scot who is banned from Monaco for life? Or the smart-ass British brewer who is already back in London counting his money? Or the Madison Avenue hack from the Pampas? Forget it—only **I** can find out what is going on here. It is bloody well time you got that into your head."

"Vladimir, I don't need this. And I wonder what ever possessed me to think I needed you. I don't need you or your filthy tongue. We are obviously not right for each other."

Vladimir rose to his feet and placed his alcohol-sodden face as near as he could to hers.

"Look, you Mexican whore, go downstairs, get into the master bedroom, get undressed, and wait for me. We'll see who needs who. You know you need me. You always have."

"I am going, Vladimir. And going forever—right out of your life. That's how much I need you."

Vladimir jumped up and placed himself between Paz and the gangway blocking her exit. But with his back to the wharf, he could not see someone about to board.

"Listen, bitch, you go down into that bed NOW or you'll feel my hand across your face."

Vladimir now sensed someone creeping up on him. He whirled around ready for confrontation. But the vodka was already having its effect, and the dramatic whirl destabilized the Russian and he landed flat on his rear end with his back to the life raft box, still miraculously holding the vodka glass about a quarter full.

"You heard the lady, Vladimir. Get out of her way."

Vladimir looked up at his aggressor, his face contorted with jealously and rage. He tried to get up, but Sverdlov's right foot kept him down.

"Mr. Sverdlov, what are you doing here?"

"First, making sure you behave, and second, ensuring you get your arse back to Moscow as you agreed and wait for me there. Give you both time to think things through."

Sverdlov stood back allowing the Russian to find his feet. It was a bad decision. Vladimir immediately lunged at him, but Sverdlov easily saw it coming and moved aside. The enraged Russian rushed past, tripped hard on the shore rope, smashed Paz against the saloon door, and fell hard onto the starboard cleat. He collapsed in a heap, blood oozing from his forehead. He did not move.

"Jesus, I think we may have killed the poor man!" whispered Paz.

She rushed to feel his pulse but was stopped dead in her tracks by a shouted command.

"DON'T TOUCH HIM. FINGERPRINTS. GET OFF THIS SHIP NOW. I'll handle this. Go home, pack, and get that Hamish fellow ready to take you and your kid to the airport later in case we have to... Where is he now anyway?"

"In Menton, I think, with his friend Helene and her fisherman father."

"Shit, you are right. He can't come into Monaco. Not allowed. He knows that fishing family well, right?"

"Yes, very well. They are great friends."

"OK, good. Look, get him on the phone and tell him to meet me at the Marriott in thirty minutes. You and your daughter stay in Monte Marina until I call. Do not leave for any reason. Got it?"

Paz looked at him stunned and shaking.

"Paz, did you get what I said?" Paz nodded affirmatively. "OK, do it. Call Hamish. Tell him I'll be at the Marriott in thirty minutes. And thank the Lord you called me. He could have hurt you badly."

Paz jerked herself into action and left the ship.

As she walked down the gangplank, she saw Sverdlov drag the dead Vladimir behind some awnings.

Hamish put down the phone.

"What's the matter, Hamish?" asked Helene.

"Don't know, but there appears to be some problem in Monaco. I gotta go. Maybe see you tomorrow?"

CHAPTER 32

SVERDLOV SNAPS INTO ACTION

As soon as Paz disappeared out of sight, Sverdlov called Pallazza.

"Mr. Pallazza, I need your help—confidentially. Can we meet tonight at the car park below the Country Club? You are dining until about eleven? OK, what about eleven thirty? At your house? Fine, I'll be there. I appreciate it."

He cleaned up the deck as best he could and slowly made his way to the Marriott where he chose a dark corner booth in the bar easily seen from the door but still far enough away from any curious eavesdropper. He ordered a glass of rose wine and allowed himself a self-satisfied smile.

"Funny," he said to himself, "how solutions to problems always seem to present themselves automatically if you just relax and let Lady Luck take over!"

He had just enjoyed the first sip of the tart, cold wine when an ashen-faced Hamish arrived and sat himself quietly opposite the smiling Russian.

"Paz told me about Vladimir. Did he die?"

"Yes, I am afraid he did. Very soon after Paz left."

"Nobody did it, right? He tripped himself?"

"True, but then again everyone in town knows he and Paz had a number of violent rows. I just do not know if anyone saw the one on the boat—or heard it. I don't even know if anyone saw him back in town. As far as the authorities are concerned, he is safely back in Moscow. Good thing Paz called me before she went on board, as there is no telling what might have happened. He was out of control—and on drugs I'm afraid."

"Shit. What the hell do we do now? I could be a prime suspect as well," wailed a confused Hamish. "Everyone knows we also had a few bitter fights. Should we all just run away to and get the hell out of town?"

"I think not. If you do that their suspicions will be immediately aroused. Do not change your routine at all. Be as natural as you can be."

"Then what?"

"Well, I have been thinking about that. You know, Hamish, no one in Monaco really gives much of a damn about Russians like us, and especially not illegal residents and occasional drunken workers like Vladimir. Personally, since he appears to have found a coke habit, I will not miss him that much either."

Sverdlov went silent for a minute as he sipped the wine and appeared to be deep in thought. A moment later he placed the glass back on the table and leant closer to the worried Scot.

"I think there may be a way out of this, Hamish. None of us needs a scandal or a ruckus. It strikes me that without a body or a complaint, no one is going to care a heck of a lot about our pal. Who will miss Vladimir? No one. They think he is in Russia. Who will find his body? No one—if we can carry out my plan."

The glass went slowly back to Sverdlov's lips.

"What plan, sir?" begged Hamish.

"Well, first of all I think we should spread the story that Vladimir and Paz have decided to get married somewhere else—that Monaco created too many problems in their domestic life. That seems perfectly believable to me in view of all the tensions lately. We'll let it be known that Vladimir went on ahead to Moscow as he agreed, and sometime next week Paz will cancel the wedding arrangements and then go home to the USA. She can decide later if she wants to marry him or not. Personally, I am sick of that silly romance. It has just brought us all trouble."

Sverdlov took another sip of wine.

"What about the Cantina? Who will run that?" asked Hamish.

"I already have that covered. The wife of a friend can do it; it would even save me some money. We could prepare a little farewell party and make it all look oh-so-natural! As far as the authorities are concerned, and unless someone saw Vladimir those few hours he was back here today, everyone thinks they've safely gotten rid of him."

"That takes care of the story. Now the body. It is lying wrapped up in the hold of my boat. No body, no suspicion. We have to get rid of it. We have about twenty-four hours to act before it starts to seriously decompose. That means we have to act tonight."

"WE have to act? WE? Who's we?" queried Hamish.

"Actually, mainly you. *You* have to act. You are the only one who can make my plan work. Here is my idea. How close are you with those fisherman family friends of yours in Menton?"

"Pretty close…"

"Well I suggest you go back there now, find the father, and explain what happened. He never liked Vladimir, as you know. My boat used to be docked in Menton whilst we were awaiting a berth here. Vladimir kept complaining about the noise the fishermen made returning in the morning. There were rows, and I think they almost came to blows. Don't really know the full story. But anyway, that fisherman pal of yours helped get us thrown out of Menton. Luckily our berth here came through at about the same time.

"Anyway, get him to take the fishing boat out tonight. Doesn't he come to Monaco from time to time? To deliver fish?"

"Yes, often. The prices are better here."

"Fine, make sure he pops over to Port Hercule fishing pier tonight and delivers some fish. I will have a new set of fishing nets delivered to the Port Quay at about 2:00 a.m. in a Hertz rental truck. I have a whole stock of nets below in the hold. Vladimir will be in the middle of those nets. You load the nets and dump the dumb shit out to sea. End of story. No one will suspect the fisherman of anything. They know him. You will be on the boat, hidden of course, to help him off-load the carcass cargo."

Hamish whistled softly.

"Wow! What a plan. Will it work?"

"That's up to you, Hamish. Can you get the old fisherman to cooperate?"

"I think so. I'll get his daughter to help me. She's an old friend."

"OK, Hamish. Go to Menton and call me as soon as you have a "go" agreement. Just say 'dinner is on or off'—nothing more or less. Calls are monitored here in Monaco, you know. And take the train. The Rolls is far too obvious."

"What do I tell Paz?"

"Nothing now. Let's see if our plan works. We can fill her in tomorrow if all goes well."

The two men shook hands and parted each to his own project. Hamish scurried to get to Menton.

Sverdlov hurried back to his boat. There was a lot to do and a lot to be done. If this was all to go as he planned, each detail had to be right.

First he had to find the drugs—the drugs he knew Vladimir had been stealing from him and hiding.

He went down into the cabin Vladimir usually used and carefully looked around him. He tore the bedclothes off the bunk and examined them. Nothing. Then he carefully removed the TV, the radio, the books, the tapes. Nothing.

He emptied the medicine chest in the bathroom and carefully combed through the drawers of the wardrobe and the clothes in the cupboard.

"Shit," he said to himself. "If the stuff is not in his cabin, it could be anywhere." That could take him all night to discover.

He sat down in Vladimir's chair to think, leaning his back on the head-rest. Then he saw it. One piece of the skirting board was loose. That must be it.

He bounded up the gangway into the galley and grabbed the box of rubber dishwashing gloves. Putting one on each hand, he carefully pried the board from the wall and peered inside. There by the ship's pipes and wires lay Vladimir's bum-bag—the type tourists take on vacation to keep valuables tight on their bodies.

Hand still enclosed in the gloves, he opened the bag. Presto! It was full of little brown envelopes of cocaine.

Next, he placed a call to his captain at home in Villefranche and told him to bring the hire (Hertz) van he was using to Monaco, park on the port, and await another call. Next, he grabbed a bunch of polythene food bags and raced back down the steps to Vladimir's cabin where he forced one foot each into a plastic bag and then carefully selected a pair of Vladimir's sneakers—the special ones from Gucci he had loved so much and Sverdlov had given him for Christmas in happier times.

It was a tight fit—Sverdlov's feet were a full size and larger—but necessity forced the discomfort.

Finally, he selected one of Vladimir's fuller ski parkas with hood, and stuffed a bunch more polythene bags into each jacket pocket.

Now he was ready. He sat down to await the call.

Sverdlov was excited. He loved danger almost as much as he loved intrigue. There had been too little lately. And now there was almost too much. But then how could there ever really be too much?

He was just dozing off when his cell buzzed. It was Hamish. "Dinner" was on. Sverdlov breathed a deep sigh of relief as he read the text message again and again.

He called Pallazza and confirmed the meeting for 11:30 p.m. at his house. Then he called back the captain and told him to be ready in about thirty minutes to deliver their spare fishing nets to a fisherman who wanted them that night.

Job done, Sverdlov set his alarm and settled down for a few hours' sleep.

CHAPTER 33

LAST VISIT TO MENTON

Helene was waiting at the station as the train from Monaco slowly groaned to a halt. Hamish waved to her happily and they hugged warmly as they met. Funny how this woman could still turn his heart after all those years.

"Hamish, what is so urgent that it can't wait a few days—or at least until morning?"

"Helene, can we talk in your house? Did you call your father? Is he coming to see me?"

"Hey, slow down, man. Yes, he is looking forward to meeting you. What the hell is going on?"

"Please, let's just get home."

Once in the cozy little house with its chintzy sofas and lace curtains, Hamish told his story. Helene loved it and read it slightly differently than he told it. No matter, thought Hamish, it is the result that counts, not the details.

"So, Hamish, you are so in love with this Mexican lady that you are doing this thing to rid her of that lout? What a romantic story. I am so happy that you finally found your true love."

And she hugged him so tightly he could feel the firmness of those breasts he still remembered so well.

"Of course Father will help you. He hated that Russian boor!"

As if on cue, the old man walked in. Hamish let Helene tell the story. The old man listened intently. Hamish watched anxiously.

When Helene had finished, the old man stroked his chin and answered, "I don't give a shit for that Russian bastard, but the plan is risky. Monaco is full of police at all times of the day and night."

"But Papa, they all know you. Why would they suspect anything? You are always there."

"Yes, but never at two in the morning. I deliver between six to seven *after* I have caught the fish, not before."

"Papa, that's the beauty of Hamish's plan. You are collecting new nets. You need nets before you go out to sea, no?"

"Since when do my lazy French compatriots deliver material in the middle of the night? Come on—that's just not believable."

The meeting went quiet, the old man slowly lighting another of those obnoxious yellow cigarettes. After a puff or two, he placed the glowing smoke on the ashtray and started to grin.

"The Port of Monaco has been closed all this week because of work to the foundations of the new yacht club. Of course I could not take delivery during daylight. The cops will know that."

"So you'll help, Papa?"

"Oui," the old man replied, "we'll do it. You are right, Helene. Why would anyone in Monaco suspect me? Anyway, I like Hamish and I hated that arrogant Russian. We sail at one. Now we drink a Pernod together. Helene, glasses please."

A few minutes later Hamish excused himself and went in the hall to place the text message Sverdlov was waiting for.

"OK for dinner tonight" it said.

CHAPTER 34

PALLAZZA MEETS SVERDLOV... AGAIN

At 11:00 p.m. Sverdlov woke to the cell phone alarm. Ready for action, he laced up the painful Guccis and placed the yellow rubber gloves on his hands again. He donned the bum-bag, put on the parka, raised the hood over his head, and made his way down the gangplank to the yacht's scooter ready to make the 11:30 p.m. rendezvous.

Dressed in Vladimir's clothes, on Vladimir's scooter, and with Vladimir's rare and costly Guccis on his feet, he hoped he would be easily mistaken for the missing Russian if anyone happened to notice.

Pallazza let him in after the first knock: he was extremely curious as to the purpose of this urgent need to talk. He led Sverdlov immediately into the kitchen and clicked on the electric kettle for some communal tea.

Seated at the table, Pallazza poured two cups. Sverdlov did not touch his nor did he take the gloves off his hands.

Pallazza, now noticing the strange gloves, nodded nervously toward the plastic mittens.

"Sorry, Mr. Pallazza, but I developed an acute eczema this evening and I don't know if it is transmittable. I will check at the hospital tomorrow. These were the only hand coverings I could quickly find. Monaco is not exactly the climate for gloves!"

Pallazza relaxed again.

"Mr. Pallazza, I am here to tell you that I have persuaded Paz to leave the Cantina. She will probably follow Vladimir to Russia and marry him there, the silly fool. That marriage can't work. Tough—but that's their problem…By the way, have you heard anything from Vladimir after you guys booted him out and sent him to Moscow? I have not heard a peep!"

"No, why should I hear from that idiot? Good riddance, I say. He'd be crazy to come back. They'll incarcerate him for sure and forever. It was not easy to get the judge to let him go, you know; the silly man flashed a gun. That drives the police crazy. But in a way it helped me talk them into releasing him; they don't want any publicity that anyone ever bandied a pistol around. Scares the poor little billionaires, you know!"

Sverdlov breathed a sigh of relief. If Pallazza had not seen Vladimir, or heard of his arrival today, probably nobody noticed. If anyone had spied him, for sure this ferret and gossip monger would have been among the first to know.

"Mr. Sverdlov, I am delighted that we will be doing business. I will inform my wife in the morning that she will take over the Cantina—actually, ex-wife. But we are still good business partners. She will run the restaurant well; probably much better than that dumb Latina."

He spat the word "Latina" out with palpable disgust.

"Good, that is one problem solved. Now, Mr. Pallazza, I'd like to return to our conversation on dope, if you don't mind."

"Mr. Sverdlov, you do not have to admit anything. I know your business and as I said before, it is none of my affair nor does it bother me. If people are too stupid to know what they are paying for and playing with, well, then more fool them."

"No, no, Mr. Pallazza. It is not my business in dope I want to talk about but yours. I did not know *you* were a heavy user."

"Me, dope? You crazy—never touch the stuff."

"That's funny because Vladimir asked me—as a farewell gift—to give you this pouch."

Sverdlov handed over the little canvas bum-bag full of the dangerous white powder. Pallazza took it gingerly, unzipped the top, and peered inside.

"Oh, it's cocaine all right. Top quality. From Afghanistan. We Russians still have good contacts there, you know!"

"Well, I don't want it. Take it back. I told you that fellow Vladimir is totally crazy…"

"Mr. Pallazza, my new friend and partner, Vladimir wants you to have it, so take it. In fact, why not take a snort now? Here, I'll lay out a few lines on the table…"

"NO, NO, NO…I do not want any trace of that stuff in this house. The palace is dead against drugs."

"But you allowed me to frame that dishonest gallery man and place a bag in his painting? I do remember that right, do I not?"

"That was different. That was business. Mr. Sverdlov, take that stuff out of this house immediately."

Sverdlov finished laying out three lines of the gray-white powder and then smiled sweetly at Pallazza.

"Don't deny an old friend a favor. Vladimir wanted you to have a snort free—now do it. Snort Pallazza. Snort."

Pallazza started to reply but froze as he found himself looking at the muzzle of an old German Luger pistol.

"The cocaine will blow your mind or this Luger will, Pallazza. Take your choice."

Pallazza looked at his tormentor in abject astonishment and then slowly did as the Luger instructed. He snorted deeply, coughed, spluttered, and ran to the sink to blow out his tortured nose.

Then he was violently sick, all his good dinner now covering the kitchen sink bottom.

And that was the last Pallazza remembered. He slumped to the floor.

Sverdlov laughed and, after making sure the cocaine dust on the ground clearly showed the Gucci sneaker sole pattern, he exited the house.

Then he waited patiently outside for the Hertz truck to transport him and the scooter and some very heavy fishing nets back to the ship.

CHAPTER 35

COLLECTING THE NETS IN MONACO

At precisely 1:00 a.m. the little fishing boat eased its way out of its Menton mooring and 'pop-popped' its diesel-engined way to Monaco. The sea was calm and the night clear. From his hideaway in the bow, Hamish watched the stars drift by. He was scared, but he was excited as well.

At about a quarter to two, they slowly and quietly entered Monaco's Port Hercule Harbor and docked at the fisherman's pier just opposite the Quai des Artistes restaurant. Two bored and beefy Monaco policemen met them. The elder saluted, "Andre, you know we don't like late-night ship movements. It disturbs our sleepy billionaires!"

"Pierre, how are you? How's crime tonight? And f–k the billionaires. You and I have to make a living. Thanks to you guys closing the port today I had to take delivery tonight of some new nets; they were delayed from Marseille, so we decided to meet here rather than in Menton."

"Why take delivery here? We don't like fishing boats polluting the quiet at night, and we like trucks even less."

"Pierre, you are a prize con. What silence? Listen to the jerks yelling and dancing at Stars 'n' Bars and the Rascasse. Anyway, if you had been alert, you'd know there's some problem on the A8 motorway tonight. They closed part of it, right?

"Ah oui," remembered the older cop. They mentioned that in our briefing tonight."

Thank the Lord for the radio, thought the old fisherman. They had warned listeners about that fracas on the Autoroute. A truck had overturned and shed its load of Italian tomatoes. The information came in handy right now.

"Yeah," added the younger policeman. "I heard about that mess. Well, be quick will you? Before HQ gets annoyed and starts hassling me to get you out of here. Night, Andre!"

As the two cops turned away, the Hertz truck arrived. Sverdlov and his captain unloaded the big roll of nets and manhandled them silently into the boat. They shook the old fisherman's hand and drove off. The whole transfer took less than five minutes.

Andre started the engine again, and the little boat headed back out to sea.

As they rounded the new floating Digue (or dock)—the home of the huge new cruise liners that visited Monte Carlo—Hamish stiffly rose from his hideout, stretched, and said, "So far so good, mon Capitaine!"

"Si, so far so good."

It was about 2:30 a.m. and the air was fresh. Hamish watched the net-draped corpse rolling on the floor at his feet and could feel the nausea overtake him. The old man kept on going determined that the body of Vladimir Koschenko would meet his watery fate as soon as humanly possible.

CHAPTER 36

PAZ PACKS UP

At about 7:00 a.m. Hamish strolled as nonchalantly as he could into the Marriott. He collected his newspaper and entered the dining hall as he had done on countless previous mornings. He ordered his breakfast at the same table and at approximately the same time as was his wont. Act One was over.

Breakfast completed, he walked onto the pool deck and called Sverdlov.

"Mr. Sverdlov, I hear you wanted to have coffee with me and Paz this morning? Good. You know I can't enter the principality, but I will await you here at the hotel. About ten o'clock? Fine, I will be here."

At a few minutes after ten, Sverdlov strolled into the Marriott with Paz. The three happily greeted each other and then moved out onto the comparative privacy of the terrace to have coffee.

When the waiter had taken the order, Sverdlov asked anxiously, "Was the package delivered, Hamish?"

"Delivered and fully paid for," answered Hamish, smiling as if he was discussing the arrival of a bag of groceries from Carrefour.

"Good. Now, Paz, let's you and me walk over to the seawall there and take a look at the boats."

Paz was puzzled. But she was also curious. What package were these two men talking about?

As the mismatched couple leant over the seawall, ostensibly examining the expensive array of marine hardware in Cap d'Ail Harbor, Sverdlov held Paz's shoulder and whispered.

"Paz, I have grave news to tell you. Do not react. Do not cry. Just keep looking at the boats. OK?"

Paz felt a cold knot forming in her stomach and slowly oozing up her spine.

"Paz, Vladimir is dead. He did not survive that fall. The cleat broke his skull. Hamish and his fisherman friend buried him at sea last night."

Sverdlov felt Paz's shudder.

"Paz, do not let go. Please keep a grip on yourself. Obviously after what has happened here over the last weeks, Hamish would be a prime suspect. That is why I had to act. I am sorry, but frankly it is probably all for the better. Vladimir was a coke head and rapidly getting out of control. I think you know in your heart of hearts that a long-term relationship between you two was doomed. Anyway, be that as it may, what has happened, happened. Now we have to minimize the damage. Paz, listen carefully. We have a plan, so don't worry."

Sverdlov laid it out as gently as he could. Paz would announce that Vladimir had gone back to Russia, which would be totally believable as the Monegasques had already sent him off to Moscow via Paris. For now, no one knew he had turned right around and flown straight back. Paz would then cancel all the wedding plans and announce she was following her 'fiance' to Moscow—also totally believable. Sverdlov would give her $50,000 for her efforts in establishing the Cantina, and the head waiter would take over. Hamish and the Lady would drive back to Scotland in a few days in the Rolls. Game, set, and match.

Paz said nothing for a few minutes and then, holding back her tears as well as she could, sadly answered, "Wherever I go trouble seems to follow me. The only true peace and happiness I ever had was those few years in Florida with my much older husband."

Slowly the tears welled up and she could no longer hold back the rising tide. Sverdlov held her tightly until she stopped shaking.

"Go home, Paz. Take Natasha and go home where you belong. You still have your old house, correct?"

Paz nodded adding, "At least Natasha will be happy—happy to see her old friends again. And that awful dog. You know, Mr. Sverdlov, I really did like Vladimir. But you are right. It would never have worked out. Never. I know that now."

They looked at the water a little longer and then rejoined Hamish on the terrace to finish their, by now, rather cold cappuccinos.

A few days later, the papers were full of the disappearance of Mr. Pallazza. Drugs had been found all over the house. The story reported the shock of those who knew him and their surprise that he seemed to have had such a severe and secret drug problem. Nobody knew the exact story and the police were not forthcoming. At least, not yet…

Sverdlov smiled as he read. Now he had to get them all out of Monaco fast before the police got wiser.

CHAPTER 37

REUNION IN FLORIDA

The return to Florida had been happy for Paz and Natasha. They retrieved 'Dawg' from the neighbors, and he went totally wild. Natasha was equally elated to rediscover her old school and her old friends.

Paz asked the renters to relinquish their lease on her property before lease end, and soon the two girls were happily reestablished in their old and familiar life along the Loxahatchee River in rural Jupiter.

She hoped Natasha had not realized all the mayhem surrounding Vladimir and his death. She herself tried to wipe the half year or so of Monaco right out of her consciousness.

True, Paz was lonely, but relaxed. Old memories of her life there with Peter, her husband, kept her content in the lonely weekend evenings. During the week, she went back to managing Pedro's Mexican Restaurant, which effectively helped keep her busy and allowed sad thoughts to be kept somewhat under control.

Then one morning, a few months after they returned, came that phone call. It was Sverdlov calling from London. Hamish and he were flying down to spend a few days with her next week to have a reunion and tell her some news.

Paz was nervous as she waited at Palm Beach airport. After the initial euphoria at the thought of seeing old friends wore off, she became worried. Why open up the Monaco story once again? What news could Sverdlov possibly have? Were they all in trouble?

Paz saw the two men through the 'meeters and greeters' window long before they saw her. Sverdlov looked a little older and grayer than she remembered him. But Hamish looked bronzed and healthy. Strangely, because she had never been romantically attracted to the Scot, his arrival stirred a longing she found hard to explain.

They chatted small talk on the thirty-five-minute ride home avoiding, as if by unspoken mutual desire, any mention of Monaco or the recent events there.

"My little house is not really large enough to house all you big men, so I got you a special business-to-business rate at the Jupiter Resort. It's right on the shore. You'll love it."

Paz dropped them off and arranged a pick-up for dinner at her house at about 7:30 p.m.

As she collected the desert plates, Paz could stand it no longer. They had again avoided any talk of Monaco all through the meal.

"Well, you are fed, rested, and I hope happy, so now tell me why you are here…please," begged Paz.

"Let's go onto your terrace and we'll talk," answered the Russian. "Your girl is not likely to interrupt us, is she?"

"No, no, she is overnighting with her girlfriend in Juno. I thought that might be more suitable."

Comfortably seated in the lanai, with the frogs croaking and lazy river slowly washing by, Sverdlov let out a deep sigh and started.

"Paz, Vladimir is not dead. He is in Russia in rehab. It will take months and months to cure him of his addictions, if we ever can."

Paz's hand shot to her face in shock. Her eyes widened in horror. She turned to Hamish for some sort of confirmation, but Hamish just looked away.

"Paz, the police in Monaco blamed him for the murder of Mr. Pallazza. They found a pouch of cocaine with Vladimir's fingerprints on it in Pallazza's house. Vladimir's shoe prints were all over the kitchen floor and entrance. It appears Vladimir was selling Pallazza dope and some sort of argument ensued—probably about payment. You know how unstable and mercurial Vladimir was."

"But, but…" stuttered Paz.

"Wait, Paz, hear me out. Suspecting foul play and finding all those clues indicting Vladimir, they started looking more closely into what happened after they let him out of prison.

It did not take them long to work out that he never went on that plane to Moscow and returned to Monaco. People remembered seeing him at the Rascasse and on my boat.

So they assumed he came back to Monaco to settle some score with Pallazza and then fled to Moscow again—which they know is where he is today."

Paz stared at the Russian in disbelief.

"Whatever happened, the Monaco Police have closed the case. It is not worth them trying to extradite Vladimir from Russia; it would never succeed. Anyway, without a body, murder conviction is always difficult. Remember also, the Monagasque do not like to admit that murder could actually occur in that gilded land !

Furthermore, the Monegasque are embarrassed that they should never have let this obviously unstable man out of prison or have allowed an undocumented resident such freedom to live in their principality. They would rather the whole sad story just float away and be quietly forgotten.

It also appears Mr. Pallazza was not as important or as well respected in the principality as he thought. No one cared much of a damn about him either. They thought he had just upped sticks and run back to his native Rome. In the end life is very cheap. Most of us create some sort of a ripple in the pond of life, but when we go the ripple dies with us. Worth remembering just how small we all actually are!"

Paz turned in panic to Hamish.

"But, but…Hamish, you buried Vladimir at sea. Hamish, answer me. Please…"

"No, Paz, apparently we did not. I thought we did, but I never looked deeply into those nets."

"Then who? I know you dumped a body—somebody's body. Whose was it? For heaven's sake, somebody tell me?"

Nobody answered.

A sudden thought hit Paz.

"Jesus, you guys dumped Pallazza? Vladimir killed Pallazza and begged you to dump the body and then you sent him to Russia? He was only knocked out when he fell on that boat? Or was that whole fall staged for my benefit too?!"

Paz started to sob uncontrollably.

Despite Paz's obvious discomfort, Sverdlov smiled inwardly. She had come to the exact conclusion he had hoped for.

Vladimir got all the credit. Vladimir had killed Pallazza and got the heck out of town. Great! End of story. Sverdlov could keep his business dealings in Monaco alive and free from the meddling, annoying little Italian.

"Paz, I am afraid it was something like that. Yes. And that is why Vladimir can never leave Russia—even if he gets cured, which frankly I doubt, because he would be picked up by Interpol immediately for the murder of Mr. damn Pallazza."

"How could Vladimir have been so crazy? He could be such a loving man at times…" moaned Paz quietly.

"Paz, he was a slave to drugs. And you also have to remember that he had a very traumatic past as an agent in Russia and Chechnya. In fact, it was in Chechnya where I first met him. He saved my life. So I owed him—owed him big time. That's why we helped him get out of Monaco and why I am helping him now."

The room went silent again.

"Gentlemen, I think I need to be alone for a bit. Would you excuse me?"

"Paz, do you have navigation in your car?" asked Hamish.

"Yes, why?"

"I suggest I take your car to the hotel and bring it back tomorrow when you feel better. Would that be a good idea?"

Paz said nothing, but she rummaged in her purse, found the car keys, and gently threw them over to Hamish.

"What time should we come back? The plane leaves at three o'clock or thereabouts."

"Hamish, please call me in the morning, OK? Will you guys be all right?"

"Sure," answered Sverdlov. "We'll be fine. Good night, Paz. Sorry about the shock, but we felt we owed you an explanation. If ever Vladimir improves, he might try to contact you. It's none of my business, but I would leave him alone. That's a permanently flawed personality, I am afraid."

Hamish showed Sverdlov the car and, out of habit as a chauffeur, opened the door for him. He switched on the Sat Nav and slowly drove up the gravel path.

"That went better than I thought, Hamish," offered Sverdlov. "She is convinced Vladimir bumped off that scumbag Pallazza. And I think we should leave it at that. What point is there in telling her the truth?"

"Why bother her anymore?" replied Hamish.

"Well, it troubles me a little that she now believes her old fiancé is a murderer. That does not appear entirely fair."

"You did not tell me until a few months ago. I never told Andre the fisherman. We both thought those fishing nets contained Vladimir Koschenko's body."

"True, but I was worried the fisherman might baulk if he knew the truth. Then we would have been in a pretty mess."

"No, *you* would have been in a mess," replied Hamish with just a touch of malice.

"Whatever. Now—one way or the other—you have a free run at that Mexican beauty, don't you?"

Hamish stopped the car. Although Hamish had secretly admitted to himself many times before what Sverdlov was insinuating, he still did not like hearing it.

"Sverdlov, my hands are soiled because of what you did, not because of any feelings I might have had, or have, for Paz. You know that. Anyway, if we are now being honest with each other, tell me exactly what happened that night at Pallazza's."

Sverdlov peered into the night sky for some minutes debating with himself if he could really truly trust this Scot.

"Hamish, when Vladimir cracked his forehead on that cleat, I knew right away he was not dead—only concussed. I brought him round and helped him to my cabin where, frankly, I chloroformed him. But I also knew I had a golden opportunity to ensure he could never marry Paz, which you know would have been a disaster. And it gave me a way to get even with that loathsome toad Pallazza who threatened me and black-mailed me. Hamish, don't ever do that to a Russian."

Hamish stared at him in the gloom.

"I donned Vladimir's clothes and shoes and found his bag of cocaine and planted his prints all over Pallazza's house. I knew the police would eventually find out that Vladimir had returned that day to Monaco and would assume what Paz also immediately assumed—that Vladimir had killed him. Everybody knew they disliked each other."

"Yes," insisted Hamish, "but how did Pallazza die?"

"I forced him to snort three lines of cocaine, which made him immedi-ately sick. He rushed to the sink to vomit. As his head came back up, I hit him as hard as I could with my Luger. It has the weight to do real cranial damage. I have to tell you, Hamish, I felt deep satisfaction when I heard that rat's skull crack. He was an insult to Monaco.

"I then wrapped him in the hall carpet and waited for my captain to collect me. Together we carried Pallazza's corpse and the scooter up into his Hertz van. In the van, we unwrapped the body out of the rug and covered the head with a plastic film so that the face would be distorted enough for you not to recognize it and thus realize you were not burying a Russian but an Italian. Finally we just rolled the body in an old sheet and then buried everything in the nets before delivering our 'package' to your boat. The rest you know. I'm sorry I had to dupe you, but I could never have continued to do business in Monte Carlo with that turd around my neck. And, as I said, Paz is now free of Vladimir and he—my good friend and savior in Chechnya—is hopefully being cured in Moscow."

"And the rug? Where is the presumably blood-soaked rug?" asked Hamish quietly.

"Burnt. I included it with a bunch of junk from the apartment I bought and was clearing in Beausoleil and had taken to the Monte Carlo incinerator."

Hamish turned to Sverdlov and said sadly, "I don't think I'll ever go back to Monaco again—even if they allowed me."

"Hamish, your place is here, in Florida, with that girl. Be a man and go get your woman. Lady L wanted me to tell you that as forcefully as I could. She knows you love her.

"Vladimir is now well out of the picture—he can never leave Russia. As I told Paz, Interpol would pick him up immediately. He was totally wrong for her anyway—we all know that. No, Hamish, Paz is yours to win—or lose. It's as simple as that!"

"Lady L told you that? That I love Paz? Is she still making deliveries for you? I heard you ordered another spare wheel or two for the Rolls and that she still has the car."

"Hamish, some things are better left unsaid. What I *can* tell you is she regularly holidays in Monaco—and often on my boat!"

Disgusted and shaking his head, Hamish started the engine.

⸺◦⟨◉⟩◦⸺

In the morning Hamish called Paz after breakfast and by ten thirty two cars were grinding the gravel on the access road to the little cottage by the river.

"Paz, I hired a car—Hertz. Mr. Sverdlov followed me here in your car. I plan to take him to the airport in Miami and then drive down to Key West. I always wanted to see it. I loved reading Hemmingway at school. Can I come back in a week or so and see you again when maybe you have had a little time to digest all these difficult things? There is a little more to the story you might like to know."

"Yes, Hamish, I'd like that," she said with more enthusiasm than she expected. "Please do it. You can stay in the spare room if you like. Call me. Good-bye and thanks for coming down. I appreciate it. But don't you have to get back to Lady L in Scotland?"

"No, I don't work for her anymore. I'll tell you when I see you, OK?"

Paz was still too much in shock to register, so she just pecked Hamish on the cheek and closed the door.

EPILOGUE

It was Natasha who opened the door. She whooped for joy when she saw the familiar face.

"Uncle Hamish! Welcome to Florida. How nice to see you."

She jumped into his arms and hugged him tightly.

Hamish had no idea what to do, so he just stood there grinning widely.

Paz came out of the kitchen wiping her hands on a cloth as she walked to meet him. She also hugged him tightly.

"How was Key West? I've never been there."

"I loved it. Full of crazy tourists trying to get as drunk every night as Hemmingway was reputed to have been. But it was fun. Allowed me to sort of wrap up the past. And how are you, Paz?"

"Oh, I'm fine. I have come to terms with things. I am just sorry we ever got involved with all that Monaco stuff—with him," she added softly.

"We are NEVER leaving here again, right Mummy? You promised?"

"Yes, Natasha. I promised, and I promise, but at least you speak French now, plus Spanish. That's quite a plus for a pretty young miss!"

Natasha smiled and whooped back, "I am never leaving here. When I grow up, I will marry a Florida orange farmer and have lots of dogs and children—all girls. I hate boys—except for Hamish, of course."

Hamish grinned again and picked up the girl and hugged her tightly. He was surprised by how good that felt.

"Hamish, I am taking you down to Panama Hattie's on the Intracoastal for lunch. It's Natasha's favorite place, and she is off on a school trip to Washington tonight. Is that agreeable to you?"

"Absolutely, but it's on me. I am an old-fashioned Scot and women are not allowed to pay. It's the law—at least it's my law!"

"I think I'll move to Scotland!" laughed Paz.

Natasha heard that and ran back to her mother in fear.

"No, no, Natasha. That was a joke. I told you, we are staying here. Forever!" Natasha ran off happily again to her room.

After lunch, Hamish unpacked his few things in Paz's spare room and watched Paz get Natasha ready for her culture and heritage class experience in Washington.

"Good-bye, Uncle Hamish! I love you. Why don't you marry Mummy and come live in Florida? You were good at helping run that awful Cantina in Monte Carlo. You can help run Pedro's."

Hamish blushed a deep red, and, of course, didn't know what to say. So he said nothing, as usual. Paz laughed heartily.

"Natasha, Hamish is married…aren't you, Hamish?"

"No, I am divorced. For about six weeks now."

Paz couldn't help showing a little jolt. But she pretended not to hear and just waved Hamish good-bye as she bundled Natasha and her suitcase in the old Chevy ready for the trip to the airport.

When she returned about two hours later, they retired to the lanai and shared a peaceful moment and a Mexican Cuba Libre (Mexican rum and Coke).

"Now tell what it is you promised to reveal on your return here."

"Oh, you mean about Lady Lothmere? Well, you remember how she hated that art dealer Prentice and how he tried to cheat them over those Jacoby pictures? Well, she kept going back to the gallery to rant at him, but the more she ranted, the more they seemed to get on. She even testified at his trial on that cocaine-in-the-picture case. He got a suspended sentence as no one could see any connection between the man who purchased the painting in Bulgaria and drugs. There is a suspicion that Pallazza was someway involved, as he was noticed in the warehouse on the night the cocaine seemed to enter the picture. But as we all know, Pallazza is dead and dead men tell no tales."

Hamish took a sip of the drink.

"Yes, and then?" prompted Paz.

"And then, would you believe it, they got married. Prentice sold the business and moved up to Scotland. Just like that! Amazing isn't it?"

"I'll say it's amazing. I thought he was a Monaco fixture. He's been there for decades. What could have changed his mind?"

"Love. Sex. I dunno!" snickered Hamish.

"No, be serious, Hamish. What's your best guess?"

"Well, I don't think he ever quite got over the cocaine accusations and the scandal, plus bumping into Sverdlov in Monaco from time to time was becoming just too painful for him.

"One other possible factor that could have influenced the greedy Mickey-boy is money. The Lady is much richer than you think. She is in a very lucrative business with Sverdlov."

"Sverdlov?" repeated Paz incredulously.

"Yes, Sverdlov—Prentice's enemy and the possible reason for him leaving Monaco—*is her partner*. Can you believe it? And I don't think Mickey, her new husband, even knows it. What a wicked spider's web they weave!

"Anyway, whatever finally enticed Prentice to move, the two old rogues are now happily manipulating art auctions together and bickering every day. I think it keeps them young. But Prentice doesn't dare cheat her any-more that's for sure!"

Hamish thought that hilarious and almost spilled his drink in mirth.

"But heavens above, Hamish, she must be twice his age, no?"

"Yes, she is older, but I bet no more than a few years at most. Prentice is much more, shall we say, 'mature' than he looks. Had that gallery for over forty years—you do the math. Anyway, there is plenty of life left in that old lady, I can tell you."

"So where did that leave you, Hamish?"

"Out on me ear, as they say. She used me so much that my taxi business went to heck. And, frankly, I did not feel like building it up again. I sold the house and car, gave half to my ex-wife, and with the money the old lady gave me, I now have some £120,000 in the bank."

Paz stared at her glass—goodness how fast things change.

"Oh, and one other thing. It was her idea to send Sverdlov and me down here to talk to you. She insisted you know the truth. I wasn't going to go, but she paid my ticket and that sort of was that…"

Paz was crestfallen.

"Why, didn't *you* want to come? Didn't you want to see me?"

Hamish did not answer.

"So you'd rather not see me again, is that it?"

Hamish jumped up at that.

"No, no—heavens alive. No, no, no. I love you…I mean, I love seeing you, but, but…"

"But what, Hamish?"

"But I don't want to say good-bye again. It seems my life is all good-byes."

Suddenly Paz understood. She went over to Hamish's chair and knelt beside him.

"Hamish, look at me right in the eyes. You don't have to say good-bye. You can stay here as long as you like. Natasha would love it. And she's right. You'd be a great help at the restaurant. Short-term or," and she hesitated, "…or long-term."

As she got up again, she kissed him lightly on the cheek.

"Let's go to bed and tomorrow we'll think of happier things."

Paz could not sleep. She was now pretty sure Hamish loved her. But could she love him back? Should she? He would make an excellent husband—like Peter did. And she had not really been 'in love' with her ex-husband. But she had loved him and made him happy.

Maybe she was asking too much of life. Good men don't grow on trees, and bad men usually make lousy life companions. That much at least now seemed abundantly clear to her.

Then she heard it. The first rumblings of one of those famous Florida thunderstorms you read about. She started to shiver. She hated thunderstorms, even though it was a thunderstorm that had originally brought Paz and her husband together. Was fate playing a hand again?

She smiled and said softly to herself, "Silly Paz."

Another lighting flash and another thunderclap—this time louder and almost above her head. She let out a short scream of fright.

Hamish rushed in as naked as the day he was born.

"Are you all right, Paz?"

"I just got a shock. I am scared to death of storms. Will you stay with me until the damn thing passes?"

"What—like this?"

She had been so frightened she never noticed his nakedness. She threw him her bathrobe and he hastily tried to put it on. But, of course, it was far too small, and no matter how he tried, Hamish could not get the thing to cover his vital parts.

Paz started to laugh at his confusion. And then there was another crack—this time loud enough to shake the house.

Petrified, Paz jumped into Hamish's arms, her face buried in his chest—exposed manhood or not.

She stayed there until the storm passed—a good six or seven minutes in all. When the moon appeared again through two thunderclouds, she raised her head to look at him. As she did so, her nightshirt loosened and one breast slowly caught the light.

Hamish tried to look away, embarrassed at his own exposure and trying hard to avoid looking at hers.

She dropped her arms from holding Hamish, shook her shoulders, and let the nightshirt slide silently to the floor. Then she held him tightly again.

"Hamish, kiss me."

"Paz, Paz…I don't know…"

"I do—I know. I know you love me—at least I think you do. Only if you kiss me will I know for sure. So Hamish, kiss me!"

He kissed her. Lightly and with his lips pursed tightly together. Paz grabbed his head and pulled it down. Now she kissed him. Fully, passionately, and erotically.

She felt him respond against her belly.

"Come to bed, Hamish. I am getting cold."

He followed her sheepishly.

"I have not been with a woman for a long time."

"Neither have I. Not with a woman—or even a man!" giggled Paz. "But like riding a bike, they say you never forget!"

It did not take more than a few moments for Hamish to get over his shyness, and—to his pleasant surprise—he found he remembered pretty quickly how to 'ride that bike'!

Now it was Paz's turn to be amazed. She had not expected such passion from the dour Scot.

When it was all over, she held him tightly and happily.

He turned his head and murmured in her ear, "That was even better than I imagined it—and I imagined it a lot I can tell ye, lady!"

"Glad you liked it, *sir...!*" she replied mimicking him.

Hamish sighed the deep sigh of the satisfied man and drifted off to sleep—as 'satisfied' men have a habit of doing.

Paz did not sleep. She could not help but wonder at the events of this night. Hamish's ardor she had not anticipated. True, he was no Vladimir, carefully orchestrating both bodies to a dazzling and well-timed conclusion.

But she had been well pleased on how he seemed to fill her so completely. Remembering this, curiosity now got the better of her. She had, of course, noticed his nakedness, but modesty had forbidden a closer examination.

With Hamish snoring lightly at her side, she gently extracted one arm and reached down to touch him.

She started at the bottom and slowly shifted her attention to the tip.

"That was it. That's why it felt different," she said to herself. "He's uncircumcised. An unclipped man—a first for you, Paz."

Out loud she added quietly, "A first for number three!"

"Number three what, Paz?" groaned the half-asleep Hamish.

"Nothing, Hamish," she replied, embarrassed that he had overheard her private thoughts.

"No, tell me—three what? Men?"

"Yes, Hamish. You are number four!"

Suddenly a thought seemed to hit Hamish. He sat straight up and switched on the bedside light.

"Paz, number four will be your last. I want to be your husband. I really do. I love you so much!"

After Paz had recovered from her shock, she answered quietly, "To be my husband, you have to marry me. To marry me you have to ask me to be your wife…"

Hamish thought about that for a moment and then got up to his knees, one leg on either side of her.

"Paz, will you marry me?"

"Not if you ask my breasts. Look me in the face and try again."

"Can't. Those are the most beautiful breasts in the whole universe. I have never seen such cute brown nipples."

"Hamish, please!" But her eyes were laughing.

"Paz, it's true. You are really beautiful. Up there."

"OK, OK then, my breasts will marry you. The rest of me will answer you over breakfast."

She brought his head down to her bosom and that is where he spent the rest of the night, happy (as they say in Scotland) as a pig in shit.

Paz slept soundly too, even though the storm rumbled back and forth. It seemed as if the whole weight of the world had left her body and morphed into his. She had a man around the house again. Someone to look after her. Someone to love her. Someone to live for. Someone to make her happy. Someone to share the day. Someone to excite at night. Stability. Peace. Completeness.

If that is the best love she could find, it would be more than enough for her. She'd save the heart-pounding flushes for the romantic movies or novellas.

At breakfast, Hamish ate his huevos Mexicanos (spicy Mexican eggs) in total silence. When Paz had finished hers, she looked at him and said, "We have unfinished business. Ask me again what you asked me last night—and without looking at my breasts!"

"So you weren't fooling with me? Last night was real?"

"Of course it was real," she snapped. "Last night was the first time I realized you loved me. You never showed it. Was I supposed to guess?"

'OK, Paz, forgive me. It was all so sudden and unbelievable. My wildest dreams came true."

He paused and cleared his throat.

"Paz, will you marry me? Will you let me look after you, love you, and protect you as long as we both shall live?"

Tears welled up in Paz's eyes. She ran over to him and sat in his lap. She kissed him several times.

"That's the nicest proposal I ever heard. Here is my answer. Yes to being looked after *(kiss)*. Yes to being loved by you—and loving you back *(kiss)*. Yes to you being my protector *(kiss)*. And even yes to allowing you to stare at my breasts all night long if that turns you on! *(longest kiss of all)*.

"And no man number five?"

"Of course not. What kind of girl do you think I am?"

"Well, what if Vladimir shows up again, Paz? He has a habit of turning up, wanted or not. What would you do? I'm not sure I could handle that scenario!"

Paz jumped onto her feet like a rocket was tied to her back.

"*Vladimir?* Are you joking? He's history. I do not love him anymore, especially not after what Mr. Sverdlov told us about him murdering that Italian.. I am not sure I ever did love him. It was all purely physical. I know that now. And if he should somehow find us, I will not let him into this house or into our lives. You have my word on that. It is you that I want, and if you want me, that's it. The rest is over. Spelt O.V.E.R."

But it wasn't over. Once again Vladimir would appear. Once again Paz's peaceful life would be disrupted.

But that is yet another story.

Made in the USA
San Bernardino, CA
08 April 2014